Adventures
of a
Salsa Goddess

JoAnn Hornak

BERKLEY BOOKS, NEW YORK

THE BERKLEY PUBLISHING GROUP
Published by the Penguin Group
Penguin Group (USA) Inc.
375 Hudson Street, New York, New York 10014, USA
Penguin Group (Canada), 90 Eglinton Avenue East, Suite 700, Toronto, Ontario, M4P 2Y3, Canada
(a division of Pearson Penguin Canada Inc.)
Penguin Books Ltd., 80 Strand, London WC2R 0RL, England
Penguin Group Ireland, 25 St. Stephen's Green, Dublin 2, Ireland (a division of Penguin Books Ltd.)
Penguin Group (Australia), 250 Camberwell Road, Camberwell, Victoria 3124, Australia
(a division of Pearson Australia Group Pty. Ltd.)
Penguin Books India Pvt. Ltd., 11 Community Centre, Panchsheel Park, New Delhi—110 017, India
Penguin Group (NZ), Cnr. Airborne and Rosedale Roads, Albany, Auckland 1310, New Zealand
(a division of Pearson New Zealand Ltd.)
Penguin Books (South Africa) (Pty.) Ltd., 24 Sturdee Avenue, Rosebank, Johannesburg 2196,
South Africa

Penguin Books Ltd., Registered Offices: 80 Strand, London WC2R 0RL, England

This book is an original publication of The Berkley Publishing Group.

This is a work of fiction. Names, characters, places, and incidents either are the product of the author's imagination or are used fictitiously, and any resemblance to actual persons, living or dead, business establishments, events, or locales is entirely coincidental.

Copyright © 2005 JoAnn Hornak
Cover design by Rita Frangie
Text design by Tiffany Estreicher

PRINTING HISTORY
Berkley trade paperback edition / October 2005

Library of Congress Cataloging-in-Publication Data
Hornak, JoAnn.
    Adventures of salsa goddess / JoAnn Hornak.—Berkley trade pbk. ed.
      p. cm
    ISBN 0-425-20548-7 (pbk.)
    1 Americans—Peru—Fiction.   2. Women travelers—Fiction.   3. Peru—Fiction.   I. Title.

    PS3608.O7623A65 2005
    813'.6—dc22

                                             2005048301

PRINTED IN THE UNITED STATES OF AMERICA

10 9 8 7 6 5 4 3 2 1

To everyone who has been touched by the magic of salsa.

Acknowledgements

This book would've never been written without an inspirational brainstorming session with my dear friend Janet Protasiewicz. A special thanks to Gail Hoffman for her devoted friendship and steadfast faith in me. Gail and Janet were also brilliant editors and I'm eternally grateful for the countless times they encouraged me to keep writing when I was on the verge of quitting.

Thank you to the readers of my rough drafts, my brother Steve Hornak, Dick and Penny Podell, Rebecca Vaughn, and Jane Zien for their insightful comments and suggestions. I am grateful to Susan Byrnes who inspired several of the funniest lines and scenarios in this novel. Thank you to Beth Braun and Nancy Chochrek who were excellent sounding boards and a constant source of support. I want to thank my mother, Grace Hornak, my family, and all of my friends for always being there.

I'm indebted to Mary Linn Roby for her tremendous help and advice in transforming my "final" rough draft into a publishable manuscript.

I'm also grateful to my editor Christine Zika, whose gifted judgment for plot and eye for detail improved this novel beyond measure. Thank you to my agent Paige Wheeler and the staff at Creative Media Agency.

And finally, to all of my dance partners with whom I've shared the joy and passion of salsa, thereby making my life far richer than I could have ever imagined.

I'm Not Too Picky—I Just Want a Sexy Hero

By Samantha Jacobs

Is it possible to be too picky when choosing a mate? Must we end up with the comfortable pair of plain white sneakers bought during a Kmart blue-light special, when we'd prefer the five-hundred-dollar strappy Versace's with the impossibly high, cigarette heels, bought on a whim during a spring trip to Paris?

And just how much longer can I hold out?

Recently, a former boyfriend and I reminisced over lunch before the subject turned to the black hole of my life, dating, which for much of my life has consisted of sporadic blips of romance on an otherwise flat Saharan desert of singlehood.

"You're too picky," my ex-lover said, something my mother had also told me too many times to count.

"But you're happily married to a great woman. Why shouldn't I wait for the same?" I countered.

He confessed that although he loved his wife, she had never been his dream woman. Going on, no doubt to make himself feel better, he predicted that at some point, I would follow the road much traveled and do the same.

"You'll settle," he told me confidently.

This was all I needed, Father Knows Best *advice from my ex, who had become one of* Bridget Jones's *insufferable "smug marrieds."*

Must I really fall in with the rank-and-file and sacrifice passion for the it's-Tuesday-so-it-must-be-meat-loaf routine that smug marrieds call contented domestic bliss? Has holding out for the man of my dreams really made me too selective?

And who is he? Does he even exist?

After I saw the movie Gladiator, *I finally found the man I've been searching for my entire life—Maximus, the general who became a slave, the slave who became a gladiator, and the gladiator who has become my ultimate soul mate. Some might say my standards are a bit high, but he's the perfect man for me: patient, humble, courageous, dignified, intelligent, and fair. A rock of moral strength, loved by his men, feared by his sole enemy, Maximus, some might say, is a man's man; but I like to say, Maximus is the ultimate woman's man by virtue of one quality: fidelity.*

Never has a man so virile, so steeped in testosterone, been able to persuasively convince me that he is devoted to monogamy and to the sanctity of marriage. Maximus is no James Bond who beds women with the nonchalance of one changing his boxers. No, Maximus lived, breathed, fought, and died for the memory of his wife, his one true love. And, has anyone else in history ever made a casually draped dead animal skin look so appealing? So necessary? So GQ?

But, is it even rational to believe that a real modern-day man could combine the qualities of inherent goodness and wisdom of the fictional Maximus with the raw animal sexuality of the very real Russell Crowe? Aren't virtue and sensuality mutually exclusive in the same way superior intellect and physical beauty so often are?

Is the choice then, between a hero and a hunk?

Like most single women I know, I don't want to choose. I want it all: a breathtakingly handsome man who changes diapers, cooks gourmet dinners, reads Keats, has a fifth-degree black belt in karate, slays the dragons of doubt that creep into his wife's mind, joyfully embraces monogamy, and is an animal in bed.

Is this really too much to ask for?

I'll admit that it's a bit awkward searching for perfection when I'm far from flawless myself. But I can get over that. It's time, though, that I gave myself a dose of tough love and faced the far more troubling fact that gorgeous, exceptionally virile, intelligent, and highly virtuous heroes might not actually exist. In fact, I probably have a better chance of tripping over the Holy Grail in my breakfast nook than I do of ever meeting my heroic hottie.

Margaret Mead once said that marriage worked well in the nineteenth century because people only lived to be fifty. It also worked well when people lived in tiny villages, confined by poverty and harsh mountainous terrain, and were forced to marry their second cousins with mustaches—both the men and the women.

To put it more succinctly, particularity wasn't an alternative then. But today in our highly mobile global community we have so many options we can all afford to be choosy.

But is it possible that my ex-boyfriend and mother are right? Am I too picky? Perhaps. Then again, shouldn't I hold out? After all, my Maximus, my sexy brave soul mate, my perfect match, may be just a date away.

One

Late-Bloomer Cinderella

"You slept with my husband, you bitch, and I'm nine months' pregnant!"

The shrill tear-choked voice screamed out of my speaker-phone with biting clarity. This was definitely not the best way to start my first day back at work after a fabulous two-week vacation to Peru. I stabbed the button and switched off the speaker, but it was too late.

I looked out the glass wall of my office and saw two coworkers bow their heads in unison, making it painfully obvious that they'd heard every word of this woman's rant. Janet, my editorial assistant, was now furiously pounding away on her keyboard, while, at the next desk, Doreen picked up her Palm Pilot and pretended to stare at it with rapt attention, still keeping one ear cocked in the direction of my office.

I got up and closed my door.

"I found your card in his wallet," my unknown caller sobbed into the receiver, revealing a Southern drawl.

After listening to five minutes of excruciating detail about her husband's cheating ways, I'd managed to piece together that she must be the wife of Wayne Lockwood, an entomologist working for a natural history museum in Atlanta. Wayne, whom I'd met on my trip to Peru, looked nothing like an entomologist, but since he was the first I'd ever encountered, it would be more accurate to say that he looked nothing like my stereotype of a man who studies bugs for a living. A passionate, philandering entomologist had never crossed my mind.

"He used to love me, before I got fat," she continued, sniffling loudly. "But when I had the twins ten months ago and Rachel a year before that, I gained eighty pounds."

This was going to be Wayne's fourth kid in two years? My God, the man was a walking sperm bank.

Sixteen days ago, I'd strolled into the airport lounge in Atlanta on my four-hour layover from New York to Lima, Peru. The second I'd spotted Wayne, my weirdo radar signaled loudly, "avoid this man with every fiber of your being." Detouring around him, I'd found an empty table at the farthest corner of the bar and opened my book. A minute later, I got that gold-chains-Old-Spice-polyester-bald-spot-comb-over-feeling you get when you know a man whom you want nothing to do with is ogling you. Peering over the top of my book, I could see that Wayne had turned around on his stool to face my direction, while leaning his elbows back onto the bar. He just kept staring at me, like it was his job or something. A few minutes later he slithered up to me.

"Excuse me, miss, do you mind if I join you?" he said in a slow, sexy voice, holding a beer out for me. I kept my nose tight inside my book until I realized I couldn't get rid of him that easily and decided to give him a good looking-over.

He stood there tall and lanky, in his tight, beat-up jeans and a leather jacket, which had seen a lot of dusty towns that weren't on any maps. His big tan cowboy hat had a rattlesnake curled around the brim with the head of the snake jutting out, front and center, like the prow of a ship.

If he had tried a pick-up line, I would've told him to get lost, but Wayne was a little bit Indiana Jones and I was a little bit lonely.

I was on my way to Peru to meet Andre—my traveling buddy, my platonic kindred companion seized as I was by wanderlust, who I'd always thought of as the big brother I didn't have—to climb Machu Picchu. Wayne was taking the same flight, on the way to Peru's Amazon rain forest to collect bugs. An insect lover and a women's magazine editor might sound like a match made only in beach novels or made-for-TV movies, but there was something about my yearly trips abroad that freed me to temporarily suspend my real life in an alternate universe. My traveling persona took over the moment I stepped into the airport, and then I would inevitably end up doing crazy things I'd never dream of doing in my real life, like eating cuy frito, a Peruvian delicacy better known as crisp fried guinea pig, something Wayne had talked me into trying just two hours after we'd landed in Peru. We'd had three days together in Lima before we'd gone our separate ways.

Something caught my eye and, looking up, I saw my assistant, Janet, holding up her left wrist and tapping furiously on her watch. I saw from the clock on my desk that I had exactly one minute to get upstairs for a meeting with my boss, Elaine Daniels, founder and editorial director of *Très Chic* magazine.

It was time to cut this call off, but I don't believe that Emily Post or Ms. Manners has written about the appropriate way to end conversations like this. I didn't have the heart to hang up on the woman, but what should I say? Why doesn't your husband wear a wedding ring? I'm sorry, Mrs. Lockwood, but he told me he was divorced and had no kids? We only did it a few times and the sex was only middling on a scale from tepid to volcanic molten rock?

I mouthed the word *help* to Janet, who punched into my line. "Excuse me, ma'am," she said smoothly. "This is Ms. Jacobs's assistant. Ms. Jacobs has . . ." She paused, looking at me for guidance. I walked out of my office and stood over Janet's desk.

"Tell her I died," I whispered.

"Ms. Jacobs has been called away for an important meeting, can I take a message?" asked Janet with a smile.

I sprinted to the elevator, pushed sixty-five, and leaned back against the wall, willing myself to stifle the nauseous feeling I had in the pit of my stomach. Getting a furious phone call from a lover's wife was not the kind of call I got every day, or ever before, for that matter. One minute you're going along with your life, thinking you're a pretty good person, doing the golden rule thing and all, and in the next moment you find out you've inadvertently shattered someone's life.

Normally, travel flings don't count, the same way calories don't count when you're sampling cookie dough batter or eating appetizers instead of a meal. I'd had my fair share of travel romances before Wayne. There was Helmut, a German psychiatrist who'd rescued me from a crevasse, while skiing in the Italian Alps last spring. I'd met Guy, an Australian architect, on the beach in Bali about five years ago. And I could never forget Pierre, a thin, brooding, darkly handsome man who liked to discuss Nietzsche and quote from *The Egyptian Book of the Dead*, whom I'd met during my undergrad year abroad in Paris when I was nineteen. Pierre had way too much angst, but we were in Paris, and I was young and in love for the first time in my life.

But sleeping with a married man was nothing I had ever intended to do, and it made me sick to think that I had, even though Wayne had deliberately lied to me.

I got off the elevator and purposely slowed my stride, as if I'd had every intention of arriving fashionably late for a meeting with my boss.

"Sam, where have you been?" asked Sally, Elaine Daniels's executive assistant. "She just buzzed, looking for you."

"Do you know what this meeting is about?" I asked Sally. Although she'd never married or had children, Sally reminded me of the kind of mothers who bake everything from scratch and wouldn't dream of using a mix, even in an emergency.

Sally, a matronly redhead, could be counted on to always look out for us peons. She'd give us the heads-up if we were facing the chopping block, getting a promotion, or being exiled on assignment to Pennsylvania Dutch country to uncover the sex secrets of the Amish. Sally, who knew more than the CIA and Interpol combined, looked to the right and left, and leaned forward over her desk.

"I don't know," Sally told me in her gravelly whisper, "but Elaine said that if everything goes according to her plan, it's certain to boost circulation by at least twelve percent."

Very bad indeed. I couldn't think of a single thing that would have that kind of impact on sales other than an exclusive scoop that Madonna was really a man. I think I'd rather get fired.

"She had me get out your personnel file yesterday to check your birth date and how long you've been working here," continued Sally in a low voice, as I sat down in a chair across from her desk.

Elaine wanted to know how long I've been here? Let me see, had it really been fifteen years? I remember walking down Broadway for my interview with her as though it were yesterday, dressed in my one and only interview outfit, a Chanel black wool bouclé tunic dress and matching cropped jacket. For luck, I'd worn the real pearl necklace from Tiffany that my mother had given me on the occasion of my graduation from Fordham University, where I'd managed, just barely, to eke out the requisite thesis so I could earn my master's degree in Comparative Literature. I'd entered graduate school at twenty-three, thinking that getting a Ph.D. and becoming a professor sounded like a pretty good idea. But, I'd quickly learned that I was about as scholarly as a trashy romance novel. Luckily for me, my master's thesis—"The Role of Female Sexuality in the Literature of Anaïs Nin: Prose or Pornography?"—had landed me this job. As it turned out, Elaine loved Anaïs Nin and had read everything she'd ever written.

"You can go in now," said Sally, suddenly jerking me back to the present.

I wobbled my way up to a standing position.

"How do I look?" I asked Sally, painfully aware that I was shaking from my knees up to my lips. Add to this my nervous habit of raking my hand back and forth through my short blond hair, and I'm pretty sure my calm, cool air had frazzled to that of a sweaty punk rocker with a coke problem.

Sally grimaced slightly and then gave me the thumbs-up. Just then Elaine's door burst open.

"Samantha, you look fabulous!" said Elaine, her voice high-pitched and unrecognizable. "Where did you get that adorable . . ." She looked down at my skirt and raised a thin eyebrow. ". . . outfit?"

"Um . . ." I looked down and saw that my linen skirt was clinging to my thighs like a pink dishrag. I was wearing a suit I'd bought at a consignment shop in SoHo a few years ago, a retro Jackie Kennedy lipstick-pink, tailored Yves Saint Laurent. I loved fashion, but my days of dropping wads of cash on new designer clothes had ended when my mother announced that she was cutting me off after grad school. As a lifestyle editor at *Très Chic*, I made a decent salary, but only enough to splurge occasionally.

"Good to see you, my dear," Elaine said, as she escorted me into her office with her arm around my shoulders. "Have a seat."

I sat down in a high-backed zebra-print upholstered chair and waited while Elaine settled herself behind her colossal teak desk. Perching her black-frame reading glasses on the edge of her tiny nose, she leaned back in her chair and picked up a manila folder with "Samantha Jacobs" typed on a neat label on the cover. As she slowly flipped through the documents clipped inside my personnel file, I noticed that her pale blond hair was swept, as usual, into a perfect up-do, topped with a mass of neatly pinned curly tendrils that showed off her graceful, nearly unlined neck.

Elaine had decorated her office after a safari to Kenya a couple of years ago. Cowry shell–beaded masks were arranged in a diamond shape on the wall behind her head. Several tiny African stools sat here and there around her warehouse-sized office, as if a third-world vendor had accidentally wandered in and dropped them here. And the chair I was sitting in was on top of what looked like a real leopard skin rug.

The only sounds I heard were the turning of pages and the faint whir of a helicopter buzzing over Manhattan.

As I waited, I wondered which Elaine I would encounter today. It was a little game everyone on the staff played, since her personality fluctuated more than an oscillating fan. A movie montage of all of the Elaines I knew might look something like *The Three Faces of Eve*, only with a dozen more faces.

"Can you keep a secret?" she asked, finally breaking the yawning silence with a question I believe I last heard at a slumber party when I was fourteen.

"Of course."

"I have good news for you, Samantha. Maya Beckett is giving up 'La Vie.'"

I couldn't believe it. I sat there stunned. For years I'd been hoping to hear those very words. Features was considered the pinnacle for staffers at our magazine because they worked on the sexy gigs like movie and rock star interviews and serious pieces bordering on actual investigative journalism, such as "Could the Next Love Canal Be in Your Backyard?" But I had always coveted the seven-hundred-word humor column, the last page of our semimonthly magazine called "La Vie," which had belonged to Maya Beckett for the last eight years.

"She's giving up her column? Why?" I asked.

"Maya is burnt-out. She plans on staying with *Très Chic,* but will probably be moving back to Features," said Elaine.

Had Maya Beckett lost her mind? Giving up that column would be like discovering the fountain of youth only to abandon it, because you've decided that getting old and decrepit wasn't so bad after all. Maya was the star of *Très Chic*. She had more devotees than your average cult and received mailbags full of fan letters each month—not surprising since she'd been nationally recognized as an exceptionally talented humorist.

Subject to Elaine's final approval, Maya had complete freedom to choose the subjects she wrote about in "La Vie"—everything from the usual trials and tribulations of being single, to a satire of Bill Clinton that she'd written at the height of the Lewinsky scandal to tongue-in-cheek pieces such as a column from last year called "The Goatee Rule" about why men with goatees were sexier and more desirable than clean-shaven men.

I had spent years hoping that Maya Beckett would move on to another magazine, *The New Yorker* or Oprah's magazine or *Feed Lot Weekly* for all I cared, as long as she moved on. In order to be in a prime position should that wonderful day ever arrive, I'd actively lobbied for "La Vie," writing a dozen essays and sending them up the pipeline, hoping they'd reach Elaine's desk. But, for all I knew, they were at the bottom of a landfill, unread and molting.

"I've read all of your manuscripts, Samantha," Elaine said. "You have an excellent way with words. And you've been a loyal employee. I reward loyalty, as you know," she said, dropping one perfectly shadowed eyelid.

Oh no, she's winking. I'm getting the I'm-your-best-friend-not-your-boss Elaine.

" 'La Vie' is yours," Elaine said.

"Really? Wow! I mean, thank you! You won't be disappointed, Elaine. So when do I start?" I asked.

"September. But there's a very minor little assignment I'd like you to take care of first," she said, meaning exactly the opposite. Whatever she had in mind would no doubt change my life forever.

My heartbeat slowed to normal as I steeled myself, gripping my armrests with a death hold.

Elaine stood up and began pacing. I've always felt like a giant sloth next to women like her, whose miniscule size-two bodies couldn't possibly hold all of the organs that normal-sized women like I have. Women like Elaine must somehow get by without intestines and livers.

"Samantha, you've been with *Très Chic* for fifteen years now. In your opinion, what are we selling?"

Was this a trick question?

"Magazines?" I finally ventured after a long pause.

"Dreams!" she said like a cheerleader on speed. "We're selling dreams to our nine hundred thousand readers, women who want it all—the career; the smart, sexy, caring husband; a great sex life; motherhood. You've captured that with your essay, 'I'm Not Too Picky, I Just Want a Sexy Hero.'"

"I have?"

"Yes, precisely. Although why a successful professional woman would actually want to get married is beyond me," she said with a flip of her hand.

I quickly closed my gaping mouth. Elaine was currently on marriage number six, to a real estate investment tycoon who was at least a decade younger than she. I wouldn't be surprised to learn that Elaine was on a first-name basis with all the city clerks in the Marriage License Bureau and that they had a pre-printed license form all ready for her to simply fill in the name of the husband du jour.

"Nonetheless, the surveys we've conducted show most of our readers are single and want to get married," she said, shaking her head as if she were an anthropologist recounting the bizarre rituals of a remote tribe of Stone Age people.

"Samantha, you're forty-one and never married, is that right?" she asked, as she turned to face me. "Tell me, how does that make you feel?"

If someone had told me in college that I'd still be single at this age, one thing was certain, I wouldn't have wasted countless weeks, months, and nearly every hour of the past quarter century of my life agonizing over men.

Will he call? What did it mean that he called but didn't set up another date? Is this relationship going anywhere? Can I even call it a relationship when we've only gone out twice, and I haven't heard from him in over a week? Has my Mr. Right permanently moved to Uzbekistan, a country I'm not even sure I can spell correctly? Should I talk to my travel agent about booking a trip to Uzbekistan on the off-chance that he's there? Am I destined to remain single because my Mr. Right was killed in a car accident when I was five years old and no one has had the decency to tell me?

But then I'd met David and everything had changed. I'd finally found the man I was going to spend the rest of my life with. I'd never have to spend another Valentine's Day alone watching sappy movies while picturing my solitary future. That is, until David broke off our engagement just three months before our wedding date. And for the past thirty-seven months, two weeks, and five days, I've mourned the loss of that perfect life I'd pictured with David—companionship, children, a family that I could relate to.

"Um, being single at forty-one, I don't really . . ." I stammered.

"Does it make you feel fabulous?" she asked. "It should, because I'm about to offer you the opportunity-of-a-lifetime assignment never before tackled by anyone."

I could practically hear the *whoosh* of my brain releasing the adrenaline that was now coursing through my nervous system screaming, "Run!"

"Samantha," Elaine continued, "do you remember the statistic from *Newsweek* about a forty-year-old single woman being more likely to be killed by a terrorist than to ever be married?"

"I think so, but I remember that I didn't pay much attention to it because I was only in my twenties when that came out," I said. My twenties—that seemed like a million carefree years ago.

"That's correct, it came out in 1986," Elaine agreed. "But as you know, our world has become a much more dangerous place since then. That statistic has recently been updated."

"It has?" I asked, wondering what the hell any of this had to do with me or the fabulous assignment Elaine was about to thrust upon me.

"The new stats will be all over the news by the end of this week, which is why we need to jump on this opportunity before someone else thinks of my idea," she said. "Do you know what you're going to be doing this December thirty-first, Samantha?"

Hopefully not what I had done last year on New Year's Eve, one of the most depressing nights of my life, the occasion of my third and final date with Seth, a forty-three-year-old divorced architect.

I had presented myself at his apartment as arranged, wearing a new silver-sequined, mid-thigh-high dress. Smiling sheepishly and wearing ripped sweatpants and a faded Rolling Stones T-shirt from their Voodoo Lounge tour, Seth had told me that his buddy who worked for the Neil Simon Theater hadn't been able to get us tickets to see *Hairspray* after all. So, he had suggested we stay in and watch his favorite movie, the original 1933 version of *King Kong*. I left before the movie ended, and at the stroke of midnight, when I was supposed to have been in the midst of a champagne toast kissing a handsome man, I was crying in the back of a cab, trying to remember the address of the party that my friend Elizabeth said she'd be at.

I jumped when Elaine brought me out of my sad reverie with a loud slap of her hand on the edge of her desk.

"This New Year's Eve, Samantha Jacobs, you will be at the Plaza Hotel getting married!" she announced. "It's all arranged."

I couldn't have been more astounded if she'd told me I'd been assigned to go back in time to interview Joan of Arc.

"Getting married? To whom?" I asked.

"Exactly!" Elaine said, hands on her nonexistent hips. "I want our readers to not just dream the impossible dream, but to believe they can have it too. And you, my dear Samantha, are going to give it to them!"

Impossible dream? Elaine didn't believe in impossibilities, but I did. Portent of doom. I could almost see the floor opening up into a cavernous abyss as I toppled down into the fiery pits of hell.

"Late-Bloomer Cinderella Finds Her Prince Charming! Older Pretty Woman Weds Rich Successful Businessman, or doctor or lawyer," she said with so much fervor I thought she might spontaneously combust. "Can't you see it?"

I could imagine what it might be like to be with Mr. Right, but as much time as I'd spent trying, I just couldn't picture him.

"You'll hand our readers the dream on a silver platter by Labor Day. I'm planning the announcement of your engagement to coincide with National Singles Week, which is September sixteenth."

We have our own week? What the hell for?

"Isn't that rushing things a bit?" I asked her, beginning to count the months off on my fingers, May, June . . .

"Do you know where I'm going to send you to find this wonderful man?" she interrupted, clearly on a one-way conversational roll that didn't require me to be here at all.

Pluto? An undiscovered solar system?

"The city with the absolute worst, most abysmal marital statistics for single, professional women in this entire country, Milwaukee!" she said flashing me a huge grin.

Milwaukee? Milwaukee? Was that in one of those *I* states—Indiana, Iowa, Illinois—all clumped together in the middle somewhere?

"And do you know why I want to send you there to find your husband?" she continued.

"Because you want me to fail?" I suggested, although my chances had to be better than staying in New York. Between my single friend Elizabeth and I, we'd pretty much tapped out the entire Eastern Seaboard.

"No, no, no, silly girl. Because I want each of our readers to know that if you can find a husband in *Milwaukee*, then she can do it anywhere."

"I see," I said, seeing nothing, now certain that Elaine had gone insane and that my best bet was to agree with everything she said until it was time for her to take her meds and, hopefully, she stabilized enough to tell me that this was all just a joke.

"I want to make one thing absolutely clear, Samantha," Elaine continued, as she turned away from her floor-to-ceiling windows to face me. "There are some professional women who seem to be beating the odds by marrying men with blue-collar jobs. But under no circumstances will you end up with an uneducated man. I want you to marry the dream man, the perfect man, the man our readers want to marry: professional, college-educated, and preferably drop-dead gorgeous."

Sure, no problem, Elaine. Would you like me to throw in a cure for cancer and a peace treaty for the Middle East while I'm at it?

"By the way, Elaine," I said, deciding to humor her, "what is the new updated statistic for single women over forty?"

Ever prepared, she handed me a copy of a press release announcing the imminent publication of a book written by Harvard-educated sociologist Dr. Victoria Huber, titled, *The Single Professional Woman Over Forty: The Hopeless Search for Happily Ever After.*

A single sentence on the press release had been highlighted in pink: *A never-married single professional woman over forty now has a better chance of winning a seven-figure lottery jackpot than ever marrying.*

I felt my jaw drop.

"Don't worry about those silly numbers," Elaine said with a wave of her hand as if she were holding a magic wand that had just made this dire pronouncement disappear.

I scanned the rest of the press release, my eyes landing on another sentence: *Of the fifty most populous cities in the United States, Milwaukee, Wisconsin, has consistently ranked last, in all age groups, for the percentage of single professional women marrying.*

"You just need to focus, Samantha," said Elaine briskly. "Now, remember, this is a top-secret project. During the summer you'll send your articles about your dates directly to me for editing. You leave in two weeks."

Two weeks? Wait a minute. I *don't* have to worry about these statistics or Elaine's outlandish scheme.

"I'm not sure I'm the right person for this assignment, Elaine," I hedged.

Failing would be disastrous not just for my career at *Très Chic* but also for my self-esteem. After a broken engagement, more than a few failed romances, and scores of bad dates over the past twenty years of my life, I could be declared a hazardous romance site. And despite my grim track record, I keep trying. I'm not one of those women who believe she can't be happy without a man. Lord knows most of the men I've been involved with have either bored me to a stupor within minutes or driven me temporarily insane. But growing up seeing how happy my parents had been, I've never been able to picture any other future for myself.

My mother and father had been one of the giggly, gooey-eyed couples who embarrass the hell out of everyone around them. I remember them constantly holding hands and looking dreamy-eyed at one another at the dinner table and the movies and melting the frozen food sections of grocery stores. And then my dad had died of pancreatic cancer when I was sixteen. He was diagnosed one day and gone within five months. And after that, my mother had never been the same.

Elaine perched on the edge of her desk directly in front of me. I could feel her breath on me as she put her hands on my shoulders.

"I know you can do this, Samantha," she said, ignoring the real issue.

How could I possibly find someone I wanted to spend the rest of my life with in just one summer? Not just any man would do. I wanted exactly what my parents had had—absolute blissful happiness; in other words, the type of marriage that eluded 99 percent of the population. But knowing Elaine, true love wasn't part of her agenda.

"But what if I fail?"

"You won't," she said, with a flash of concern in her pale blue eyes. "You won't fail, promise me."

"Okay, I promise." What the hell? I'll throw in my first-born son too.

Two

Brew City

"There's supposed to be a lake out there somewhere, but I can't see a thing," I said into the cordless telephone.

I thought I had landed in the Bermuda Triangle. All I could see out my new patio doors from my eighteenth-floor vantage point was pelting rain and swirling mists of fog. Just before I left New York, Sally, Elaine Daniels's executive assistant, had given me a copy of the real estate ad that described my two-bedroom apartment as being "on the fashionable East side of Milwaukee with expansive views of sunny, scenic Lake Michigan." The thermometer attached just outside the door read forty-two degrees.

"Have you met any men yet?" asked my best friend, Elizabeth, who I called the second I'd arrived in my new apartment.

Elizabeth liked to cut through all the chitchat and get straight to the point, which I suppose she couldn't help since she lives and breathes the law, working sixty to eighty hours a week for Hobson, Dwight, and McKenzie, the third biggest law firm in

New York, since graduating from UCLA law school fourteen years ago.

"Not since the plane landed forty-five minutes ago," I said. I was in a city with almost 600,000 people and I only knew one of them. I was already feeling very lonely.

"I'm disappointed in you," she said, a smile in her voice.

Elizabeth and I had been friends since we were both three years old, having met in a preschool ballet class. Although I have no memory of our first acquaintance, a photograph that I've carried in my wallet for years, taken at our first recital, shows the two of us in our little pale pink tutus, our arms around each other's shoulders, with my golden-blond Barbie doll shoulder-length hair leaning against Elizabeth's dark brunette Audrey Hepburn pixie. I have a vague memory of asking Elizabeth if she wanted to be my best friend and her saying yes, and here we were nearly thirty-eight years later, still best friends.

While I talked to Elizabeth, I did a tour of my new apartment. The living room had a tacky starving artist's landscape painting above a plain brown couch. A wood veneer coffee table sat on powder-blue dentist's office carpeting. Bedroom number one—queen bed, dresser, straight-backed chair, graying walls, gray carpeting, and a gray bedspread. I took two steps across the hallway to bedroom number two—black laminated computer desk, black metal filing cabinet, and a door leading out to the balcony. My apartment had all of the warmth and charm of a mental institution.

"Just think, your future husband is in the same city as you," said Elizabeth.

I had my doubts, but, if he was here, chances were excellent he was intoxicated. According to the guidebook about Milwaukee that I'd read on the flight over:

Milwaukee is a great city on a great lake with countless ethnic festivals and nonstop flowing taps of beer. With its large German population and a reputation as one of the friendliest cities in the United States, you'll often hear Milwaukeeans speak of their famous *gemutlichkeit*. At its zenith, Milwaukee had close to sixty operating breweries. With a tavern on almost every block, it's no wonder this thriving metropolis has garnered the nickname "Brew City."

When my plane had landed, I'd half expected to see throngs of drunken men in lederhosen and serving wenches with heaving bosoms spilling over low-cut tight-fitting dresses, all of them swilling beer and dancing gaily on the tarmac. Instead, I'd landed in the midst of a monsoon with all of my checked luggage having apparently taken a side trip, probably to a warmer destination. The airline assured me my bags would be delivered tomorrow or in three days, after the Memorial Day weekend.

"You know, your husband might even be living in your building," Elizabeth said. A split second later, a mighty crack of thunder sounded, the deafening, biblical kind of thunder, loud enough to scare all dogs within a hundred-mile radius under beds and bring sinners to their knees.

"Did you hear that?" Elizabeth asked. "It's a sign. I'm sure your husband is there. I can feel it."

Once Elizabeth had received a sign—thunder, a black cat walking under a ladder, crop circles—she couldn't be dissuaded even if God herself came down from heaven, shook her by the shoulders, and told her to get a grip.

"I just want to get through this summer," I said, looking out my patio doors. It looked as though the storm was subsiding. I could now see a horizontal gray line that had to be Lake Michigan.

"Be positive!" Elizabeth urged me.

It had only taken me a few minutes after leaving Elaine's office two weeks ago to decide that I would do this crazy assignment after all. It was certainly time for me to shuffle the deck of my life. I was bored not just with my job as a lifestyle editor, a position I'd held for the past four years, but with everything. Besides seeing Elizabeth a couple times a week and the occasional date, I had no social life in New York. I lived for my four weeks of vacation a year when I could travel with my pal Andre. I loved my younger sister, Susan, her husband, and of course my new niece, Matilda, but Susan and I had never really connected. My father, whom I'd been very close to, had been gone now for almost twenty-five years. And every time I saw my mother, a woman who could drive the Pope to take a hit off a crack pipe, I wasn't myself for days afterward.

Of course it would be a dream come true to get "La Vie," my own humor column, but what had actually convinced me to come to Milwaukee was very simple: I wanted to see if finding a man I could fall in love with and marry was even possible. I had nothing to lose and potentially everything to gain by doing this assignment. Elizabeth was right as usual, I needed to be positive and take this assignment seriously.

☆　☆　☆

The next morning I walked out onto my balcony under a perfect cloudless sky and turned my face up to the sun. White sailboats dotted the sapphire blue water. I could see weeping willow trees bent over a pond in the distance and a few colorful kites hovered over a huge expanse of green. Rubbing my arms, which had broken out in goose bumps, I took in the spectacular view, which made me feel as though in the middle of the night I'd been whisked away to a commercial set for a feminine hygiene product.

After taking a quick shower, I slicked a comb through my hair and put on my favorite pink lipstick and a thin coat of mascara. I slipped on a red halter dress and a bright yellow sweater and was out the door in twenty minutes. Grabbing the Saturday paper I found on my welcome mat, I took the elevator down to the ground level and stepped outside to take my first sunny breath of Milwaukee. The smell of freshly cut grass hit me, reminding me of summer visits to my mother's house in Scarsdale, New York.

In search of my morning caffeine fix, I walked by redbrick and brownstone mansions, twenty-story apartment buildings, the construction site of a new condo building going up, the Wisconsin Conservatory of Music, and a small art museum. The sidewalks were filled with people walking dogs, jogging, and strolling hand in hand. Outside a retirement home I passed, old men and women sat on benches, chatting in a broken language full of harsh consonants, probably Yiddish or Polish.

A few minutes later I saw the sign THE JAVA JUNKIE and knew I'd found the perfect spot. Anything that implied unhealthy excess when it came to coffee was my kind of place. I ordered a latté and a blueberry scone and took them outside to the only free black, wrought iron sidewalk table.

Two sets of dewy-eyed hand-holding couples with the we've-just-gotten-out-of-bed-after-a-night-and-morning-of-amazing-sex looks on their faces were sitting at tables on either side of me. Post-bonking hormones swirled through my airspace like unwanted secondhand smoke, and I felt my early-morning good spirits slowly sinking into emotional quicksand.

Not a good way to start the summer. I packed up my scone, grabbed my coffee cup, headed back to my new apartment, and spent the rest of the day trying to do as little as possible. I unpacked my carry-on suitcase, finished reading the paper, and went out to my balcony, where I must've dozed off, since the downstairs buzzer woke me at six.

I opened the door to a stunning woman with a pierced navel and a blue and gold shooting-star tattoo soaring over her belly button. Her wild auburn, strawberry, and cherry hair was gelled into crazy two-inch spikes, and big silver hoop earrings dangled from her ears.

"Can I help you?" I asked, thinking it might be the apartment manager or a neighbor wanting to share some of that famous Milwaukee *gemutlichkeit*.

"Sam, don't you recognize me?" she said, throwing her arms around my neck and giving me a hug, which was followed by one of those awkward it's-good-to-see-you-and-I-want-to-look-you-over-to-see-how-three-years-have-changed-you-but-don't-want-to-be-impolite-and-stare moments. I couldn't get over how different she looked.

"Lessie, wow, you look fantastic!" I said finally, not wanting to bring attention to her weight loss directly.

"You do too!" she assured me cheerfully. "You haven't changed at all except, what happened to all your hair?"

I'd had shoulder-length straight blond hair my entire life up until three years ago when, in a post-ex-fiancé-David-break-up-frenzy, I'd had my hair chopped off the very day that we were supposed to get married. I'm sure it had nothing to do with the fact that he loved my long blond hair and had told me that several times a week for the entire three years we'd been together.

"I have the same question for you," I said, looking at her short spiky locks, which seemed to change color as the sun hit them when she walked across my living room.

The first time I'd seen Lessie had been in the bathroom of our dorm during our freshman year at Brown University. I'd noticed her hair immediately. She'd had magnificent hair, the kind that was capable of launching a thousand ships—waist-length, thick as molasses, golden blond, and perfectly straight. Lessie had always been pretty, but I'd never seen her wear makeup and her weight had always been a problem. Every year she'd added another five to ten pounds, and by the time we'd graduated, she must have been close to two hundred. But Steve, her fiancé, at six foot five and probably fifty pounds lighter, had loved her exactly as she was. After graduation, they moved to Milwaukee, Steve's hometown, and were married six months later. Three years ago, just before David and I had broken up, Lessie had come to visit me in New York just after she'd filed for divorce and when she'd still looked like the Lessie I'd known in college. It was the last time I'd seen her, but we'd been in constant contact via e-mail and telephone since that visit.

Lessie, a high school art teacher, stood in the center of my living room and looked around, hands on her narrow hips. She wore a cropped white halter top, white Capri pants encircled by a hip-hugging silver chainlink belt, and white sling-back sandals. I glanced down at her hipbones jutting out through the thin material of her cotton pants.

"When I lost all my weight after my divorce, the biggest thrill of my life was discovering I actually have hipbones just like everyone else," she said. "But I have to be careful, if I so much as think about ice cream, I gain five pounds."

Men don't know how easy they have it. If one of their buddies whom they hadn't seen in a few years had lost a lot of weight, they'd either avoid the topic altogether (impossible among Venetians) or say something like, What the hell happened to your fat ass and beer gut? Women on the other hand must follow the unwritten rule of never calling attention to physical imperfections, former or present, because when we look into the mirror, we see every facial hair, trace of a wrinkle, and cellulite molecule beginning to form on our thighs. But bald, chinless men with guts that could qualify for their own zip codes look in the mirror and think "stud" before going out to try and pick up a woman half their age.

"Great apartment!" Lessie said, stepping out onto the balcony. "What a view!" She turned and flashed me a huge smile. "So, Sam, you were all mysterious on the phone about why you're in Milwaukee. What's up?" she asked me, her blue eyes expectant. "You're on assignment, aren't you?"

I handed Lessie a copy of the May 27 issue of *Très Chic* with a silhouette of a woman's head on the cover carrying the lead story: "Will Our Mystery Woman Defy the Statistics and Find Mr. Right?"

"Holy shit, are you the Mystery Woman?" she asked, gaping at me as though I'd just announced the date for my sex change operation. "I heard something about this on the news yesterday."

I shrugged. "I'll tell you the whole story over dinner."

★ ★ ★

"So this whole thing isn't just a publicity stunt for *Très Chic*?" Lessie asked me a half an hour later. She stabbed a forkful of greens with her right hand while she grabbed a French fry off my plate with her left, swiped it through the ketchup, and popped it into her mouth. "You're not going to get a quiet annulment a few months after everything dies down?"

"No scam. I'm here to find true love," I said. I cut another slice of my filet mignon, taking full advantage of my healthy expense account. "And my wedding is already set for this New Year's Eve at the Plaza."

I had also finagled a three-week honeymoon to Europe from Elaine once I realized I had some leverage. Unless Elaine wanted to go with a freelance writer, and I knew that for this type of assignment she preferred to keep it in-house, I was the only choice, being the only woman over forty and never married presently working at *Très Chic*.

"Wow, this is just like those reality TV shows, only I guess it's reality magazine?"

It was real enough I suppose, although nothing before in my life had ever had such a bizarre, surreal quality to it. It was difficult to grasp the concept that it was now my "job" to find a husband, something I'd thought I wanted since I was a teenager, except that now I was no longer sure.

"You've picked a hell of a city to try and find a husband," Lessie continued, shaking her head. "I know that's why you were sent here, but . . ."

"Is it that bad?" I asked her.

"The first words that spring to mind when I think of Milwaukee's dating scene are *black, soulless wasteland of loneliness and despair*," she said in a voice, serious soft, like a mother explaining that the hamster isn't sleeping, it's dead.

My face must've collapsed at that point, since she immediately broke out into a huge grin. One of the things I'd always loved about Lessie was her wicked sense of humor, which was so disarming and unexpected coming from someone who'd grown up on a dairy farm in the middle of Minnesota. At least she used to look wholesome. Her sense of humor fit her new looks perfectly.

"The problem is that we have an epidemic of un-dating," she said.

"Un-dating?"

"You know, men who don't really ask you out. They suggest meeting them at a bar, maybe buy you one drink, and then expect you to jump into bed with them."

"Yeah, we have that in New York too. I guess I was hoping the Midwest was a little more traditional," I said.

"Or maybe they do ask you out, sort of, but then make the women do all the work," she said.

Lessie recounted a story about meeting Kirk at a summer festival the year before. I exchanged my own un-dating experience, telling her about Brad, a wealthy entrepreneur whom I'd met weight lifting at my health club a couple years ago. Our first date had been great, but then he'd followed up with a lame e-mail wanting to know if we were going to have a second "meeting." I made a mental note to write about un-dating in my journal later. I wanted to have ideas and columns ready for "La Vie" when I started in September.

"For the first two years after my divorce, I was looking for a real man who would treat me well. But over the past year, I've downsized my criteria. Now I'd be happy with a man whose picture isn't hanging on the wall of the post office."

"So the dating scene here is bad?"

"It's not great, but I suppose it all depends on what you're looking for," she said. "Let me see if I have this straight. According to your boss, you're supposed to find a college-educated, professional guy, attractive, but preferably movie-star handsome since it will make for a better cover shot, never married, or if divorced, no kids or skeletons in the closet, right?"

"Basically," I said. She made it sound like I was in the market for a luxury sedan with all the standard equipment plus all the options.

"Good luck," she said, as she played with her left hoop earring.

If gorgeous, smart, and sexy Lessie had been looking for three years without much luck, I'd be lucky to have one good date this summer.

"I'm going to be publicly humiliated. In September I'll be revealed to the nation as the loser who couldn't find a husband."

"Your boss doesn't seem to have a clue what it's really like out here in the bowels of singlehood," Lessie said.

She didn't know Elaine Daniels. Of course Elaine didn't have a clue, and if she did, she wouldn't care.

"So what's your plan of action?" Lessie asked.

"I thought I'd go through the white pages alphabetically," I told her. "Hello, my name is Samantha. If there's a single man in your household between the ages of eighteen and seventy-five, could I speak to him please?"

"Aren't you limiting yourself a little with that age range?" asked Lessie.

"Okay, I'm supposed to do the video dating thing, Internet dating, personals ads, three-minute dating, singles volleyball, a singles' cooking class, baseball games, stuff like that," I said.

"Are you going to have time for any fun this summer?" she asked.

The waitress came by and Lessie ordered another glass of wine. A toddler in a high chair at a nearby table gurgled happily at his parents.

"Do you still want to have kids?" I asked her.

I knew that the kids issue had been the main reason Lessie had divorced Steve. After years of trying, Lessie hadn't gotten pregnant so she'd gone through all of the tests, which she'd passed. Then, after begging Steve for years, he'd finally gotten tested. They'd found out he was sterile due to a case of mumps when he was fourteen. Lessie had wanted to use a sperm donor or adopt, but Steve wouldn't even discuss it or go to marriage counseling.

"I'm not sure I want to have kids anymore. I think I'm getting too old," Lessie said.

The waitress brought her glass of wine. We both passed on dessert.

"How about you, Sam, do you want kids?"

"Yes," I said, "but I don't see myself as a single mother. Every time I go to the gynecologist's office, I get that look from my doctor like 'what are you waiting for?' I want to tell her, I'm waiting for the whole package and in the usual order, the husband and then the kids."

I used to think a lot about the children I would have. David and I had had it all planned out—two kids and then maybe adopt one. But then, everything fell apart because of a chicken wing.

Just three months before our wedding, David and I were having dinner when I'd made the fateful mistake of wondering out loud how many eggs I had left. I was only thirty-eight at the time, practically up to my eyeballs in eggs, but I thought I was getting too old to have a child. When I told David I wanted to get pregnant right after we got married, he inhaled a chicken wing and started choking. He grabbed his throat and turned beet red. I watched in horror while the waiter saved him with the Heimlich maneuver.

Having a chicken wing temporarily lodged in his throat turned out to be a life-transforming experience for David. First, he started talking about giving up his partnership and quitting Ernst & Young to travel to India and stay for a while at Swami something-or-other's ashram in the Himalayas. If you knew David, you would understand that a declaration like that would be a little like Hugh Hefner announcing that he was giving up women, sex, and his publishing fortune to pursue a life of asceticism. Not only had David given a new definition to the word *workaholic* (he'd slept at his office two or three nights a week), I'd begged him since we'd first started going out to take some time off to travel with me. But David had always claimed that he couldn't get away from work.

Next, he was no longer sure he wanted to have children and had suggested postponing the wedding. I'd thought he was just getting a normal attack of wedding jitters. But it wasn't the usual case of cold feet. His had become encased in glaciers that wouldn't thaw until the next millennium. And a week after that, David had told me he didn't love me anymore and wasn't sure that he ever had, and then he'd broken off our engagement.

When the bill arrived I pulled out my *Très Chic* American Express card and put it on top, waving Lessie off when she reached for her wallet.

"I think we should do something special to inaugurate your arrival in Milwaukee," said Lessie with a devilish smile.

＊ ＊ ＊

"You can open your eyes now, ma'am."

I'd just suffered the ultimate in humiliation, being called ma'am in a tattoo parlor by a kid young enough to be my son.

Part man, mostly tattoo and metal, the tattoo artist had a face that could launch a nuclear attack. He had so many piercings, I couldn't tell where his skin ended and the metal started. Eyebrows, nose, forehead, cheeks, lip, and chin were lined with dozens of tiny silver hoops, while his arms were swathed with snakes, dragons, and what looked like a mermaid being swallowed whole by a whale. A scorpion was tattooed on the front of his neck, and a U.S. flag dead center on the back.

I've had my share of zany moments, and I suppose this was one of them, although I hated to admit that I might actually be one of those women who refused to acknowledge the fact that they were—although technically only in the numerical sense of the word—middle-aged. You know this kind of woman. She still shops for clothes in the juniors section and gets Botox injections and face-lifts until her head hovers a few feet above her shoulders. She dates much younger men, pierces her navel, and lets someone she hasn't seen in three years talk her into getting a . . .

"Let me see your tattoo," said Lessie, who'd stepped back into the room as soon as the needle had fallen silent.

The three of us looked intently at my stomach as if peering into a still, very deep pond. The delicate wings, the tiny bow, the quiver of arrows, the cherubic face . . . What the hell had I been thinking?

"It's a beautiful Cupid!" said Lessie.

"Thanks again, ma'am," the tattoo artist said to me as we left.

Ma'am. I wouldn't go near a magnet if I were you kid, not unless you wanted to have your face sucked off your skull.

But the night was far from over. Fifteen minutes later I stood with Lessie outside a two-story caramel-colored brick building in downtown Milwaukee. The music blasting from the upstairs out onto the second-floor patio above us was so loud, the building seemed to pulsate like a giant beating heart in rhythm to the music.

Lessie stood on the first step with her hand on the brass door handle. She lowered her voice, trying her best to be serious.

"This may be the last oasis of sexy, sinfully delicious single men left on the face of this planet," she told me. "I must warn you, this is not a place for amateurs. I met a prime specimen here myself a couple weeks ago, and he's supposed to be here tonight!"

The downstairs of Club Cubana wasn't much to look at. A few guys in suits were at the bar smoking cigars and drinking. We ordered two frozen margaritas and headed straight upstairs past a brightly painted wall mural of the heart of Havana—fifties cars, the Bacardi factory, and the name of a bar I thought I remembered as being one of Hemingway's haunts when he'd lived there.

As we reached the top of the stairs, the music hit me physically, like a G-force. Couples were spinning and twirling to salsa music on the packed dance floor.

"There he is!" said Lessie, waving to a handsome Latino man dressed all in black who was standing on the other side of the room, next to the patio doors. As soon as he saw her, I could almost hear the deadbolt click shut as their eyes locked. Skirting around the dancers, he slowly made his way over to us, seemingly oblivious to everyone in the bar except her. When he kissed her on the cheek, Lessie giggled like a high school girl being introduced to the star quarterback.

"Sam Jacobs, I'd like to introduce you to Eliseo Lora," she said as we shook hands.

"Eliseo is a fabulous salsa dancer," gushed Lessie, who immediately latched herself to his arm like a vise—not that I could really blame her since Eliseo's looks were the kind that typically graced the covers of romance novels. He was handsome in a way that made me want to stare and look away at the same time.

Eliseo explained that he and his family came from the Dominican Republic to Miami when he was six and that his entire family had moved to Milwaukee five years ago when his younger sister got a scholarship to Marquette University.

As Eliseo talked, Lessie stared. Her cheeks had flushed to a delicious apple red, and she kept giggling, at nothing, both obvious signs of a woman who had already entered the dangerous deep crush phase that preceded finding out if he was a ladies' man, a rebounder, or if the planets had magically aligned themselves in just the perfect order and she'd landed herself a real catch.

Once the introductions were over, Lessie and Eliseo entertained themselves by gazing deeply into each other's eyes while I stood there feeling invisible. I took a sip of my margarita and licked the salt off my lips.

The dance floor was filled with couples—black, white, Latino, Asian, young, old, clumsy, graceful, and everything in between. And they all looked happy. The brassy horns and the quick drumbeat were so irresistible that I tried a twirl, tripped, and spilled the rest of my margarita down the front of a stocky man about my height, who grabbed on to my arms to steady me.

"Oh! I'm so sorry," I said. Without thinking, I dove in, trying to mop up the damage with a napkin that shredded, leaving little clumps of white tissue sprinkled down the front of his black nylon shirt. I felt his breath on me and looked up into his face. A hot flush rushed through my body like a surge of electricity. Suddenly, everything seemed different. What was I doing with my palms on the chest of this total stranger who seemed so familiar to me? My heart was pounding inside my chest and my legs felt like jelly, but I forced myself to remove my hands from this man who I wanted to touch for the rest of the night, and I took a step backward.

"I see you've met my baby brother, the salsa teacher," said Eliseo, who'd walked up to his side holding hands with Lessie. Brother? They shared the same coloring, dark chocolate eyes and hair, and skin the shade of a medium roasted coffee laced with a generous dose of cream. But beyond that they looked nothing alike. While one was tall and lean, the other was short and stocky. And where Eliseo was dangerously handsome and unsmiling, his brother was cute with a disarmingly friendly expression. Not my usual type, so I couldn't understand why my heart was flip-flopping and beating wildly.

A waitress came up with a towel and handed it to Eliseo's brother, who nodded toward my empty margarita glass. He held his shirt out from his body with one hand while brushing it off with the towel.

"Good as new," he said with a big grin, exposing one dimple on his left cheek. Oh God, I love dimples. I had to grab both of my hands to prevent myself from reaching out to touch it. He greeted Lessie with a kiss to her cheek, and then turned to me.

"Hi, I'm Javier Lora," he said, kissing me on the cheek as well, provoking a delicious quiver to jolt through my body.

"I'm really sorry," I said to Javier, pointing to his shirt. "I'll pay for the cleaning."

Actually, I wouldn't have minded taking the shirt home and washing it by hand, but standing next to a fully clothed Javier seemed dangerous enough. I couldn't picture a shirtless Javier. Well, of course I could, but I'd better not.

Suddenly, there was altogether too much going on. The waitress appeared and handed me another margarita. It took all the self-discipline I possessed not to drink it down like a shot and ask for another.

"It's nothing," he assured me. "But you could do something for me."

A myriad of possibilities came to mind.

"Like?" I asked.

"Tell me your name," he said.

"Samantha Jacobs, but everyone calls me Sam." Oh God, I hope he doesn't notice that my hand feels like a dead trout, although this was probably wishful thinking, since Javier seemed like the kind of guy who missed very little.

"Eliseo is going to teach me some more salsa," said Lessie, as Eliseo pulled her out to the center of the dance floor. Lessie stood in front of him on the balls of her feet, about to float off the floor.

"Would you like to dance?" Javier asked.

"I'd love to, but I don't know how," I said. My heart picked up tempo again at the anticipation of his touch.

"I'll teach you," said Javier, who proceeded to demonstrate the basic salsa steps. A step back with my right foot, together in the middle for two counts, and then forward with my left foot. Sounded easy, but I wasn't getting it.

"Quick, quick, slow," he said over and over again to explain the rhythm. I felt like a circus clown on stilts, but he just kept flashing that one-dimpled smile and I responded with a giggle. I hoped he didn't think I was a blond airhead.

After twenty minutes, we took a break and stood at the bar rail running alongside the dance floor.

"How did you learn how to salsa?" I asked him, but was really wondering what it was about Javier that made me feel completely comfortable and at ease around him, despite the fact that I'd only known him for thirty minutes.

"I used to hang out at the Miami clubs from the time I was fourteen. One of the dishwashers would sneak me in the back door and I'd watch the dancers," he said.

"So you've never had a lesson?" I asked. "And you're the instructor here?"

He shrugged in a good-natured way and ran his hand through his brown hair. I couldn't believe that something that seemed as complicated as salsa dancing could be picked up by simply watching.

We went back out to practice, and I started to get it. The next thing I knew he twirled and dipped me. Wow! Looking up into his face, my heart hammering and the blood in my veins flowing like lava, I realized that salsa dancing might be contagious. Or was it Javier? Would it feel this incredible with just any man who could dance?

"So how long have you known Eliseo?" I asked Lessie later on the drive home.

"Two weeks," she said. "Lisa, who teaches pottery at my school, talked me into coming here after I'd had two martinis. Eliseo asked me to dance, and at the end of the night he asked for my phone number. We went out last weekend. And," she added barely able to contain her excitement, "he asked me out again for this Saturday night!"

I could understand her elation. After a wonderful first date, a man had actually asked her out for a second date instead of running away from her in a commitment-phobic frenzy. It almost sounded like a fairy tale.

"Younger men are definitely the way to go," she said. "The last guy I dated who was my age complained about waking up every day with a new ache or pain and talked incessantly about getting hair plugs. The one before that had to take medication for high blood pressure and couldn't get it up."

I'd never dated a younger man before. All of the significant men in my life, starting with Pierre in Paris, had been at least a few years older. But now, a few years older meant getting dangerously close to AARP cards and early-bird buffet dinners.

"How old is Eliseo?" I asked her.

"Thirty-five," she said, letting out a big happy sigh.

"That means Javier must be thirty-two," I said, doing the arithmetic. Eliseo said he was six and Javier was three when they moved to Miami from the Dominican Republic. Oh no! He's almost ten years younger. He'd never be interested in me.

When Lessie dropped me off at my apartment it was almost midnight. I took off my clothes and dropped into bed exhausted. I was too excited to fall asleep immediately. But eventually, when I did, I dreamt of being in Javier's arms, both on and off the dance floor.

Three

The Demise of Courtship, The Era of Un-Dating

By Samantha Jacobs

A close friend, let's call her Lisa, forty-two, met Kirk, thirty-nine, at a summer festival. He was tall, friendly, and shared his pretzel with her. They talked about politics, books, and music. He asked for her number and actually called three days later.

It all went downhill from there.

"We should get together sometime," said Kirk toward the end of their first telephone conversation.

Lisa readily agreed, but Kirk was unable to respond with a suggestion for where they might meet, what they might do, or even a date for a possible rendezvous. Finally, after much hemming and hawing, Kirk arranged to meet Lisa at his favorite dive bar, where he bought her a fifty-cent tap beer and then asked her to go home with him.

Another friend, Mary, forty-one, had a post–first date experience that was also troubling. She went out to dinner with a divorced businessman in his forties, father of a ten-year-old boy, owner of a two-seater airplane and a Jaguar. Mary first heard from him a week after their date.

"He e-mailed me and asked me if we were ever going out again. An e-mail. Can you believe it? I wonder if he likes women?" Mary pondered.

Indeed one would assume that a successful entrepreneur who had previously taken the vows of matrimony, procreated, and made major consumer purchases could have done a little better than sending off a flaccid e-mail that suggested nothing. I seriously doubt that Donald Trump courts women via e-mail. But perhaps Lisa and Mary should count themselves fortunate, since a far more ominous dating situation faces the typical twenty- and thirty-something woman.

When a generation Y or X man and woman do get together these days, it seems to be a joint project, patchworked together with hints and obscure references to the future. A man's initial attempt to woo a woman typically starts with an amorphous statement, such as, "I might be at ABC bar tomorrow night." Silence follows this statement and the prospect of spending time together is left floating in the telephone or computer cables until the woman responds with something more definitive, such as, "I will be at ABC bar tomorrow night. Should we meet?" But, alas, today's typical bachelor is not ready to commit to anything more serious than a tee time. Thus, he is likely to respond, "Well, then again, I might not be there. But if I do show up, maybe we could have a drink, if we happen to run into each other." Thus, a chance encounter (for it really would be a gross exaggeration to call it a date) is set.

What is going on here?

Sadly, we have entered the era of un-dating. Un-dating is characterized by nebulous, half-hearted missives suggesting some sort of activity, which are never quite explicit enough to be mistaken for an actual romantic invitation. Modern courtship has evolved into a form of tango dancing in outer space. The male partner stays on the mother ship, while the woman floats in her bulky and unflattering spacesuit, tenuously tethered to the hull of the vessel, desperately hoping to be reeled back inside, as she catches glimpses of her would-be suitor twirling and dipping himself on the bridge of the craft.

Un-dating is a frustrating and gloomy state of affairs, but I think I have the solution, based on my theory that women have forgotten what the real man of yesterday was like. A refresher course is in order. I propose a nationwide one-week marathon film festival, mandatory for all unmarried women over eighteen. I'm proposing the following films be shown, although other suggestions are welcome:

Cary Grant in North by Northwest, Richard Burton in Cleopatra, Clark Gable in Gone With the Wind, Humphrey Bogart in Casablanca and the ultimate man, Steve McQueen, in any movie. These are men that make us pant with lust. We blush just thinking of five minutes in a bedroom with them. In short, these are men who know how to pursue women and ask them out on actual dates.

I'm hopeful that after the Real Man Film Festival, single women will politely turn down our typical bachelor of the new millennium when he suggests that he and his would-be date bump into each other with all the deliberation of electrons in a cathode tube. I'm confident that with persistence, in the not-too-distant future un-dating will be undone. In time, women will recapture the era our female ancestors inhabited—an age when men gallantly fought in duels for the women they loved, a time when men buried their emotions and drank themselves to oblivion over a lost love in a faraway Casablanca nightclub, a time when men told women, "I'll call you," and actually did.

It was with zero enthusiasm and a feeling bordering on actual dread that, bright and early Tuesday morning, after an emergency jolt of two cups of organic Dark Sumatran coffee, I drove to the address of Single No More, the largest video dating service in the country. I entered a narrow two-story wood-frame building on the near west side of town. Fifteen minutes later I felt close to committing the first truly violent act of my life.

"Yes, but how much does the service cost?" I asked for the third time. Bunny Woods bounced up from her chair and leaned her manicured hands on her desk.

"We have a special price just for you if you sign up today!" she said, repeating the same response she'd given the other three times I'd asked. When I'd called yesterday with the same question, I was told that they never discuss prices over the phone. Apparently they don't discuss them in their office either.

Bunny sat down again, her big seventies, blond hair flouncing with her as she waved her arm Vanna White–like toward the video room, where I saw a barstool, a camera on a tripod, and bookshelves filled with video tapes.

"But Ms. Woods," I began, "I really need to know the price of . . ."

"Samantha, please call me Bunny. I insist," she said, flashing a saccharine smile.

Bunny's overenthusiastic personality, in contrast to the shabby surroundings, made her stand out like a Las Vegas showgirl at a wake. The tan carpeting was frayed and balding and soiled with assorted dark brown and yellow stains, the furniture had apparently been collected from cheap outlets, while the walls were covered with faded posters of arm-in-arm couples with plastic smiles against backdrops of fabulously fun and romantic sunset beach and Ferris wheel scenes.

"What kind of screening of prospective clients do you do, Bunny?" I asked her, feeling stupid calling a grown woman Bunny.

She explained that Single No More did a standard criminal background check, verified education and employment history, and if there were any doubts or discrepancies, turned those applicants away.

"I can assure you Samantha, that Single No More has only the highest quality members—well-educated professionals such as yourself."

I wondered where the rejects went? Single Forevermore? Or worse—to the online personals? I'd spent valuable minutes slashing and burning my way through twenty pages of profiles on MilwaukeeDates.com earlier in the week and had felt afterward as though I'd been accosted by a roomful of men, each with the same bad pick-up lines. I couldn't believe how many profiles mentioned the stomach-churning, "I love 'hugs' or 'cuddling' or 'sunsets.'" Who the hell doesn't? It's like saying you like breathing, food, and water. And I was highly disappointed to find that not one man had the guts to cut through the crap and share some really valuable information like, "Haven't scrubbed out bathtub for five months," or "Have 7K in credit card debt."

I'd never placed a personal ad or done the Internet dating thing myself, but how was I supposed to find the man of my dreams based on an autobiographical profile that is: a) de facto not neutral since no one, not even Buddha or Gandhi, was capable of describing themselves that way, and b) intended to conceal faults and highlight assets that probably didn't exist?

Finally, I'd tallied up the grand total of profiles that claimed to be professional, college-educated, and over thirty-seven and under fifty. That left two, both without photos posted: The first, a divorced man, 46, 6', 185, college-educated, self-described hopeless romantic who enjoys movies and dining out; the second, a never-married, 47, 5'11", nonsmoker who likes music, books, traveling, outdoor cafes, romantic evenings, and summer festivals.

I nixed Bachelor #2 immediately. Although I had to give him credit for saying he's 5'11" since most guys would just fudge it up to the nice, round, six-foot number, his profile stated that he was looking for a "possible close relationship."

As Dr. Laura says, to date an over-forty never-married man was a major red flag. I couldn't agree more. If dating a never-married guy in his thirties was like taking a short walk over a bed of hot coals, dating a never-married man over forty was the equivalent of trekking across the Mojave desert barefoot and without water. Bachelor #2, Mr. "Possible Close Relationship," was screaming through cyberspace, "I'm commitment-phobic and will never get married!" That had left Bachelor #1, whose profile I responded to two days ago.

Bunny jumped up and darted to the other side of her office, giving me whiplash.

"Before I sign up, could I see your book of photographs?" I asked Bunny. I was starting to be amused by the number of my questions and requests that she skillfully evaded. "I'd like to see what kind of men are available before I commit my time and money . . ."

"I can see that you are a smart, discerning woman," she said. Bingo! Bunny scores again.

"Can you tell me how many men are available in the age range I'm looking for?" I persisted.

Bunny looked around and lowered her voice as if she were about to impart answers to the mysteries of the universe. "If I were still single and not an employee, I'd be tempted to break the rules and dip into what I like to call *the vault*," she said, reverently stroking the cover of a thick photo album as if it were an original fifteenth-century Gutenberg Bible. "The men in here are to die for!"

I noticed that her hand was interestingly devoid of rings of any kind as she faked a swoon, brushing the back of her left hand across her brow.

"Yes, but how many . . . ?"

"I'd be shocked, shocked if your husband wasn't in here, Samantha!" she interrupted.

Bunny had her sales pitch down to a science. On the one hand, she made it sound as though if I didn't sign up at this very moment, my soul mate would surely slip through my fingers and tie the knot with a less ambivalent woman who'd had the good sense to sign up immediately, no questions asked. At the same time, Bunny implied that there were so many extraordinary men overflowing the books and videos of Single No More that I could be busy dating all of them until the end of time.

Against my better judgment, but having no choice since it was the only video dating service in Milwaukee, I mustered the minimal amount of enthusiasm necessary to convince Bunny that I wanted to sign on the dotted line and discovered that the "special price" was two thousand dollars for six months, which sounded suspiciously like the special price for everyone all of the time. I filled out the forms, claiming to have been self-employed as a freelance writer since grad school. Next came my Single No More video debut: directed by Bunny Woods, produced by Bunny Woods, and written by Bunny Woods.

First, she forced me to primp in the bathroom, and sent me back in twice to "fix my face," which as far as I could see looked fine, but then, I'd only been looking at it for forty-one years so what did I know? We practiced, doing so many takes that I lost count, until she insisted on writing out an actual script. I'm fairly certain the filming of Cecil B. DeMille's *The Ten Commandments* had taken less time to make than my Single No More video.

"You won't be disappointed. See you on Friday," said Bunny, giving me a wave, which I returned halfheartedly, like a flag signaling distress. In three days, after my background check had cleared, I could finally be initiated and allowed entry into the vault and the video room. I could hardly wait.

Four

Date Rescue

Is dating getting you down? Are the personals profiles you're responding to more fiction than fact? Have your recent rendezvous been more ordeals than orgasmic? Then contact Date Rescue! The next time you find yourself on a horrendous date just dial our toll-free number. Date Rescue will respond within minutes to your location—strip mall restaurants, budget movie cinemas, NASCAR events—wherever you may be. Our crack team of rescuers made up of former Armani models and Chippendale dancers is trained in CPR and mouth-to-mouth resuscitation. They will whisk you away and take you to our nearest safe house where you will be revived with a pep talk assuring you that Mr. Right is right around the corner.

Within a second of seeing Trevor, Bachelor #1, "Mr. Hopeless Romantic" from MilwaukeeDates.com, I knew that the hopeful flutter I'd felt just before I'd entered the bar where we were meeting would soon become a distant memory, like the after-effects of a migraine headache or a bout of botulism. In Trevor's e-mail to me, he'd said that he'd be wearing a blue shirt, and although there were three men with blue shirts, I knew him in an instant. He was the one in the bowling shirt with ivory-colored buttons shaped like bowling pins and the name *Trevor* embroidered in big white letters above his breast pocket.

I forced myself to approach him. Trevor had either sent a stand-in for our date or had mysteriously shrunk four to five inches and his weight had ballooned fifty pounds or so. His skin had the flaccid, doughy consistency of someone who has spent their entire life in a dark windowless room, only allowed out on holidays and special occasions.

I followed him to the suburban strip mall restaurant. When we were seated Trevor launched into a conversation about his job as a computer technician, relating in excruciating detail last year's near "thermo-nuclear meltdown" in accounting because doddering old Mrs. Phillips hadn't de-fragmented her computer in nine months.

"Can you believe she'd never even heard of de-fragmentation?" he asked, sitting across from me in a corner booth at a chain seafood restaurant.

"Shocking," I mumbled.

Next our conversation had moved into the area of international intrigue. Trevor believed that a group of local high school computer geeks was plotting to hack in to the new website that he'd designed for his company, Mutual of Michigan Insurance. Sounded plausible. What group of teenagers wasn't completely captivated by the insurance industry?

"Ahoy mateys, what can I get you two landlubbers for dinner?" asked the waitress in a weary voice, as if she'd been swabbing the deck for three days straight without any sleep. She had bags under her eyes and a white sailor's hat bobby pinned to her head at a jaunty angle. I couldn't help thinking that making a human being who was probably someone's mother dress and talk like Popeye the sailorman was a cruelty that should be reserved for terrorists and child molesters.

A few minutes later, when she brought our appetizer plate, Trevor made a perfect deep-sea dive onto the plate with his fork, leaning forward to shovel several hush puppies into his mouth. Trevor didn't bother with a little nicety like swallowing before speaking as he asked me the sole personal question of the evening.

"You don't watch TV?" he asked after I'd given my reply. He looked stricken, as though he'd just been harpooned.

And then, as usually happens in times of my greatest stress, I was struck by divine inspiration. What the single women of this country needed was Date Rescue. As surreptitiously as possible, I pulled my journal out of my purse and scribbled down a few notes about this idea under the table. I don't know why I was worried about hiding this, since Trevor was staring at his hush puppies with rapture.

"How long have you been divorced?" I asked Trevor during a particularly painful lull, remembering that fact as a plus in his profile.

"Oh, I've never been married," he told me while still eating. "My mom told me to say that because she thinks some girls might think I'm a loser if they find out I'm forty-six and never married." Trevor had never been to college either, but I guess those little details were extraneous in the eyes of his mother, who was no doubt eager to have her baby bird finally leave the nest after nearly half a century.

★ ★ ★

I'm on a beautiful country road in Wisconsin lined with towering one-hundred-year-old oak trees, passing white clapboard farmhouses with dilapidated red barns, and herd upon herd of black and white cows grazing peacefully in sunlit green pastures. Grabbing the reins tighter, I feel the ostrich moving smoothly between my thighs as it picks up speed to a gallop. I look over my shoulder and there they are, a pack of men and women also riding ostriches and carrying ray guns, chasing me. Just as a death ray whizzes dangerously close to my left ear, I'm lurched to the middle of an empty field where I land in a swivel chair behind a desk. The black rotary phone on the desk starts ringing, and ringing, and ringing . . .

"Hello?" I said, still 90 percent asleep. Six A.M. Oh God!

"Good morning, Samantha," Elaine said cheerfully. "Still sleeping? Or perhaps you're busy with an overnight guest?"

There was a hopeful lilt in her voice.

Yes, Elaine, I'm in the middle of amazing sex and stopped to answer the phone. "No," I said, "I was still sleeping."

"Glad to hear you're catching up on your beauty sleep. So," said Elaine, all business now, "how many dates have you had so far?"

This made me think of Trevor, whom I'd done my best to strike from my memory bank, although over time that might be impossible since he holds the record for the worst date I've ever had in my life.

"One," I admitted, blinking at the bright slivers of light sneaking in through the mini blinds that fell across the gray quilt on my bed like prison bars.

"You need to pick up the pace, my dear," said Elaine in a dry voice. "A three-hundred-pound trailer park mother with eight kids and a goiter the size of basketball could do better than that."

I'd only been in Milwaukee for four days, but if I expected Elaine to be even marginally pleased with my efforts, I was doomed to eternal disappointment.

I heard a loud *whoosh* and the machine-gun staccato of helicopter blades slowly increasing in speed.

"I don't understand what you're doing wrong," she shouted, as I held the receiver a foot away from my still-dreaming left ear. "I'm on my way to Martha's Vineyard for the weekend. Dinner with the Von Strobels. Write up your first date and make it sound good. Fax me your weekly report and article by Monday morning. And remember, the dream! We're giving our readers the dream!"

Unable to fall back asleep, I dragged myself out of bed and made a pot of strong coffee before shuffling over to my computer to type out my weekly report about applying to Single No More and the date with Trevor, an exercise that proved to be cathartic since the report only took five minutes to write. But writing an article about my date with Trevor and making it sound good would be about as easy as making an ad for septic cleaning services read like the greatest love story ever told.

After gazing at the blank computer screen, I zoned into a trance. My mind conjured a horrible apocalyptic vision that Trevor and I were holed up in an underground shelter, the last man and woman alive after a nuclear holocaust, burdened with the awesome responsibility to repopulate the earth or let our race die out. I chose death.

Another idea for my humor column sprang easily to my mind and I grabbed my journal from my purse to jot it down. I would call this column "Is Asexuality an Option?" This piece would be succinct and to the point: "No."

I drank more coffee and urged myself to get those creative mental juices flowing so I could focus on my immediate assignment. For goodness sake, surely a person armed with an undergraduate and a master's degree in literature could dredge up something positive to write about Trevor or that would at least indicate some commonality between the two of us. Many minutes of intense concentration later, I came up with the following exhaustive list:

1) Trevor has a vigorous enthusiasm for computers and deep-fried seafood;

2) Both of us are in our forties and never married; and

3) Both of us are carbon-based life-forms that breathe oxygen.

Finally, I gave up writing about Trevor and wrote an article called "The Mystery Woman's Strategies for Sifting Through Online Personals: How to Read Between the Lines," including such tips as: "When he describes himself as a 'hopeless romantic' focus on the word *hopeless* and move on to another profile."

I pressed SEND and thought, Screw it. If Elaine doesn't like this, she can send me to a city where I might actually have a chance to meet someone.

★ ★ ★

The next night I stood in my bathroom getting ready for Milwaukee date number two. Bad dates were like getting a root canal. You're stuck in a chair for two excruciating hours, and then when it's finally over with, you have nothing to show for it. I didn't know one married couple who had met through a blind date and the few cool single guys I knew, like my traveling friend Andre, would sooner take up embroidery than agree to go on one.

I had a sudden urge to slather my makeup on really thick to make myself look like a Kabuki dancer just to see the reaction of my date, whom I'd chosen from Single No More.

Services like Single No More took little away from the blindness of these dates. Yes, you saw a photograph, watched their videotape, and learned a thimbleful of "facts"—and I use the term loosely—about your date's life. But there could be any number of alarming oversights lurking behind that well-pressed suit, great job, and commitment to saving the manatees or fighting homelessness. Halitosis for example. Or worst of all, he could be an emotional midget, a man with the IQ of a snail who was incapable of thinking about anyone but himself for more than five seconds at a stretch.

I'd gone back to Single No More a few days ago after my background check had cleared. Bunny Woods had reverently led me to the vault, placed her hand upon the cover, and hesitated for a moment before launching into the most revolting cliché ever uttered by a married person to a single person.

"They say it happens when you least expect it . . ." Bunny paused as my stomach turned. ". . . but, at Single No More, we say, it happens right here, right now."

Yeah, right, whatever, Bunny. The fact was, I never expected it. I found myself in a nearly constant state of expectation-less anti-anticipatory limbo when it came to romance. It was the ultimate catch-22. Either you were expecting it, a state of mind that men could sense with their amazing radar that detected the slightest amount of interest in them, or you could project an air of indifference, which also scared them off because then they were afraid you'd turn them down. It seemed as though you couldn't win unless you found that fine line between giving them enough encouragement to ask you out and also making them think that you didn't need them at all.

Casually flipping open the Single No More album, my eyes had landed on a photo of a certain Robert Mack. Was I seeing things? Had his photo been airbrushed? Included as a cruel joke? I liked his face immediately. The intelligence and trace of sadness in his eyes suggested that he'd experienced much more than your average forty-four-year-old. His only physical flaw as far as I could see were his ears, which stuck out at an obvious angle. The poor guy had probably been taunted with "Dumbo" as a kid, but I thought they were kind of cute. As for his half a grin, it told me he could be interesting as well as dangerous. Divorced. Law degree from the University of Chicago. Runs his own business. Wow!

Bunny had searched, but couldn't find his video, for which she'd apologized, explaining that maybe it had been misfiled, and then adding with a wink that it might have been stolen.

"You're lucky he's still available," she said when I filled out the sheet officially making him one of my selections. The service would then e-mail Robert to notify him that a client was interested in meeting him. I'd hoped when he received it, he would make the effort to come into Single No More, check out my photo and video, and be interested enough to call.

Robert must have called me the day he got the e-mail, since here we were, just three days later, at a delightful Italian restaurant drinking Chianti and noodling about with our pasta and flirtatious conversation. I thanked the powers-that-be that I'd restrained myself in applying my makeup, was having a good hair day, and that my premenstrual zits had disappeared, because I found myself gazing into a set of gorgeous blue eyes framed by the impossibly long lashes that God seemed to bestow only upon the males of our species.

I could feel so much chemistry pulsating across the white tablecloth that I pinched my thigh, hard, to remind myself to slow this down. Gasoline, fire, third-degree burns!

I'd decided that my Peruvian travel fling with Wayne the entomologist, which had ended disastrously with the tearful call from his pregnant wife, should be an important wake-up call for me to stop jumping into bed with men before I really got to know them. It was clear that I'd fallen into a bad pattern: the occasional travel fling mixed with a disappointing string of monogamous relationships, all of them started by the same common denominator, lust.

Before Wayne had been another big mistake: Chuck. For some guys, cockiness seemed to be in direct proportion to the number of initials on their resumes, and Chuck, a Wall Street broker with an M.B.A. from M.I.T. was no exception. He had excelled at letting me know in a multitude of subtle and obnoxious ways that I was privileged merely to be in his presence and that that should be enough to satisfy me. How could I ever forget, for example, that little grimace he'd make whenever he pulled out his credit card (careful, Chuck, you might strain a muscle) and his complete lack of interest in the fact that I might actually have a life, which I didn't, but that wasn't the point.

I'd met him at an art gallery opening last summer. Neither of us knew a thing about art, but we'd experienced that mutual, instantaneous, visceral lust that's dangerous but incredibly alluring—akin to a pyromaniac holding a lit match directly over a puddle of gasoline. We'd dove pelvises-first into five months of blissful sex, candlelight dinners at the trendiest new restaurants, the latest Broadway shows, and after-sex Sunday brunches when we'd share the *New York Times* over endless cappuccinos.

And then, seven months ago, I'd caught Chuck sitting on the floor of my walk-in closet. It could have been one of those horrible scenes from *Harold and Maude* or *The Rocky Horror Picture Show*, except it was my life. I'd opened the door to find him staring at me with a mortified-kid-with-his-hand-caught-in-the-cookie-jar look, only it was Chuck's nose caught in the inside of my Nike. He was holding my running shoe pressed to his face like an oxygen mask with his left hand, while feeling up a pair of my black lace panties with his right. Worst of all, he had an enormous erection.

The panties I could understand, but for some reason Chuck had chosen my sweaty gym shoes over my Stuart Weitzman slingbacks. Obviously, the man had no class.

I had known it was time for a change, but that was easier said than done when you were not two feet away from a gorgeous, sexy man like Robert. I'd much rather fall for a nice guy, but they were usually about as exciting as a case of foot fungus.

I caught Robert's eye and felt a momentary flutter. I gave myself another pinch. No, Samantha! No more jump starts after David the ex-fiancé who dumped you after a brush with death, Chuck the man with the shoe fetish, and Wayne the wandering two-timing entomologist.

But then again, surely there was something more substantial going on here than mere chemistry. After all, both Robert and I hated jazz, loved garlic, and preferred mindless action movies to artsy films. Not that any of these things were necessarily the basis for a long-term relationship, but they couldn't hurt, right?

Normally the heavy stuff doesn't come out on a first date,

but I took it as yet another good sign that this time it had. Surely after discovering we shared so many essential values, it was natural for the conversation to turn serious. He didn't ease into it; his approach was more in line with, "Lovely weather we're having, I really should clean out the gutters tomorrow, and by the way, I have terminal cancer"—all in one breath.

"I'm a widower," he said simply. His wife, Sarah, had been only thirty-three when she'd died in a car accident while driving to meet Robert for their third wedding anniversary dinner celebration.

As if reading my mind, Robert quickly apologized for saying that he was divorced in his Single No More bio.

"Now that I've been around the block a few times with these dating services," he explained, "I've learned that 'widower' is a magnet for the savior-types, or worse, the ones who mix up maternal instincts with healthy sympathy and then want to mother me to death."

I refrained, with considerable difficulty, from assuring him that there was no danger of me mothering him, since I couldn't stop my mind from leaping to the conclusion that, so far, at least, he'd make the perfect husband. I had no doubt that both my mother and Elaine Daniels would give Robert an immediate stamp of approval. Damn this intense chemistry that was doing its best to suppress that little voice in my head that said for every one lie uncovered, there were a dozen and one others that I didn't know about, yet.

Robert went on to explain that after earning a law degree from the University of Chicago when he was twenty-nine, he'd met Sarah a year later in Milwaukee. He'd opened up a one-man general practice law firm here, which he'd sold after she'd died five years ago. Both his parents had died when he was a kid, he had no siblings, and the grandparents who'd raised him were also gone.

"After Sarah died, I fell apart for a while and didn't do anything. Then three years ago I saw an opportunity to invest in a recruiting firm," he said. "I needed a change so I did it."

Why couldn't I make myself stop thinking about kissing this guy? And shouldn't I feel guilty for thinking about making out with him when he was in the middle of telling me about his dead family?

"But enough about me," he said, reaching across the table for my hand. I felt a thrill run through my body. "I want to hear all about you, and I hope you will forgive me for getting morose and agree to see me again."

I told him a bit about my travels and then felt the need to delve into some of the serious stuff in my own past since Robert had shared so much with me. Thankfully, I was able to avoid altogether the topic of my real mission in Milwaukee and my job in New York.

"You seem too good to be true," he said out of left field during a pause in the conversation.

I didn't think I'd told him much of anything that would qualify for a statement like that. I looked into his eyes. He seemed sincere, but I managed to keep myself from reciprocating the compliment because my common sense kept shouting, "Why would a guy this great ever need to join a dating service?"

When Robert dropped me off at my apartment, he didn't try to finagle an invitation to come inside. One gallant kiss to my hand, another on my cheek, and he was gone, leaving me wanting more. Was Bunny Woods right after all, that Single No More was a bastion of wonderful single men?

* * *

Early the next morning I sprinted to a bookstore for coffee and a copy of the June 10 issue of *Très Chic*. There it was on the cover, "Mystery Woman Goes on Her First Date." The article, together with my byline "The Mystery Woman" was right there on page thirty-eight, between an ad for the ultimate antiwrinkle cream and another for a magic potion claiming to reduce cellulite by 70 percent:

If someone had told me a year ago that I could meet a handsome, interesting single man through the online personals, I wouldn't have believed it. But that's exactly how I met my first date in the Mystery City.

My date, I'll call him Paulo, a computer whiz and affluent entrepreneur, took me to an elegant restaurant where our conversation sparkled over a bottle of sparkling wine and candlelight . . .

I stopped reading. I couldn't believe Elaine had done this. Thousands of our 900,000 readers were probably causing computer crashes on personals websites across the country at this very moment in a rush to place profiles, all to meet men like Trevor. What in the world had I gotten myself into?

Leaning my head against the magazine rack, I mumbled a prayer to the divine powers-that-be, "Please deliver me from this never-ending singles hell." The woman standing next to me flashed me a worried look and scurried away.

Five

Dipping Addict

WARNING: Salsa Dancing may involve dipping, a highly addictive dance maneuver known to create feelings of euphoria, an artificially enhanced sense of self, delusions of grandeur, and extreme impairment of mental reasoning capabilities. For your own safety, please limit the number of dips per dance to one. Club Cubana will not be held responsible for any dancer exceeding five dips per evening.

Lessie and I were going to Club Cubana tonight after attending a Brewers' baseball game, one of the events on my boss Elaine's summer schedule. I couldn't wait to see Javier! Just the thought of being with him tonight made me nervous and excited. But I'd also been hoping he would dip me again! I couldn't get him or that dip out of my mind. Really, clubs should have warnings posted.

Since I had a few hours to kill before meeting Lessie, I decided to take a walk along Lake Michigan, which I'd only seen from the eighteenth-floor patio of my apartment. Fifteen minutes later, I was walking out onto Bradford Beach. Two bored lifeguards in red suits perched high above me, their megaphones hanging unused on the sides of their chairs. No one was in the water, but a dozen sun worshippers were scattered about, soaking up the early June rays on beach towels and lawn chairs. The sand felt cool and moist on my feet as I kicked off my sandals and walked to the water's edge.

Elaine's executive assistant, Sally, who had an aunt and uncle who lived in Wisconsin, had mentioned a couple weeks ago that one of Milwaukee's best features was its lakefront. My response had been, "It's on a lake? What lake?" picturing one of the small lakes that dotted northern New York where you could swim from one end to the other without getting winded. Lake Michigan looked as vast as an ocean. I stuck my big toe in and pulled it right back out.

"It doesn't warm up until August."

Turning to the voice, I saw a tanned face, primary blue-colored eyes, and a body that looked like a Michelangelo sculpture come to life.

"Hi, I'm Zack," he said, holding out his hand.

Men this good-looking shouldn't be allowed to roam free. They should be on display in special stores with viewings by appointment only. I tore my eyes away from his face to do the oh-so-subtle left ring finger reconnaissance. No wedding ring and no tan line. Wow, things were suddenly looking up in . . . Where was I again? Oh yeah, Milwaukee.

"No, I'm not married," he said.

Whenever I'm embarrassed, my knees, chest, and face, in that order, turn a lollipop red that gives most people the impression that I'm having a seizure that requires emergency medical attention.

Zack and I spent the next hour and a half together, the conversation flowing effortlessly as we walked along the beach and eventually meandered over to a picnic table under a big oak tree. It was perfect. He was perfect. We were perfect.

Except for one thing.

"Why didn't he ask for my number?" I asked Lessie later. The two of us were seated in prime second-row seats behind the Brewers' dugout at Miller Park stadium—seventy-fifty dollars a pop, compliments of *Très Chic.*

Taking a big unladylike swig of a Milwaukee brew, I wiped my mouth with the back of my hand. Okay, I was feeling sorry for myself. I couldn't help but picture my inevitable fate: a hardened woman who hung out in dark, smoky bars, drinking bourbon or scotch and chain smoking Marlboros, hoping some man, any man, would buy me a drink and take me home for the night.

"His good-bye hung in the air until it was sucked out to sea, across the waves, never to be heard again," I continued, knowing I'd lapsed into one of my ridiculous moods.

Lessie sighed and crossed her arms. "Why didn't you just offer him your number or—here's a crazy idea—ask for his?"

"Have you lost your mind?" I demanded. "Let me say just six words: *He's Just Not That Into You.*"

"Don't tell me you're one of those women," groaned Lessie, as she slapped her hands on her thighs. Lessie's baseball game attire, a red sleeveless T-shirt and ultra-short blue jean shorts did double duty, showing off every muscle in her toned arms and thighs. "You don't see men reading self-help books about how to catch a woman or how to know when a woman isn't interested."

"That's because they don't have to!" I argued. "They're the ones doing all the pursuing, or at least they should be. It may be the twenty-first century, but men still want to club women over our heads, drag us into their caves, and have their way with us."

"What kind of guys were you dating in New York?" asked Lessie with a sideways glance.

"Well, come to think of it, the last few liked to beat on their chests, swing from vines, and had foreheads like Cro-Magnon men."

I took a bite of the first bratwurst of my life. Not bad. Not as greasy as an Italian sausage and much better than a hotdog.

"My philosophy is, if a woman meets a man she likes, she should go after him," said Lessie. "I don't agree that there are rules about who can pursue whom. It's just a load of crap."

"Crap! Crap? How can you say they're crap?" I cried. The woman seated in front of me turned, glared, and tipped her head in the direction of her son, apparently warning me to watch my language. The kid looked about fifteen and probably had a better sex life than I did. Then again, at the moment, sea slugs had a better sex life than I did.

"Are you sure the guy on the beach was flirting with you?" asked Lessie. "Maybe he was just being friendly? Remember, you're not in New York anymore."

"He held hands with me," I told her, "and then he did that thing where he looked into my eyes and brushed the hair from my forehead with his index finger, and he told me he thought I was beautiful."

"That's serious below-the-belt flirting," Lessie agreed with a nod. Just then, I heard the sharp *thwack* of the bat hitting a ball, which was caught on a fly by an outfielder. The Brewers' second baseman had just struck out for the third time. The sixth inning was over.

Then I saw something strange, something very strange indeed. Four giant sausages emerged from a gate at the far end of third base line, their elfin arms waving at the crowd, which cheered wildly and rose to its feet. My bratwurst had come to life in the form of a giant lumbering foam casing that had sprouted human legs and arms.

"It's time for the sausage race," said Lessie, grabbing my forearm and pulling me up. For the next few minutes we cheered and shouted as the giant wieners with tiny legs careened around the baseline for a thirty-second marathon rounding home plate and finishing directly in front of us. The Brat crossed the finish line by a casing, just in front of the Italian.

We sat back down to continue our in-depth analysis of the situation, a situation, I might point out, that was completely hopeless since I was never going to see Zack again. If men only knew how much time women spent analyzing them, their gonads would shrivel, and they'd all move to cabins in the woods, swear a life of celibacy, and write self-help books for men.

"Maybe he was married?" Lessie suggested.

"Definitely not," I told her. And then, suddenly, I wasn't so sure. Thanks to Wayne the bug man, I now know that if a man tells you he's not married, he may be single, but that could be only on a part-time basis, strictly in his fantasies and while geographically estranged from his wife.

"Cops don't wear rings," Lessie suggested. "I've dated a couple. One turned out to be married but he justified it because he said fifty percent of them cheat on their wives. So I guess that made it okay that he did it too."

"Zack said he was a pilot for Midwest Express," I said.

"He could tell you he is the heir to the Miller brewery fortune. How the hell would you ever know?"

"When did you become so cynical?" I asked, and looking closer saw that Lessie's eyes had become all watery. "Is everything all right with you and Eliseo?"

"He hasn't called," she said sadly.

How many times a day are those three words uttered by women across the planet? A trillion? I used to think getting rid of your telephone would solve the problem until a friend of mine who'd volunteered for the Peace Corps in Africa a few years ago told me that no one there had telephones, which meant that her prospective dates would promise her they were going to stop by her house and then just not show up. I remember being devastated to learn that it wasn't just North American men that promised an "I'll call you" and didn't deliver; it was universal, maybe even genetic?

"You saw Eliseo two nights ago, you have a date with him this Saturday, and you're going to see him in a couple hours," I reminded her.

"Maybe he's met someone else?" she said, looking really worried, and I could certainly sympathize. I did the same thing when it came to men I liked. The worst-case scenario leapt instantly to mind. If he didn't call, he'd either become engaged or eloped in the twenty-four hours since I'd last seen him.

"That's impossible," I said confidently, knowing of course that when it came to relationships, *nothing* was impossible. But that's what I would want Lessie to tell me if I were in her situation.

"But they're not like us! They don't have emotions!" Lessie put her palms over her face, leaned her head back, and groaned. "Why do we even want men? They just drive us insane!"

✳ ✳ ✳

Two hours later, Lessie and Eliseo were standing smashed up against the balcony of Cubana's patio, sneaking the occasional kiss mixed with long minutes spent gazing into each other's eyes like two war-torn lovers finally reunited after continents and decades spent apart. A troupe of naked circus performers could have waltzed by and I doubt they'd have noticed.

I couldn't help but feel a twinge of jealousy. This could be Zack and me, except that clearly Zack was a cad with no qualms about using his Adonislike magnetism to lure women into lusting after him, and then sadistically cutting them loose, leaving them frothing at the mouth, mere helpless puddles of goo.

"It's too bad they don't like each other."

I turned and saw Javier behind me. I thought I might have imagined my visceral response to Javier from the other night, but once again, just the sight of him sent my heart into overdrive. He nodded in the direction of Lessie and Eliseo.

"Yeah, they would've made such a nice couple," I said smiling.

Javier kissed me on the cheek and then paused, lowering his face to my neck for a second before straightening up. During that second, which seemed to last an hour, I willed him to kiss my neck; I could feel his lips caressing my . . .

"What perfume are you wearing? Wait, let me guess." He grabbed my right hand, and led me out to the dance floor. "Obsession, right?"

"Are you an expert on women's fragrances as well as an expert salsa instructor?" I asked him, feeling my legs going weak.

"In this line of work, I'm forced to smell the necks of a lot of beautiful women," he said, adopting a serious look.

"Sounds terrible," I said, assuming an expression of deep concern. "How do you manage?"

"I'm not sure," he told me. "Some days I think about getting a more pleasant job—exterminating cockroaches, cleaning urinals at the Greyhound bus station, making deliveries to toxic waste dumps. But I guess a sense of duty keeps me here. It's a rough job, but somebody's got to do it."

I'd only been in Milwaukee a short time and had already found myself intensely attracted to two men (three if you counted Zack). But being with Javier felt so different than my date with Robert. Everything was lighter, easier, and more fun. And then there was Javier's dimple. I can't explain my utter infatuation with dimples. It's like asking someone why he or she loves chocolate—they just do. For me it was dimples. And chocolate. But alas, it was my fate thus far in life that I'd never even kissed a be-dimpled man.

We started dancing. Actually, Javier started dancing while I flailed about like a puppy sprinting across a newly waxed floor, co-ordination not being one of my strong points. This could explain why I was chosen last or next to last for every team sport in school. It was either me or Naomi Hertsgaard, a girl with Coke-bottle eyeglasses who was so uncoordinated and spindly she looked like an octopus on roller skates when she walked across a room.

Javier suggested as tactfully as possible that my steps needed to be smoother, my arms were too stiff, and my torso was angled too far forward. Then there was my footwork—going north with the right when I should've been going south with the left. Or perhaps it was east and west?

But I admired Javier's patience as he went over the basic steps again and again, until I finally started to get the hang of it. I advanced to a double twirl and when he dipped me and held me there for a moment, I felt like Vivian Leigh gazing into the face of Clark Gable in *Gone With the Wind*. As he held me, bent backward in his arms, our eyes locked together. I felt myself falling into his deep brown eyes, which radiated so much warmth they could melt a glacier. I wanted to run my fingers through his straight black hair and kiss his perfect mouth. I wanted to . . . do dips normally last this long?

Slowly straightening up with me still snug in his arms, Javier suggested that we take a break. Excellent idea. I wondered if he could feel the heat my body was generating. I was so hot, I felt almost feverish. We wandered over to the balcony where a tall Latino man was talking with Lessie and Eliseo.

"Sam, this is my good friend Sebastian Diaz," Javier said, giving the stranger a quick manly slap on the back. Sebastian stood a head taller than Javier and it was clear from his thick neck, bulging biceps, and thigh muscles that could barely be contained by mere synthetic fibers, that he spent a lot of time in the gym. But he'd managed to package all of it into classy casual attire, a sky blue oxford shirt tucked neatly into a belted pair of black pleated trousers.

"So, Sam, Lessie tells me you're from New York," Sebastian said. "What are you doing in Milwaukee for the summer?"

It wasn't just the intensity of Sebastian's gaze that unnerved me, along with the fact that he could have crushed my skull with a flick of his pinky finger, it was the sudden realization of the fact that I hadn't given a single thought as to what my Milwaukee cover would be.

"I'm a researcher," I blurted, after what I hoped no one would notice was an extraordinarily long pause. But, it was unfortunate that at that exact same moment Lessie announced I was a writer.

"Well I'm a researcher-writer," I explained. "I do both, but really more researching than writing."

"What exactly do you research and write about?" Sebastian asked, standing head and shoulders above the rest of us with his arms crossed in front of his body like the Jolly Green Giant.

"Men," Lessie announced.

"—opause. Menopause," I said without skipping a beat.

"And menstruation," offered Lessie, who'd dragged the word out to its four syllables so there could be no possible misunderstanding.

The word fell like an anvil. A painstaking silence followed as the men took a rapt interest in the shuffling of their feet.

After a break in conversation that had stretched into an eternity, I said, in an attempt to undo the damage caused by Lessie's proclivity for literary license, "I work for a women's health research institute that's doing a study on women in the Midwest. They sent me here for the summer to do, um, research and writing and you know, research and . . ."

The lies bubbled up from some inner murky depths of my soul like crude oil from the ground. This was wonderful. Now I'd have another skill to add to my resume: pathological liar.

Lessie cut in, brightly suggesting we all go out to dance. Sebastian, polite to a fault, excused himself, while giving me a piercing look that I swear said, "I see right through you, I know you're lying, and you know you're lying. But why?"

"Shit, I'm so sorry," said Lessie later on during the drive home.

"It's my fault," I told her. "I should've known this would come up. But at least you stopped the inquisition with 'menstru-a-tion.' "

The questions from Sebastian weren't the real problem. It bothered me that Javier's friend had apparently decided not to like me for some reason. I just hoped that Javier was the kind of man who made up his own mind about people.

Six

The Mammary Mirage

Men are fascinated with women's breasts. Women are fascinated by the fact that men are obsessed with lumps of flesh that are little more than fat and milk ducts. According to Freud, it all starts in infancy, but with males, the enthrallment with the mammary glands never stops. This, as it turns out, is a good thing. The only mystery is, why the hell did it take me until I was forty years old to exploit this male weakness?

Forever caught between the respectable but boring B cup and the not-quite-attention-getting C cup, I'd always felt lacking in the bosom department. And then one day last year while shopping in the lingerie department of my favorite store, I came across the amazing water bra. I lifted it off the rack. It had weight and substance and it was on sale for $39.

I wasn't expecting much when I tried it on, but I was completely transformed—Pamela Anderson, Jayne Mansfield, and all of the Dallas Cowboy cheerleaders rolled into one! I couldn't stop staring at my own chest. They were huge, beautiful, perfectly shaped, up-lifted, separated, and I could actually claim to have décolletage! I was now a C+, bordering on a D-, well within the realm of lust-provoking cup size. And all this in just the first five minutes of my new life inside the dressing room!

When I walked out of the store, for the first time in my life men were staring at my breasts. I haven't had so many men look at my chest since, well, ever. Now they don't even pretend to be looking into my eyes with the furtive glance downward that they try to disguise with an innocent glance. They speak directly to my bust as if it's a separate person deserving of its own e-mail address and Social Security number.

In this day and age of air bras, water bras, gel bras, and breast implants, it's hard to believe that in our not-too-distant past, the sixties icon Twiggy popularized the flat-chested look. But it's simply no longer fashionable to be without a bosom, and not just in L.A. This is true even in Milwaukee, Wisconsin, land of beer, brats, and now, boobs.

Of course some might argue that water bras are disingenuous, that they lure men on false pretenses. But this reasoning just doesn't hold water. First, are breast implants any less dishonest? They don't feel real and they certainly don't look like natural breasts. I have nothing against implants, but for a fraction of the cost and in just a few seconds, why not give yourself an instant boob job with the water bra?

Like my natural breasts, water bras are not perfect. There's the infamous Will & Grace episode where Grace's water bra springs a leak on a date at a very public gallery opening, an embarrassing situation to be sure but a chance I was willing to take. I assumed that in the unlikely event this ever happened, it would be worth the story value alone in exchange for the humiliation involved.

But I discovered a far more vexing problem when I found myself on a date with a man I liked very much. At the end of fabulous date number two, Seth and I were slow dancing together in my living room. He was holding me close, when after many minutes of kissing and dancing, I happened to look down and discovered he'd been caressing my breasts but I hadn't felt a thing because I was wearing a water bra. I felt like my best friend had gone to Maui and all I got was this lousy brassiere. Since I'd had no clue how long he'd been stealing second base without my knowledge, I couldn't very well start moaning with pleasure at that point. So I'd kept quiet, figuring that it was better to let him think I was frigid rather than psychotic.

Despite the potential problems with water bras, I will never go back to the standard model. Not only do I feel better about myself while wearing one, I've learned that if you make them bigger, men will come. So get breast implants, buy a water bra, an air bra, or a bustier, just don't remind men what breasts are really made of.

I woke to one of those gorgeous June days that reminds you of the summers of your childhood when every day was picture perfect. I couldn't recall a single cloud, thunderstorm, or chilly or sweltering summer day when I was a kid, because like most adults I knew, meteorological amnesia had set in long ago.

Lessie plunked a tray with her special homemade batch of margaritas onto her patio table. We were outside her two-bedroom brick ranch on her backyard deck. A young couple walked by pushing a baby stroller with a bald baby. They waved to Lessie and she waved back.

"So how was blind date number three?" Lessie asked, referring to yesterday's dating debacle, which Sally had set up through Brunches or Lunches, a service designed for "busy professionals" to meet two new people a month for—you guessed it—brunch or lunch. The name of the service was revoltingly cutesy, but the beauty of it was obvious. Lunches and brunches were a far more reasonable time commitment than dinner and a movie. If worse came to worst, at least no one would have to feel as though they'd been trapped in an eternal dating time warp.

Which it did.

"Not worth talking about," I said, visualizing Will, a man with a pointed face reminiscent of an anteater. The high point of the date was when he'd crossed his arms in front of his body and started scratching under both armpits simultaneously.

"I almost forgot," Lessie said, unfolding what appeared to be computer printouts. "I surfed the Internet this morning. You're famous."

I found myself scanning headlines from newspaper articles across the country: "Is the Mystery Woman Living in Our City?" "Are There Any Single Men Left: Can the Mystery Woman Do It?" "Mystery Woman Battles Cupid in Fight for Rare Species!" "Welcome to Topeka, Mystery Woman. Your Mr. Right Is Right Here."

A couple holding hands and walking a German shepherd strolled by, the father carrying a tow-headed toddler on his shoulders.

Most of the printouts were short filler-type articles, covering the basics about my assignment. Then I came to the last one.

"Oh no! Did you read this?" I cried, feeling as though I'd been punched in the stomach. "Listen to this, Lessie," I said, and then read aloud, "'What could explain the Mystery Woman's unmarried status: a personality disorder, a glandular problem, or is she just a man-hater?'"

Lessie snatched the paper out of my hand. "I shouldn't have printed that one," she said. "Sorry."

"The people of Bogalusa, Mississippi, think I have a gland problem! They despise me!"

"They don't despise you, they just feel sorry for you. Here," she said, handing me a computer printout from Newsday.com. "This will make you feel better."

Well-known socialite and CEO of *Très Chic* magazine, Elaine Daniels, has sent a forty-something never-married professional woman, better known as "The Mystery Woman," on a quixotic quest for a husband to a city unknown. Daniels, who is better known for her captivating wit, business savvy, and her own frequent trips to the altar, rather than in her new role as yenta, is no doubt hoping to boost lagging magazine sales with a publicity stunt that rivals the new breed of reality TV shows such as *Joe Millionaire, The Bachelorette,* and *Bachelorettes in Alaska.* Whether the Mystery Woman will succeed certainly is a mystery. But her fishing expedition has captured the interest of single women across the nation, who are pinning their hopes on her success and cheering her on.

The phrases *fishing expedition* and *quixotic quest* bothered me. It wasn't like I was searching for the lost island of Atlantis. Single men were everywhere, right? Just then I noticed a heavily pregnant woman and her husband ambling by, trying to keep up with two identical twin girls on tricycles, all of them smiling and laughing like they were the Von Trapp family.

"Is everyone in your neighborhood married?" I asked Lessie, becoming concerned that every time I went out in this city, all I seemed to come across were couples.

"I believe I am the token single woman," Lessie admitted and then ran her fingers through her short hair.

"Well, at least you've got a hot date tonight," I said, trying not to sound envious. But I couldn't help it. It had been four days since I'd gone out with Robert Mack, and I hadn't heard from him. And I'd been hoping that Javier would ask me out despite our age difference.

Lessie looked at her watch. "Yeah, I have three hours to buy a new outfit, get a manicure and pedicure, shave my legs, and get a boob job," she said.

"A boob job? You're not serious?"

"When I lost all my weight they went from double Cs to microscopic," she said, cupping her hands over her chest. "They look like peas." She peered inside her V-necked sweater, and frowned. "No, peas are too big, more like grains of sand."

Très Chic had done a story on breast implants a few months ago. So many women were getting them now that pretty soon the real thing would become as rare as raw hamburger. In the not-too-distant future, museums would have displays of A and B cup bras, right next to the Tyrannosaurus Rex skeletons and the mummies.

Why did so many truly beautiful women like Lessie think they were less than perfect just because they didn't look like Barbie dolls? I assured Lessie that she didn't need to change a thing about her appearance since most women would gnaw off their right arms to look as good as she.

"Have you tried water bras?" I asked her.

"No. Why?"

I told Lessie about my discovery last year of water bras and how they'd changed my life, along with the story of the problem with water bras that I'd discovered on my second date with Seth, the architect who I'd dumped last New Year's Eve.

"That's hysterical. You should make that one of your humor columns," said Lessie. Excellent idea!

"Now before I leave, one piece of unsolicited advice: no lace and no thongs for tonight."

"I'm not going to sleep with Eliseo," she said, looking as confident as a vase of wilted daisies. "It's only our second date."

We've all heard the stories, more like urban legends really, of women who jump into bed on the first or second date with highly eligible studs whom they later marry. But these events were exceptional, infrequent phenomena, like seeing Halley's Comet or finding the long-lost Dead Sea Scrolls. I just hoped that Lessie was being careful and wouldn't get hurt.

As I drove back toward my apartment, I thought briefly about stopping off at Bradford Beach to see if Zack was there, before deciding that even if he was, I had no interest in becoming one of his beach concubines. Who needs you Mr. Best Looking Man in the Universe? You had your chance.

I collapsed on the lawn chair on my balcony, falling asleep to the sound of motorboats and wave runners racing across Lake Michigan.

I'm seated on the back of a wave runner wearing a fluffy wedding dress that looks like a French pastry as my veil trails out behind us, floating inches above the blue water. I grip my fiancé fiercely around his trim middle. Great giant waves periodically wash over us, hitting me full in the face, causing thick black streaks of mascara to run down my cheeks and smearing my lipstick grotesquely, so that I look like one of those sad clowns that frighten children. My fiancé is wearing a black tuxedo, but I'm distressed that I can't see his face. I shout into his ear three times, "What's your name?" But he doesn't answer. The minister riding parallel to us drops his Bible in the water. I keep shouting to him, "Is it time to say 'I do' yet?" But my words die on my lips.

"I must've been temporarily deranged to agree to do this assignment," I said to Elizabeth, whom I called as soon as I'd woken up from my matrimonial nightmare. "I had more fun at my first mammogram last year."

That was almost true. In fact, I'd practically pulled my completely unrecognizable breast out of the machine because I'd been laughing so hard. The nurse had given me a strange look and then told me that most women were writhing in pain during the procedure. But I couldn't help it. To me, my flattened breast had looked exactly like a pancake with a nipple.

"Have the dates been that bad?" Elizabeth asked.

"That's a rhetorical question, right?"

"Sam, you're getting paid to find a husband," pointed out my ever-practical lawyer friend. "My advice is suck it up and just do it!"

"I'm trying to decide if you sound more like my mother or a Nike commercial," I said.

"What have you got to lose?"

"Frankly, I'm not feeling exactly positive and upbeat at the moment," I told her. "I've met two guys I like. One never bothered to ask for my number." I paused just long enough to conjure up a wistful memory of Zack. "And the other hasn't called," I added, referring to Robert Mack. For some reason I wasn't prepared to tell Elizabeth about Javier yet—not that there was anything to tell since he hadn't even asked me out.

"So call him," she said. It was just like Elizabeth to make everything sound so simple. Never one to play games, she had always told men exactly how she felt about them, taking the approach opposite to mine. But the best method for dealing with men must lie somewhere in the middle, since we were both still single at forty-one.

"Are you crazy?" I retorted and then countered with several of the salient passages I'd memorized from *Men Are from Mars, Women Are from Venus.* "If I call him and he's being a blow-torch, he might turn himself off. Or maybe he's a barely flickering candle that I'll surely snuff out by showing the slightest amount of interest in him!"

"Sam, I've been telling you for years to forget about that book. Men and women are both human and are both from earth," said Elizabeth patiently.

"But what if he's being a rubber band while hiding in his cave?" I demanded, pacing around my apartment with the cordless phone hot against my right ear. My emotions began spiraling into a tropical storm, well on their way to hurricane level, as usually happened when I engaged in the entirely futile gesture of trying to figure men out.

"Every time we turn around they're turning into a different inanimate object!" I said. "How are we ever supposed to know what the hell they're thinking?"

"Sam, I'd love to debate this longer but I have a date to get ready for," Elizabeth said.

"Really! With who?" I asked her.

This was music to my ears. Elizabeth was in an even worse dating drought than I had been in before leaving New York. During the past six months she'd had exactly half a date—so called not because the date had been extraordinarily short, but because he had thought it was a date and she hadn't. She'd told Stan, another partner at her law firm, numerous times that she thought of him like an older brother. But that hadn't stopped Stan from making the tongue lunge when he'd dropped her off after they'd gone out for a movie last month. Elizabeth, who normally doesn't fluster easily, described the moment as traumatic.

"One minute we were talking about an employee tort case I'm handling, the next he thrust his tongue inside my mouth, just like that! With no warning! It was like he was planting his flag or marking his tree!"

I myself have perfected the art of the cab-dive. Given the slightest hint that a man I'm not interested in was planning the big good-night kiss, I turned into Miss Stunt Double, ready to dive out of the moving cab and roll, if necessary.

"I'm going out with that judge I've had a crush on for my entire legal career," she told me with obvious glee.

"The one that wins surfing contests in Hawaii?"

"That's the one. Surfin' Judge Doug is finally riding the waves of divorce," she said. "I just hope I'm not the transition woman."

I wished Elizabeth well and said good-bye.

After I hung up, I stood with my arms crossed, glaring at the telephone, willing it to disappear so that I wouldn't have to decide what to do with it. I got knots in my stomach just thinking about breaking the rules and calling Robert. The last time I'd called a guy I liked after a first date, he'd been so traumatized by the idea of a woman pursuing him that I think he got plastic surgery and moved to Bolivia.

Dialing Robert's number was like having an out of-body experience. I felt as though I were lobotomizing that part of my brain that had been conditioned to believe that chasing a man was wrong, the mortal sin of dating.

His phone began ringing. What if he answered? What if he didn't? Should I leave a message or just hang up? No, I couldn't

do that because of *69 and caller ID. Shit, why hadn't I thought
to block my call with *67? I hated modern technology for having stolen the last vestiges of mystery out of romance! If I got his
answering machine, what in the world . . .

"Hello?" said a voice that sounded like it was coming from
the far end of a long tunnel.

"Hi, Robert?" I said in a disgustingly cheery voice. God, I
sounded just like Bunny Woods. "It's Sam, Samantha Jacobs."

A long, horrible pause followed. "From Single No More?" I
croaked.

He doesn't remember me because I made no impression on
him at all. He's probably dating a hundred women. As the pause
stretched into infinity, my self-esteem plummeted to that of a
dust mite.

"Sam, it's wonderful to hear from you," he said finally.
"You'll have to forgive me. I was taking a nap, and I just had the
weirdest dream."

"I did too!" Damn! The words were out of my mouth before
I'd thought about it.

"Really? What was yours about?" he asked.

"Um, well, there were wave runners, waves, lots of water,
more waves, I couldn't see very much because my mascara was
running, and . . ."

My voice trailed off as I considered wrapping the telephone
cord around my neck. Unfortunately it was cordless.

"Hmm," he said in a serious tone, "Freud would say this is a
definite sign you should switch to waterproof mascara."

Half asleep and still manages to be funny. Impressive.

"I'm so glad you called me," he went on, "and that you're not
one of those *Rules* women. I love it when a woman calls me."

"You do?"

"Sure, men need a little reassurance now and then. I think a woman who never calls a man is just playing games."

Other than the rare exception I'd just made for him, Robert had just described me to a T.

"Oh, yeah, I've heard of women like that. Game players," I said with a nervous chuckle.

"Exactly. I hate playing games, don't you?"

Yes. But at least this time I was getting paid for it.

"Absolutely," I bluffed. "Especially at our age, we should be long past that."

"I was going to call you later today. I thought since you're new to Milwaukee I could give you a little tour? Are you up for some kitschy sightseeing?"

My stomach flipped into fifth gear. A Saturday night date with a man I really liked! Luckily, it was like riding a bike.

Ninety minutes later I found myself in a cave sixty feet below the ground. The walls and floor were lined with quarry stone and three gothic chandeliers hung from the ceiling. It was the perfect horror movie set for the obligatory dining room scene where the guests find out that they're trapped in the castle and slowly disappearing one by one.

The air was ten degrees cooler down there than outside. I felt a chill and shivered. Robert slipped his arm around my shoulder just as though he'd done it a hundred times before. His arm settled around me like a warm sweater on a cool fall day.

"I don't know about you, Stacy, but it doesn't look to me like they want any beer," said one of our guides, a short blond woman standing at the top of the stairs.

"I think you're right, Penny, this is definitely not a drinking crowd," Stacy replied, in a dead monotone.

"Does anyone know what time it is?" asked Penny, pointing to her watch, at which point everyone in the room but me shouted, "It's Miller time!"

We shuffled out of the cave into a mini beer hall where my guidebook predictions almost came true. There was no lederhosen or dancing, but men and women of all shapes and sizes were doing their best to swill shot-sized glasses of complimentary beer.

"Am I the only person you know in Milwaukee?" Robert asked.

I told him about Lessie and a little about our days at Brown University.

"Now, I think it's your turn to tell me about your dream," I said to Robert after a plump waitress had dropped off two more mini beer steins at our table.

Robert gave a sly smile and a barely noticeable shake of his head.

"Not fair," I said with a laugh. "I exposed my unconscious to you and now you won't reciprocate?"

"The truth is," he said, and then leaned forward, crossing his arms on the table, "I have a lot of skeletons in my closet."

My stomach lurched. Handsome and charming he might be, but I could be with a murderer for all I knew. The criminal background checks that Single No More did were wonderful, provided the criminal had been caught before. And Wisconsin seemed to have more than its fair share of serial killers. There was that guy who made lamp shades out of people's skin in the fifties and who could forget Jeffrey Dahmer? Robert laughed just as I had begun to picture my flesh dissolving in a vat of acid.

"Bad joke," he said with a smile and then touched my arm. "I'm a headhunter, remember?"

Why was I so nervous around him? It wasn't the chemistry.

What was it? There was something about Robert I couldn't quite put my finger on, but he gave me a slightly uneasy feeling. Of course, it might be because I could no longer trust my feelings after David, who had felt so right in every way. Maybe to avoid getting hurt I was overcompensating and now going to the opposite extreme by trying to find something I didn't like with a guy who was exactly right for me?

After we finished our beers, Robert drove us to the botanical rose gardens. In the car we talked about our jobs. I was as vague as possible with my cover occupation—the menstruation/menopause researcher-writer for the mysterious New York institute. Luckily he didn't press for details.

We held hands and walked up and down rows of spectacular rose bushes. The afternoon was beginning to cloud over and the air felt very still.

"Okay, so what do I need to do to get you to tell me about your dream? Chinese water torture? The rack? Are you ticklish?" I asked him.

"You don't want to hear about my childhood? My first kiss? My favorite color instead?" he teased, blinking his eyes with a wave of those amazing lashes.

"Nope, the dream or nothing," I said.

But of course I wanted to hear everything about him. I wished at the start of every relationship I could get a complete unbiased dossier on my dates. It would certainly save endless time and heartache down the road.

We strolled by a trickling stream and through a rock garden as we talked about nothing and everything until the afternoon, which had started out a bit cloudy and warm, suddenly dropped nearly twenty degrees and the sky turned the inky blue-black of a nasty bruise. A second later, raindrops the size of golf balls began to fall. We ran to Robert's black Volvo and he turned up the heat full blast.

"We have a saying in Wisconsin, if you don't like the weather, just wait ten minutes," he said in a soft voice. I didn't mind. Any unexpected phenomenon that resulted in isolating me alone with this man was fine with me.

I sunk deep into the leather passenger seat as we drove in comfortable silence. Robert leaned forward and turned on the radio. The cure for any insomniac was the voice of an NPR disc jockey, low and smooth as silk, and the voice lulled me to sleep as Robert drove to the restaurant. I floated in and out of announcements about an infestation of alien aphids in Ontario to the Hezbollah setting up operations in Brazil. There must be something in the air in Milwaukee that produced strange stirrings of my subconscious, because I awakened to hear Robert say . . .

"Speaking of, did I tell you I spent a year in Paris during undergrad?"

"Paris?" I mumbled. I touched the corner of my mouth. Thank goodness, no drool.

"As in France, not Texas," he said, pulling into a brightly lit parking lot.

My best friend, Elizabeth, who didn't believe in mere coincidences, would have loved to have been a fly on the wall as Robert and I sat facing each other over two bowls of wonton soup and exchanged reminiscences about the city of light. Not only had Robert taken classes at the Sorbonne as I had, he'd lived in the same neighborhood and had visited my favorite bakery every morning, and then rounded the corner to the same cafe for coffee.

"Remember Madame Fournay's little bug-eyed dog?" he said, laughing. "It drove me nuts. She even bit my ankle once but of course petite Fifi could do no wrong."

Just three years after Robert's year in Paris, I'd followed in his footsteps, having, it seemed, much the same experiences. Except, of course, for my love affair with Pierre. But then, I'm sure Robert had had one or two French lovers of his own, since it was practically a course requirement for American students abroad before being allowed to board their flights home.

"I'm sorry, mademoiselle, you lived here for a year and never had sex with a Frenchman? Oh la la! We can't have that. I suggest you try a little harder. Maybe we will let you leave next month."

"Can I ask you a personal question?" I ventured finally, deciding that there were some questions that just had to be asked. "How does a great guy like you end up joining a video dating service?"

He placed his chopsticks on the side of his plate and frowned. Oh no, I've asked the wrong question and now he's insulted. But it was hard to get rid of my preconceived notion that the kind of man I wanted to end up with wouldn't join a video dating service unless drafted by the U.S. government or forced to at gunpoint by a militia of desperate single women.

"After my wife died, I didn't date anyone for two years," he said slowly. "Then my friends pushed me into a bunch of really bad blind dates. I guess I wasn't ready to meet anyone. But now I am."

He reached across the table for my hand and looked past a pile of fried rice and half an egg roll, looking straight into my eyes. A moment later, I slipped my hand away from his.

"I've never had any luck meeting women in bars, and with my

business I travel a lot," he went on, "so I don't have time to meet new people. I joined a dating service because I don't want to waste any more time. I'm forty-four, I'd still like to have kids."

Why does it make me so nervous that Robert always seemed to say the exact right thing? Shouldn't I be happy about this?

"They say it's a number's game," I said, but I didn't really believe this. If you added up every man I'd dated in the past twenty years, at a minimum I should qualify for an honorable mention in the *Guinness Book of World Records*.

"Who are *they* and who made *them* an authority on everything and what do *they* know anyway?" he said with an ironic grin.

Another perfect response. This guy should write a book on "How to Charm a Woman in Ten Easy Steps."

"Now, can I ask you a personal question? How does a great woman like you get to be forty-one and never married?"

I was used to this question. At my age, it was a catch-22. The divorced women I knew felt as though they had the stigma of failure to deal with. But if you've never been married, people naturally wondered if there was something wrong with you because no one had ever given you the seal of approval. Was she normal? Was she a bitch? Was she really a man?

"My mother and my best friend, Elizabeth, think I'm too picky," I told him. "But I'd rather be single than settle."

"A woman like you should be picky," he said, giving me the once-over, but in a nice not lecherous way.

Robert drove me back home and took the elevator up to my apartment. We stood outside my door for an awkward second before he bent down and kissed me. At first, it was one of those shy, not-really-sure-if-you-want-me-to-do-this kisses that quickly became all arms and mouths as we fumbled and pressed against the wall in the hallway.

Robert pulled away a few minutes later and said in a husky voice that he'd better leave. He thanked me for a great time, and then stepped backward into the elevator. He stood there for a moment. His hair was disheveled, and the beginnings of a five o'clock shadow showed on his cheeks and chin. I heard a buzz and the doors slowly closed on my vision.

Maybe I should call men more often?

Seven

The Three-Date Rule

The day of her tragic death, "Auntie Mary" a never-married forty-one-year-old spinster, had taken her niece to the Milwaukee County Zoo as a birthday present. The two of them were admiring the newly acquired warthogs when Mary bent over to pick up her niece's pink hair ribbon that had fallen to the pavement. Suddenly, out of nowhere, a frenzied bull elephant that had escaped only moments earlier came charging up behind her and gored her up her rump. Her last words to her niece before she expired were, "Remember, Matilda, three dates are usually two too many."

Because Mary had always been a kind and thoughtful soul, she was admitted immediately through the heavenly gates. But instead of going to the usual orientation session, she was called in for a special audience with Angel Aphrodite.

Aphrodite began by flashing Mary's entire dating history before her eyes, pointing out quite clearly that Mary had been in the habit of rejecting men after only one date. She had had her reasons of course.

The guy was unattractive, boring, didn't make her laugh, or wasn't financially settled. Then there were the men that Mary had really liked who'd never called again after a first or second date. Mary had spent much of her single years pining away for this latter group of men, elevating them in her imagination to knights in shining armor, certain that once they realized how wonderful she was, surely one of them would come to his senses and sweep her off her feet.

But that had never happened.

"Mary," Angel Aphrodite asked, "do you now remember your date with Peter when you were twenty-five, with Fred at thirty-five, and your date last year with George?"

Mary remembered that, as usual, she had turned each of these men down for a second date. Peter was gangly and awkward and laughed inappropriately during The Exorcist. Fred was a struggling musician with no assets or savings. As for George, eleven years her senior, balding, jowly, and very conservative politically, he'd made Mary wish that she'd stayed home that night to organize her spice rack instead of wasting an evening with him.

"Yes, Aphrodite, I remember them. Why do you ask?"

"George was your soul mate."

"George? Jowly George was my soul mate?" asked Mary, repulsed by the sudden image of her and George together in an intimate way. "Are you certain, Aphrodite?"

"Yes, Mary," said Angel Aphrodite. "If you'd gone out with George just two more times, you would have fallen madly in love, married him, and had three beautiful children together. Peter and Fred weren't your soul mates, but if you'd gone out with either of them just two more times, you would have seen them for the good men that they are, married one of them, had children, and been very happy."

Mary was beside herself with remorse and guilt. She could now *see the superficiality that had guided her decision-making and how it had prevented her from finding true love and happiness.*

"I'm so sorry, Angel Aphrodite," said Mary. "How could I have been so foolish?"

"My dear," the angel gently explained, "it wasn't your fault that no one ever told you about The Three-Date Rule."

Hazy cumulus clouds of cigar smoke hovered in the stale bar air as Lessie and I walked into Cubana. For a change, the downstairs was packed with wall-to-wall men. Cocktails in one hand, cigars in the other, they were all looking very Ernest Hemingway-esque as we walked up to the bar.

"Do you ladies want to try a mojito, two for one tonight?" asked the bartender.

"What's in it?" I asked.

"Sugar, mint leaves, lime juice, rum, ice, and soda water," he said. "In that order."

I looked at Lessie, who shrugged her shoulders as if to say, why not? The bartender produced two tall glasses containing a faint greenish liquid sprouting mint leaves.

"Remember to chew on the leaves when you're finished," he said.

"Why?" asked Lessie.

"I don't know. Tradition I guess," he said.

I took a sip. It was a little on the sweet side, but refreshing. With our drinks in hand, we went upstairs, where Javier was giving a group lesson to two couples. He smiled and waved when he saw us. Eliseo apparently hadn't arrived yet.

Lessie and I walked out to the balcony and I leaned against the railing, looking inside at the dance floor. I saw the usual salsa crowd, but then my eyes focused on someone new. A trim middle-aged man was dancing alone, making flamboyant arm movements and weird contortions with his face, as though his mustache were caught in his teeth.

"They call him the Lone Salsero."

I turned to find Sebastian Diaz looming behind and above me, invading my personal space. I smiled up at him, said a quick hello, and turned back to the dance floor.

"What does *salsero* mean?" asked Lessie.

"A *salsero* is a male salsa dancer and a *salsera* is a female salsa dancer," Sebastian said. "The Lone Salsero never speaks to anyone, and always dances alone."

"Sounds very mysterious," said Lessie with a giggle. "Is that salsa dancing he's doing?"

The three of us stared at him as his face contorted into spasms of apparent agony alternating with something approximating the kind of grin you see on a baby's face when he's passing gas.

"So how's the research and writing going, Sam?" Sebastian asked.

"Wow, you look great! What is that?" asked Javier, who slipped up to me, put his hands on my hips, and bent down to my waist for a closer look at my tattoo. I hoped he couldn't see that my stomach was flip-flopping like a dying fish on a pier.

"It's a Cupid," I said, trying to act nonchalant at Javier's unexpected and rather intimate gesture. It was one thing to have him touch me while he was teaching, and quite another to have it occur off the dance floor.

Under Lessie's peer pressure, I'd bought three midriff tops. The one I was wearing, a V-neck black cotton sweater, showed off more of my stomach than I was used to. I'd also splurged on a pair of tight, hip-hugging, black cotton/lycra pants and a strappy pair of black spike-heeled shoes, the kind I'd seen the really good salsa dancers wearing. If I never learned how to salsa, at least I'd look good trying.

"Nice tattoo, Sam," said Javier.

"The god of love," said Sebastian. "How interesting." I was certain that for a split second he'd been sneering, but then he'd instantly covered it up with a smile.

"Javier, where's your brother?" asked Lessie. "I'm itching to dance," she said, as she undulated her hips seductively and raised both arms in the air above her head.

"He's going to be late tonight," said Javier. Lessie froze like a statue, and Javier quickly added, "My sister has a new boyfriend. She brought him over to meet my family and Eliseo is there to translate for my parents. But by now he's probably grilled the poor guy to the point that he's sorry he ever met her."

"Oh, that's sweet," Lessie said, looking relieved, but also a little embarrassed. She'd told me on the drive over that her date with Eliseo on Saturday night had gone so much better than the first, that instead of feeling happy about it, she had become only more insecure about him. I knew exactly how she felt.

"Hey, you guys should go out and dance," she said, shooing us toward the dance floor.

Grabbing my hand, Javier pulled me inside through the double patio doors. The room was muggy, almost tropical. Ceiling fans swirled above us.

"I don't think Sebastian likes me."

"What? He told me he thinks you're . . . interesting." I didn't like that pause. That's exactly how I would struggle to describe my boss, Elaine, or my mother to a third party to avoid coming off like a bitch.

"Now I'm positive he doesn't like me," I said wryly.

"Sam, Sebastian and I have been friends since I moved to

Milwaukee five years ago," he explained. "I know him better than my own brother. Believe me, he would tell me if he didn't like you."

We started dancing. The mustachioed Lone Salsero gyrated by us, looking like Saddam Hussein with a serious case of jock itch. No one seemed to be paying him the slightest amount of attention.

"Besides, how could anyone not like you?" asked Javier, as he led me into a double twirl.

My heart bounced up to the ceiling and back. I guess it didn't matter what Sebastian thought of me as long as it didn't influence Javier's feelings about me.

"It doesn't matter," I said. "Let's drop it."

"Everything you think matters," said Javier, "to me." I met his eyes, but then he looked away from me. It was the first time I'd seen him be anything but completely in control and at ease.

Tonight I was following well enough that I couldn't help but envision Javier and I moving together so gracefully that we unquestionably mesmerized the other dancers who would form an awed circle about us, marveling at our performance. We finished with a spectacular dip as I walked off the dance floor feeling like a movie star stepping out of a limo to her throngs of adoring fans, although I had to admit, it didn't look like a single person was glancing in my direction.

My feelings of euphoria lasted precisely nine seconds until Javier went up to the DJ booth and turned up the tempo of the music. Apparently he had slowed it down to toddler level for me. I hadn't been salsa dancing after all. I'd been salsa crawling.

I stood on the side and caught my breath as I watched Javier and a stunning blond woman proceed to soar over the dance floor in one long string of dips and twirls, moving in perfect fluid motion. Their dance ended to a burst of applause.

"I want to dance like her," I said, when Javier came up to me a minute later.

"You need to practice and have a little patience," he said, flashing me his one-dimpled smile.

Patience was out of the question. As my dad used to say to me, "Patience is a virtue, possess it if you can, seldom found in a lady," and then it was supposed to be "and never in a man." But he would change it to, "and never in Sam."

"How much more practice do I need?"

"Irene's been dancing since she was fifteen and winning salsa competitions since . . . forever," he said, tilting his head in the direction of the blonde. I looked at her. She wasn't even out of breath. Not a drop of perspiration graced her forehead.

"I could give you a private salsa lesson, if you don't mind that my studio isn't fixed up yet," Javier told me. "Eliseo and I live on the top floor of a duplex. I plan to remodel the first floor into a dance studio, when I get a loan."

"A private lesson sounds great," I said breezily. I said "great" but was thinking "dangerous" as I was just beginning to realize that when I was with Javier, I no longer felt like myself. Something about Javier was causing me to lose control.

Javier put on another salsa and began dancing with another student. I stood watching him.

"A man doesn't move like that unless he's got the whole package," said a beautiful Latina woman standing at my side. She was about my height, and her shoulder-length brunette hair had blond and reddish streaks running through it. I watched her as she watched Javier. The lower half of Javier.

Javier certainly was a pleasure to gaze upon. He kept his upper body perfectly still as his hips slightly swayed back and forth, a move far more subtle than the female dancers, but still incredibly sexy.

"Have you danced with him yet?" I heard her say. I tore my eyes away from Javier's package to look back at her.

"Yeah, he's giving me lessons," I said, wondering, does she like Javier? Was she checking out the competition? Wait a minute, Sam. Stop flattering yourself. You're way too old for him. He's your instructor. You're his student. And that's all.

"They say he can make your spine melt," she said in a low purr, before taking a wide detour through the middle of the dance floor and brushing up against Javier while pretending to ignore him. I'd give her a 9.5 for that move if what she'd just said about Javier didn't annoy me so much. When she reached the bar, she met up with Sebastian Diaz, who hugged and kissed her.

I felt like an extra in a salsa soap opera, except that clearly I was the only one who hadn't been given a script, had never met the cast of characters, and had no clue what the plot was.

After Javier finished his lesson, he came up and asked me if I wanted to try a merengue, a dance that was much easier than salsa. Javier took a moment to demonstrate its simple marching beat, one two, one two, right left, right left.

Eliseo and Lessie drifted by, their pelvises fused together as one unit, gyrating back and forth to the two-step rhythm. Good thing they had clothes on, because the thin material of Lessie's cotton skirt and Eliseo's jeans were their only means of birth control.

"Who is that woman talking to Sebastian?" I asked Javier, thankful that for once I could hold a conversation while dancing since I didn't need to concentrate at all on these steps.

"Which woman?"

"The tall woman at the bar with the red and blond streaks in her hair," I said, seeing that she now appeared to be throwing all of her powers of feminine persuasion Sebastian's way.

"I don't know her," said Javier. "Why?"

Eliseo and Lessie drifted by again, still oblivious to the world. They had melded together to such a degree that nothing short of the jaws of life could pry them apart. Truthfully, I was disappointed that Javier maintained a professional pelvises-several-inches-apart distance from me.

"Just wondering who's who in the salsa scene," I said, and could see from his expression that he didn't believe a single word. Not that it mattered. I could tell that he liked me.

★ ★ ★

The phone rang at 6:30 the next morning, at least three hours before I'd planned on getting my first jolt of caffeine. Elaine Daniels was one of those people whose brains needed to be dissected and studied when they died, because she didn't need more than five minutes of sleep a night to generate her usual amount of energy, enough to power the Hoover Dam. The woman practically glowed in the dark.

"Good morning, my dear," she said so sweetly, I thought for a moment I was dreaming. "How's your love life?"

"There's a guy a like," I said, feeling an immediate flashback to the time I'd had a crush on Sal Marquardt, the star quarterback, who'd spent all of high school strutting past me as if I were something that had belonged in a petri dish.

"Tell me about him," Elaine gushed as if we were two girl-friends gossiping during lunch period, which couldn't have been further from how I felt. My preferred response would've been along the lines of, "None of your damn business," but I quickly rattled off the laundry list that I knew she'd want to hear—name, age, profession, and educational background.

"He's a widower?" she said with a merry lilt, which she tried to cover up with her next statement. "Oh, that's a shame. But it will generate a lot of sympathy. How many dates have you had with him?"

"Two."

"I don't mean to pry, Samantha, but have the two of you . . . ?"

"No," I barked, which was the same answer I would've given even if we had. I had no intention of inviting Elaine into my bedroom.

"Well, I guess it's smart to make him wait a little. But we don't want to be a prude now do we?" she said in a tone thick with condescension.

"Elaine," I said, "I'd like to tell Robert why I'm really in Milwaukee. I'm starting to feel guilty about . . ."

"Absolutely not, Samantha," she snapped. "Your assignment must be kept secret. Once the two of you are engaged you can tell him everything. Remember, 'La Vie' is yours if you pull this off. Now, our readers are going to be thrilled to hear all about Robert. Fax me your copy about him by Friday. Ciao!"

Click!

My dream job, "La Vie." Was it worth all the lying and the string of abysmal dates? And the answer had to be "yes." Maya Beckett had done a decent job of that column for the past eight years. But what "La Vie" needed was, well, me.

I kept current on world events. I read *People* magazine. I've been to really bad nude performance art shows. At eight years younger than I, was it even possible Maya had experienced that dark-night-of-the-soul feeling, in the immortal words of B.B. King, that, "Nobody loves me but my mama and she might be jivin' too"? I highly doubt it. Certainly, Maya had never suffered through the dating dry spells I had, droughts that could wither a herd of camels. I've seen the sky over the Brooklyn Bridge on a cold December morn . . .

And, I've completely lost my mind.

I made myself some coffee and went out onto the patio with a cup. Hopefully by September I'd be engaged. No I *would* be engaged, and to a wonderful man. But what if I didn't meet anyone I could fall in love with? Would Elaine stop at taking "La Vie" from me? Probably not. Next she'd fire me. Then, my failure would be exposed to the nation via a glossy cover photo compliments of *Très Chic*. But after that, the worst would come: the talk show circuit.

"Well, Oprah, I'd had such high hopes for Samantha," I could hear Elaine saying. "She's such a lovely young woman. But how could I have known she'd be too picky and pass up dozens of eligible men whom she'd met in Milwaukee over the summer."

"But what about her first date with Paulo the computer whiz and entrepreneur? What was wrong with Paulo?" Oprah would ask.

"Not a thing, Oprah. Paulo was an extraordinary man, but I guess not good enough for our precious Samantha. Apparently some women really don't want to get married after all," Elaine would add, sighing deeply.

Then I would have only one option left: run away and join the circus. Come see The Spinster, the oldest living never-married woman in the universe!

In order to avoid a career as a circus freak, I went on two more dates over the next five days, one from Single No More, the other from Brunches or Lunches. On the bright side, I didn't drop dead of boredom during these dates. The fact that I'd had to hold my hand in front of my mouth a few times to check if I was still breathing might not be enough to deter some women from going on second and even third dates with these guys. But I'm not one of those women. I've never learned how to choose practical versus passion, the dull diamonds in the rough over the exciting bad boys. And the reason for that was simple. I've never been able to follow The Three Date Rule. I got up and grabbed my journal. I was so excited by this idea for "La Vie," that I didn't even have coffee first.

I spent the rest of the day preparing my weekly report for Elaine about how my dates were going and working on my humor columns in my journal, all while trying to stifle my excitement about my private lesson with Javier. I'd debated what to wear to an afternoon private lesson, and had decided that subtly sexy was the way to go—a pair of black rayon pants with little slits at the ankles and a black V-neck sleeveless cotton shirt.

I'd arrived precisely at four and Javier greeted me with a huge smile and a kiss to my cheek.

"On these two walls I'm going to have floor-to-ceiling mirrors and a ballet bar," said Javier with a sweep of his arm around his dance-studio-to-be. "And I'm going to buy a sound system and have a special wood floor installed, the kind found in professional dance studios. And the ceiling is going to stay just the way it is."

We both looked up. I'm terrible at judging distances, but the ceiling had to be at least fifteen feet high and was covered with old-fashioned etched tin squares of the type commonly found in older buildings. That was lovely, but the rest of the room could use some work. The linoleum floor was cracked and faded, and a stained couch with a broken spine sulked against a wall next to a rusted sink with a dripping faucet.

After we had practiced salsa for about an hour, I collapsed on the couch and Javier pulled up a chair and sat across from me, taking deep gulps from a bottle of spring water. I noticed his Adam's apple moving up and down under the caramel-colored skin of his throat. Aside from the dimple, on which I was passionately and irrationally fixated, he was far from being classically handsome. In fact, if I walked by him on the street, I don't think I would notice him. But after spending time with him, I was struck by the way he radiated the inner peace of a person who was completely at ease with himself—the rock in the storm. Javier wasn't trying to impress anyone and yet he'd impressed me far more than I'd wanted to admit.

"I can tell you really love to dance," I told him, and then reached down to brush some dust off my new dance shoes, a pair of silver ankle strap high heels.

"Well, I have two people to thank for that," Javier told me. "The first was my father. He was a musician in the Dominican Republic. As a kid he worked on a farm. When he was eleven, his uncle gave him a guitar. He taught himself how to play and at eighteen he moved to Santo Domingo, worked construction during the day and at night played in merengue bands. So, I guess you could say the music is in my blood."

I could listen to Javier talk all day. He was so open, so easy to talk to, and so remarkably refreshing after David, my ex-fiancé, who seemed to have problems divulging what he'd eaten for breakfast.

"Who's the second person?"

"I saw Celia Cruz perform once a long time ago in Miami. The next day I went out and bought all of her albums," he said. He ran his hand back and forth through his thick hair.

"I don't know who she is," I said.

"She was a famous singer from Cuba. She died last year. Some people called her the Queen of Salsa, others, the Salsa Goddess," he said.

Wow! Salsa Goddess. I wanted someone to call me that, just once in my life.

"Is teaching at Cubana your full-time job?" I asked him. It occurred to me that, as drawn to Javier as I was, I knew very little about him.

"No, that's just three nights a week. My real job is roofing," he said, and then gestured as if pounding a hammer. "My father and I own a roofing and siding company. Eliseo and a few other guys work with us part-time."

I felt a stab of disappointment. A roofer. I don't know what I'd been expecting him to say, but it wasn't that. Elaine and my mother would never approve.

"It's not my first choice," he quickly added. "When I was younger, I wanted to be a professional dancer. Well, the truth is, I wanted to be a movie star. Picture John Travolta in *Saturday Night Fever* except it was going to be me starring in a salsa dancing movie. After I graduated from high school, I drove out to L.A. with five hundred dollars. I figured that was plenty since I was sure it would only take a couple weeks to get my first part."

"What happened?"

"I slept on my cousin's couch and went to every audition I could," he said with a be-dimpled grin. "The first dancing job I was offered was . . . well, this is even more embarrassing—I don't know if I should tell you."

"I swear I'll take it to my grave," I said, and could tell by his expression that he was anxious to tell me.

"A Chippendale dancer."

"Really," I said in a playful tone, looking him up and down like I was selecting a stud from the stable.

He shook his index finger at me like a kindergarten teacher at a boy who keeps pulling all the girls' ponytails. "You promised, Sam, to your grave."

"Okay. Then what happened?" I asked, assuming the attitude of mere salsa student once again. I knew I needed to stop flirting with him, but I was having problems controlling myself with him.

"I turned that job down and then nine months later I made it to the big-time. I was in a movie," he said.

"You were? Which one?" I asked excitedly.

"Calm down. It's no movie you've ever seen or heard of," he said. "It never even made it to the theaters, went straight to video. I was one of the back-up dancers. I'm in three scenes, no lines."

"What's the name of it?"

"*Salsa Inferno*," he said, rolling his brown eyes. "It wasn't even a B movie, more like a D or an F."

"I want to see it."

"Believe me, you don't," he said shaking his head. "It has no plot and the choreography sucks."

"What happened after your movie debut?"

"My father got hurt, fell off a second-story roof and fractured his back. He was in traction and therapy for months and couldn't work for almost two years. I had to go back to Miami and take over the business to support my mother and sister. And here I am, let's see," he paused and counted on his fingers, ". . . thirteen years later," he said, shaking his head. "What about you, Sam? Do you like what you do?" he asked.

"Not really," I said, which was true. But I felt a stab of guilt because Javier was someone I didn't want to ever lie to. "I want to do more creative writing," I added, staying as close to the truth as possible without blowing my cover.

"Like what?" he asked me, leaning forward on his elbows, all ears.

I couldn't speak for a moment. It had been so long since a man had seemed so genuinely interested in my hopes and dreams. He was probably just being polite. Besides, you're too old for him, Sam, and you need to stay focused on your assignment.

"My dream would be to have my own humor column in a magazine or newspaper," I said matter-of-factly.

"I'd like to read some of your stuff, Sam, if you don't mind sharing it?"

"Only if I get to see your movie," I told him with a smile. Stop it, Sam! Stop flirting with him. Next lesson I'll have to have some duct tape handy to wrap around my mouth.

"I'll show you mine if you show me yours," he quipped. "You drive a tough bargain, Miss Jacobs," he said, standing up. "I want to teach you a new dance. It's from the Dominican Republic and it's called bachata."

The steps were more difficult than merengue, but easier than salsa. Bachata had a high-energy beat, but the melody was completely different. Salsa was complex, brassy, and sophisticated, while bachata was simple and folksy.

"One two three tap, one two three tap," said Javier. I had to concentrate so I wouldn't lose the step.

"It's such happy music," I said, as the guitar twanged its upbeat melody out of a boom box on the coils of an old-fashioned radiator. "I love it!"

"This song is about divorce," said Javier. "The last one was about a man who is in love with a woman who doesn't love him back. Some people call bachata *música de amargue* which means 'music of bitterness.' "

We continued dancing to the sad songs with the happy melodies. With the slightest push of his hand or pull on my waist he was able to lead me until we were dancing with our bodies pressed together. Then, the music took on another dimension. Underneath the cheerful plucky rhythms pulsed a powerful sensuality. After a few songs, Javier stopped dancing but he still held me tight, with his right hand pressed to the small of my back.

"Sam, you are so beautiful," he said, his dark eyes suddenly intent on mine.

I wanted to respond to him, to tell him how I felt, although I really didn't know how I felt about him. And, even if I did, I shouldn't let myself get involved with Javier. But I couldn't ignore how powerfully attractive I found him, inside and out.

Javier leaned in and kissed me. I couldn't help myself—I kissed him back. I felt myself dissolving into his arms, into his delicious kisses, until I came to my senses a few mintues later and broke away from him.

"I'm almost ten years older than you," I said, not meeting his eyes. I walked over to my purse. "How much do I owe you?" I asked him, holding my wallet. But then I looked at his face and knew I had hurt him without meaning to. I felt awful.

"I'm not going to take your money, Sam," said Javier.

"Well, okay then, I'll buy you a beer sometime," I said, looking down at my feet. "See you at Cubana."

Eight

Dating Circle of Hell

"Dating sucks, sucks I tell you! I hate every goddamn minute of it," said Angie, a skeletal woman with a scowl on her face that could scare puppies. She stabbed her cigarette onto her bread plate with enough force to poke a hole through it. "I just want to be married already."

I looked around the table at our ill-fated group of five. This was a new one for me. Now I was blind dating in a pack, as if one-on-one blind dates weren't horrible enough. Thanks to the services of The Dating Circle, the five of us were here at a quaint Italian pizzeria, the kind with red-checked tablecloths, candle-light, and slightly vinegary Chianti.

According to Sally, who'd made the arrangements from New York, The Dating Circle catered only to professionals, arranging for six men and women in the same age range to have dinner together—separate checks, no obligations, no messy videotapes or photos, and no phone numbers or e-mail addresses exchanged,

unless you chose to after dinner. You were all just thrown together like shipwreck survivors in the hopes that your lifeboat
wouldn't sink and sparks would fly.

We'd just finished introducing ourselves. Angie, a legal secretary
at a law firm, sat to my right. At the far end of the table was Ned, a
shoe salesman at a department store, a short balding man who
didn't seem to meet anyone's eyes. To his right and across from
Angie was Floyd, a used-car salesman who could have been anywhere between twenty-five and fifty. He had ruddy cheeks, lamb
chop sideburns, and a chin so big it hovered over the table like a
blimp. Seated directly across from me was Steve, a manager at
a video store, a perfectly nice-looking man, except that he wore a
T-shirt emblazoned with LIFE'S TOO SHORT TO SMOKE CHEAP POT.

Angie blew a big puff of smoke over the table and took a
deep sucking drag on her second cigarette, which caused her
cheeks to cave in to such an alarming degree she resembled a
shrunken head.

"I'm allergic to cigarettes," Ned the shoe salesman said. But
his voice barely rose above a whisper. "And I think we're in the
non-smoking section."

"I wouldn't mind lighting up myself, but I don't think I could
get away with my very special brand of tobacco here, if you
know what I mean," said Steve, breaking into a loud horsey
laugh and shooting Angie an exaggerated wink. Angie rolled her
eyes and gave a long weary sigh that spoke of a thousand and
one prior bad dates.

"Do you know what I mean?" Steve repeated. He held his
T-shirt out from his body and pointed to the enormous marijuana
leaf on the front of it, I suppose in case any of the "professionals"
here didn't know how to read. Steve's laughter rankled across the
restaurant causing several diners to look our way.

"We all know what you mean," said Floyd, jutting his chin out toward Steve as if menacing a weapon. Steve's laughter stopped cold. Sparks were flying all right. Just not the kind hoped for by the Dating Circle people.

"Dating is fun, my mother says," continued Angie in a high-pitched imitation of her mother's voice. "But men were different when she dated, they were actually men."

Angie lit up another cigarette, ignoring Ned, who coughed into a closed fist. The waitress came by and brought us two more carafes of Chianti. We all dived in to refill our own glass. Clearly, it was every man and woman for himself or herself in our sinking lifeboat.

"How 'bout you guys?" Angie continued, looking in turn at Steve and then Floyd. "When is the last time either of you had the balls to punch the numbers on a telephone to ask a woman out?"

The two shrunk back, as if they were about to be castrated, while Ned covered his face with a napkin.

"It's a scientific fact that men are turning into neuters," Angie continued, holding court over the table. "I read all about it in *Cosmo*. It's the chemicals in our environment and cooking our food in plastic containers. In two hundred years, the human race is going to be extinct, thanks to Tupperware."

She picked up her glass of wine and threw it all back in her mouth like a shot of whiskey.

"Here I am, gorgeous, in my prime at twenty-nine, and I can't seem to find a man," Angie continued. "I sure feel sorry for that Mystery Woman from that magazine. At least I still have time. At forty-something, she doesn't have a snowball's chance in hell."

It took me a moment to realize that Angie was talking about me. How comforting to know that I was an object of pity in her eyes. And could she really just be twenty-nine? Was it possible that I was the oldest person at the table? I might be the oldest person in the whole restaurant? Any minute now the waitress was going to come up and offer me the 10 percent discount for seniors. And then when I walked out of the restaurant, a Boy Scout would probably offer to help walk me across the street.

"Sam?" I felt a tap on my shoulder and jumped. I turned and looked up at Javier's friend and inquisitor of decrepit old women, Sebastian Diaz.

"I hope I'm not interrupting," he said. Of course he was interrupting, but that's exactly what he'd intended to do.

"Hi, Sebastian," I said, feeling a prickle at the base of my neck. What the hell was he doing here?

Angie turned to glance at him and did a double take. Her eyes poured over his arms and muscular chest like syrup over a stack of pancakes. I hated to admit it, but Sebastian did look particularly handsome that night, wearing a black button-up shirt opened at the neck and black pants, standing there like he was James Bond and the very fate of the world rested in his hands.

"Are you here for the Dating Circle dinner?" Angie eagerly asked him.

"You're on a date, Sam?" Sebastian said, looking over the table to Ned sitting motionless, still holding the napkin over his face. "With all of these people? How interesting."

There was that word again, *interesting*. I wanted to die. It was awful enough being on a bad date with just one guy, but here I was, surrounded by the Three Stooges. Why don't I just get myself a big sandwich board that reads L-O-S-E-R and wear it around town for the summer? What if Sebastian tells Javier about this? Would Javier think that I was desperate? Pathetic? Well, what else could he think, given that he didn't have a clue about my real mission in Milwaukee?

"Just a few . . ." I paused, as I struggled to swallow, "friends having dinner."

"Then I am interrupting," Sebastian said. "I apologize. I just wanted to say hello."

"No, please sit down," Angie said. "Please, please sit down."

Angie rose and grabbed on to Sebastian's arm as though it were the last bicep attached to the last man on earth.

"Another time perhaps, thank you," he told her and, having bestowed upon me a final speculative look that spoke volumes, left.

"Is that guy a friend of yours?" Steve asked as soon as Sebastian was out of earshot.

"Not really," I told him. "Why?"

"That guy is an undercover cop," Steve said. "Believe me, I can spot them a mile away."

"A necessity, I'm sure," said Floyd.

"I could tell, the way he read my T-shirt," Steve continued. "Narcs seem to think we don't have free speech and rights and stuff in America."

"Who hasn't read your damn T-shirt?" Angie spat. "That's why you're wearing it, aren't you? To make a statement?"

Angie and Steve continued bickering as I watched Sebastian from across the room, holding out a chair for his date, a Barbie doll clone with thick blond curly hair flouncing about her silver dollar–sized waist. She was the kind of woman who caused an epidemic of whiplash every time she walked through a room. As soon as he sat down across from her, he reached out for her hand and kissed the inside of her wrist. An involuntary tingle went through me. It was those tiny, seemingly insignificant moves that had the ability to sweep a woman off her feet.

Well, let Sebastian sweep a million women off their feet. I didn't care. I just hoped he didn't tell Javier about this.

★ ★ ★

Spending time alone is a healthy and necessary part of life for any mature adult—which automatically excludes me. When I spend too much time alone my mind wanders to places that would've given even Sigmund Freud the willies. No e-mails, no telephone calls in days, and no mail, not even of the junk mail variety. Even the credit card companies have deemed me unworthy of them.

This morning, after staring at my blank computer screen for an hour, unable to write a single word, I found myself so desperate for company that I clicked on the Microsoft paper clip guy to wake him up and actually had a conversation with him. A bit one-sided to be sure, but it was crystal clear that I'd reached the very nadir of my existence.

Today, I could relate exactly to how Bridget Jones felt when she said she was afraid of dying alone and being eaten by Alsatians. Except that I was the only living, breathing, sentient higher life form in my apartment. If I died I'd simply rot away to a skeleton. Maybe if I expired under my bedspread with the dehumidifier on, I'd mummify. Centuries from now they'd unearth me and discover the last single woman over the age of forty on the planet. Then they could put me in a museum, right next to the A and B cup bras.

Of course the real problem was not that no one had called me, it was that *he* hadn't called. The rational part of me argues that this is not the end of the world. It had only been a couple of days—three days, fourteen hours, and twenty-nine minutes—since I had last spoken to Robert Mack. It couldn't possibly be that I'd broken the rules when I'd called him? Could it?

I'd been hoping for a call from Javier as well. He'd kissed me before he'd found out about our age difference and now that he knew, he was probably no longer interested, which was just as well since he didn't have the right credentials for Elaine or my mother.

And of course I was well aware of the Murphy's Law of the Telephone. The man you want to call will do so only *after* you leave your apartment. The phone will not ring if you're at home, pretending to be busy. And he definitely won't call if you're picking up your phone every so often to make sure there's still a dial tone, and listening to your voice mail for a message that you might have missed while you were in the shower, or during the sixty seconds you had the blender going to make your mid-morning fruit and yogurt smoothie.

Then again, there are other possible explanations for the non-call. Men are incapable of mentally multitasking. A woman can simultaneously think about her five o'clock deadline for a fifty page report on marketing strategies for the new millennium, the fact that her best friend is going through dating turmoil, a manicure appointment for next week that needs to be rescheduled, the latest Ebola outbreak in the Congo, her mother's latest nagging phone call, and the man she's currently crazy about. On the other hand it is a well-known fact that a man is only able to focus on one thing, whether it's clipping his nose hairs or attempting to negotiate a contract for weapons-grade plutonium.

Most important of all, men live in a different time and space continuum from women. Time for them is a meaningless vacuum filled with mysterious manly concerns, which only sporadically relate to the woman he is currently seeing. Three days to a man is like an ESPN instant replay of the last four seconds of the NBA playoffs. Whereas three days to a woman waiting for that call is a soul-sucking eternity, filled with wrenching thoughts of self-doubt and analysis of every word of every conversation, every look exchanged, while she desperately tries to figure out what must have gone wrong, all the while trying to stifle the horrible thought that he may never call again.

I stared at the telephone now, wondering if I should rip the jack out of the wall and end this living hell, when it rang. I screamed and jumped back a foot as if it were about to attack me. Please let it be Javier or Robert. Wisely I waited for the third ring to pick up, because I'm an extraordinarily busy person after all.

"Bonjour, Samantha, *ça va?*"

I did a salsa sashay out to my balcony and plopped down on my lawn chair. Robert and I talked for nearly an hour. He had been out of town on business as I'd suspected. He was remarkably blasé about almost failing to close a deal on a banking executive who'd wanted to relocate from Memphis to Palm Beach, as if a six-figure transaction didn't matter.

Before we said good-bye, Robert asked me to go out with him on Saturday night, exactly what I'd been hoping for. So it seemed odd that I had an uneasy feeling after we hung up. But why shouldn't things start going my way? After all, I'd certainly paid my dues with the other night's Dating Circle fiasco that could only be called a success because the five of us had gotten out of there alive, no small feat given the arsenal of weapons available, such as verbal assaults, butter knives, meatballs, and the like. I liked Robert, a lot, so what was the problem?

Reluctantly retreating from the warmth of the sun on my balcony, I found an e-mail from Elizabeth waiting for me, two lines saying her date with Judge Doug had gone great and that she'd call as soon as possible to fill me in on the details. Sally had also e-mailed, reminding me to get my article about Robert Mack to Elaine by the end of the week. I'd already spent most of the morning trying to write it. But then again, I'd been a little distracted. Maybe now that Robert had finally called, I could manage to plunk a word or two down about him?

I clicked back onto the blank document, poised my fingers over the keyboard, and resorted to what I called The Method. Whenever I couldn't or didn't want to write, which seemed to be all the time lately, I tried a technique I'd learned in college. Simply write for fifteen minutes straight without stopping and without editing my thoughts or pausing for even a moment, just letting it flow no matter what stream of consciousness gobbledygook landed on the page because ". . . in the morass may lie a gem," as Dr. Durant, my favorite college professor, used to say. Five minutes into The Method, the "You've got mail" voice boomed from my monitor causing my heart to skip a beat. I must've accidentally turned the volume up to maximum.

I had two e-mails. Lessie said she couldn't meet for dinner but would see me later tonight at Club Cubana, a reminder of something I had been trying to forget because of the possibility that Sebastian had told Javier about seeing me with the Dating Circle dolts, and another message from Sally, giving me another order straight from the front office.

"Don't kill the messenger," Sally wrote. "Her majesty's latest edict is that you shall schedule and report on dates with four more men by June 30. She also ordered me to remind you that FAILURE IS NOT AN OPTION! Good luck! Sally."

This meant four more dates in ten days. Good God! I'd gone through dry spells where I hadn't had three dates in six months. Did she think I was a miracle worker?

Speaking of miracles, perhaps I should check my newspaper personals ad mailbox, which was going to expire at the end of this week. Elaine was taking no chances, so in addition to doing Internet dating, she'd also had an ad placed in the personals section of Milwaukee's major newspaper. I called the nine hundred number and was shocked to discover I had a message, my first, and from a man with a voice like liquid gold, a cross between Barry White and the kind of DJs who work at smooth-jazz radio stations.

"Hi there," he said. "This is rather awkward isn't it, leaving a message for a total stranger? My name is Mark, I'm forty-three, divorced, and I'm a doctor. I love to travel and just got back from a scuba diving and hiking trip to Thailand. As for my looks, my female friends tell me I'm being far too modest when I describe myself as an average Joe. They insist I remind them of Mel Gibson but with better legs and without the kilt. You sound like an interesting woman, and I'd love to chat with you and see if we have enough in common to meet for lunch or dinner."

I was certain that no man would respond to my newspaper personals ad, at least not anyone who had been born a man. Two days before leaving New York, Sally had handed me a copy of it:

I'M AMAZED I'M STILL SINGLE!!!!!!
SPWF, 41, 5'8", 135 lbs, blond/green, gorgeous, sassy, sexy, smart, wistful, rare gem, seeks Mr. Right right now!!!!! You are S/D handsome degreed professional, 37–50, ready to commit to passionate partnership for life.

The caption alone was enough to make me vomit, but "sassy," "wistful," "rare gem," and all of those ridiculous exclamation points! Mr. Right right now!!!!! I'd burst into Elaine's office wanting to disembowel her.

"Samantha, dear," Elaine had said, peering over her glasses, "you look upset, is anything the matter?"

"I think this ad makes me sound a little desperate," I'd said, trying not to sound desperate.

"Nonsense, it highlights all your best qualities. It's not possible, Samantha, that you have," she had paused and significantly bit her lip, "issues?"

Issues? Who doesn't have issues? I didn't know a single person who hadn't been to at least one therapist and more like two or three.

"Self-esteem issues," she added.

I'd forced a smile as I'd imagined stringing her intestines from one end of Broadway to the other. "Elaine, my concern is that a normal red-blooded man who possesses a single drop of testosterone coursing through his . . ."

"Samantha, you have nothing to worry about. If there's one thing I know, it's how to capture a man," she had interrupted smoothly.

And that had been that. I hadn't gotten a single response to my ad until now. Dr. Mark was probably a eunuch, but perhaps I should at least listen to his message one more time to make sure I hadn't misheard anything. After all, in my excitement at hearing my second male voice of the day, and what a voice it was, I might have easily imagined the whole thing.

Yes, all the key information was intact—doctor, Thailand, Mel Gibson look-alike, sense of humor. Well, there was no need to get overly excited about this. Most women I'm sure would dive for the telephone to call him back immediately. Not me. I'll be cool-headed about this, wait a day, not act too eager. I'd call him tomorrow or the next day and find out if he was normal enough to meet.

I replayed his message again.

On the other hand, he might be seeing patients all day tomorrow. Or maybe he'll be performing brain surgery? Or perhaps he's going to Stockholm to accept the Nobel Prize for unlocking the gene that prevents wrinkles? Doctors were very busy.

I dialed the number and there was that voice again! I felt myself melting into my shoes. Beep!

"Oh hi, Mark," I told his machine. "I'm Sam. Well Samantha, but everyone but my mother calls me Sam. It's sort of a nickname I've had since I was a kid and this boy who had a crush on me called me Sam because his brother's name was Sam and it stuck and well anyway, you called and left a message on my personals voice mail. I'm the 'I'm amazed I'm still single' ad in case you responded to more than one ad, which is perfectly fine by the way, I mean we don't even know each other and you can certainly date as many . . . Anyway, I don't scuba dive, um, but I think it's great that you do! I've never been to Thailand either. I also think it's great that you're a doctor but that's not the only reason I'm calling you. I'm sure you're very nice . . . Well why don't you give me a call? Um, okay, bye."

The second I hung up the phone I realized that not only had I forgotten to leave him my phone number, but, if there were any way to quantify these things, I'm sure I would win the grand prize for leaving the longest, stupidest voice mail message in the history of dating.

Maybe it would be easier not to try at all, just suck it up and go through those long patches when I felt like the only person on the planet not having sex. This intense marathon with the personals ads, Internet dating, the video dating, the lunches and dinners, was nothing less than a slow death march to lunacy. And it required so much energy it could be a full-time job!

I let that last thought sink into my brain as I called Dr. Mark back, leaving him a quick message complete with my number.

What's the worst that could happen? He has my telephone messages broadcast over national TV on some new reality dating bloopers show and I have to move to Antarctica for the rest of my life.

* * *

"Here for your Javier fix?" asked a familiar voice high above my right ear a few hours later. I turned to see Sebastian soaring over me, wearing a smirk where there should be a smile.

"I'm waiting for my turn," I said, doing my best to force my facial muscles into a pleasant smile. There was something about Sebastian that reminded me of the actors who are typecast into playing the devilishly handsome character who fools everyone for a while with his charisma and wit, but then turns out to be the evil genius plotting to take over the world.

Javier had been dancing with the same woman since I'd walked in thirty minutes earlier, but to say they were dancing was a little like saying Beethoven was proficient at Chopsticks. She looked like a tiny ballerina with thick dark curly hair that fell about her shoulders and flew out parallel to the dance floor as Javier spun her about and then twirled her eight times in quick succession in a complete circle around his body as though he were twisting a lasso. On the last few notes of the song, she cascaded into his arms as he swooped her into a dip that defied the laws of gravity.

That'll be me. Next lesson. No problem.

"That's Isabella, Javier's ex-girlfriend," Sebastian explained. "They went out for two years and used to dance in competitions together."

"She's very beautiful," I said, as Javier and Isabella walked off the dance floor arm in arm. I felt as though my larynx had been shrink-wrapped.

"As you can see, they're still very close," Sebastian said, pounding another nail into the coffin.

"By the way, Sebastian," I said, eager to change the subject, because if there was anything I didn't want to hear more about, it was Javier's love life, past or present, "what do you do for a living?"

"I'm a reporter for *El Día,* a local Latino newspaper," he said. "So we have something in common. I'm also a writer. And by the way, how was the group date the other night, Sam? Any success?"

Just then Javier came up, wiping his sweaty brow with a white handkerchief he'd pulled from his back pants pocket.

"My two favorite people," he said, giving me a quick kiss on the cheek. If he was upset with me for the other day at his studio, he wasn't showing it. I was so happy to see him I momentarily forgot about my concerns.

"How goes it, amigo?" he said, rocking Sebastian back and forth with his hand on his shoulder. Then they shook hands and exchanged a few words in Spanish. Javier laughed and looked at me. I felt a rush of hot shame shoot through my body. What if Sebastian was telling him about the Dating Circle dinner?

But if he was, apparently Javier didn't care, because I saw nothing but warmth in his eyes as he led me out to the dance floor.

"It's great to see you, Sam," he said softly into my ear before leading me into the salsa that was playing.

After about five minutes of practicing, Javier stopped moving.

"I don't mean to be critical, Sam," he said. "You're doing great, but you need to concentrate more on following me."

"I'm sorry. I thought I was."

"Try not to anticipate, okay?" he suggested.

We danced for several more minutes until Javier stopped again, his arms still around me.

"Sam," he said, looking directly into my eyes, "I want you to get used to the idea of totally submitting to me."

My heart pole-vaulted over my esophagus and my stomach plunged to my knees. Other than an S&M workshop, a dance floor had to be the only place on the planet where a man could get away with making a statement like that to a modern American woman without having his face slapped or getting sued. Far from making me angry, his words made me feel . . . How? No, it wasn't what he'd said. It was being with him. Javier, like no other man ever had, truly made me feel like a woman.

I concentrated on trying to do a better job of following Javier's lead, and after another twenty minutes of practice, we stopped.

"Javier, about the other day, I didn't mean to hurt your feelings," I said. "I really . . ." I really what, want to throw my arms around you and kiss you all night?

"I'm devastated," he said, looking truly upset. I felt a knife plunge into my chest. Oh God, I really had hurt the sweetest man I'd ever . . . and then I saw a spark in his eyes and knew that he had been teasing me. "There's only one way you can make it up to me; have dinner with me tomorrow night, Sam."

"I'd love to," I said, feeling a rush of happiness.

He excused himself to give a group lesson. Javier could dance for hours it seemed without needing a break.

"I hope I didn't upset you by talking about Isabella," said Sebastian, who'd made a beeline over to me the second Javier had walked away. "Javier took their break-up really hard. The truth is, he's still in love with her. Anyway, I just wanted you to know, he's on the rebound and definitely not ready for anything serious."

It felt like a thousand-pound weight had just fallen on my chest. I forced a smile that made my heart hurt.

"Javier and I are just friends," I said to Sebastian, who I wished would just shrivel up and disappear, although not likely since he must be close to two hundred forty pounds of solid muscle. "See you later."

Downstairs a bartender stood wiping glasses. A couple of men in suits were slumped over the bar, drinking and smoking. An older couple sat at a table, unmoving, silent. I felt like I'd walked into a wake. I asked the bartender if he'd seen Lessie or Eliseo, and he jerked his head toward the back of the bar, suggesting I check the humidor.

The humidor? Lessie doesn't smoke. I walked toward a slightly ajar door with a gold cigar on the outside, and when I opened it, the pungent masculine odor hit me, taking me back to afternoons in my father's study. It had been the only room in the house my mother would let him smoke in. I'd sit on his lap as he'd puff away, pointing to countries on his world map and telling me travel stories he'd read in books. He'd never had the opportunity to travel much, but his wonderful tales had inspired my insatiable wanderlust.

In a room the size of a walk-in closet, surrounded by shelf upon shelf of boxes of cigars, were Lessie and Eliseo making out like two kids stuffed in the backseat of their dad's Pontiac at the high school prom. I cleared my throat loudly.

"Lessie," I said. They pulled apart in slow motion, as if nothing in the world were harder to do at that moment. Lessie turned her head to me with a dreamy smile on her face. When that girl falls, she falls hard.

"Hi guys," I said, feeling as though I'd blundered into someone's bedroom. "I'm leaving now, Lessie. Do you need a ride home?"

She needed something, but it wasn't anything I could give her. I drove home alone, thinking about Javier still being in love with Isabella. At least now I knew for sure, he was just on the rebound and wasn't really interested in pursuing a relationship with me after all. I should feel relieved, right?

That night I dreamt that I walked into Cubana to find Javier under the spotlight in the middle of the dance floor, holding his ex-girlfriend Isabella in a low dip. I stood on the edge of the floor waiting, expectant. Naturally, I looked breathtakingly beautiful. Javier looked up, our eyes locked, and he instantly let go of Isabella, who dropped to the floor with a loud thud. Javier walked over to me, pulled me into his arms, and we proceeded to dance like we'd been born to dance together—gliding across the floor in a perfectly choreographed series of dips, twirls, and fancy footwork. We used every square inch of the dance floor until he slowly lowered me into a dip as the song came to an end. Javier stared into my eyes, leaned down, kissed the hollow at the base of my throat and then my mouth.

* * *

I'd been looking forward to my third date with Robert ever since he'd called me two days ago. All day I'd had that tingly excited feeling you get when you think maybe, just maybe, the search might finally be drawing to a close. Perhaps, in the very near future, I could finally look forward to hanging up my silk thong underwear and permanently change into a comfy pair of old lady white cotton hipsters.

He picked me up at seven and took me to Louie's, a seafood restaurant on Lake Michigan. Robert seemed to get better looking every time I saw him. At forty-four, he was in great shape. But it was those mile-long lashes that turned women's heads. Okay, my head.

"Do you ever think about going back to the practice of law?" I asked Robert after we'd finished our crab cake appetizers. The waves softly lapped at the concrete barrier behind us. A sliver of a moon hung in the sky like an ornament dangling from heaven.

"I doubt it," he told me and tugged on his ear. "When I bought my recruiting firm two years ago, I finally discovered my calling in life. I'm much more suited to the business world."

"Two years?" That didn't sound right to me. I was sure that on our first date, he'd said he bought his recruiting firm three years ago.

"You're so pretty tonight, Sam," he said, reaching out to stroke my cheek with the tips of his fingers. "Your brow makes the cutest crease when you're thinking hard."

"It's just that I'm curious, Robert," I said. "When did you stop being a lawyer?"

A pained look flashed across his face.

"There were a few years between dissolving my law firm and starting Robert Mack and Associates when I didn't do much because I was trying to get over Sarah's . . ." he paused, blinking his eyes hard, ". . . to get over my wife's death."

"I'm sorry," I said, and I was. I didn't want to stir up painful memories for him. If he wasn't ready to talk about this yet, I didn't want to push.

"No, it's all right," he said. "Excuse me for a minute," he

said. He stood up abruptly, tossing his napkin on his plate as he walked away, looking more angry than sad. At that moment, I felt exactly like I had last year when I'd run into an editor from *Très Chic* whom I hadn't seen in a long time, and had congratulated on her pregnancy only to find out that she'd gained thirty pounds after her husband had left her for a younger woman.

When Robert returned a few minutes later, he greeted me with a warm smile. He reached for my hand and waved the waitress over to order another round of drinks. I returned the kind of nervous grin you give to the gynecologist just before he inserts the speculum. Was Robert always this touchy and moody?

But by a couple of drinks later, my anxieties had passed, and when we got to the blues bar, the awkward moment had been almost forgotten. We slow danced and swayed to the music and kissed, not caring who saw us. When he dropped me off, we did a repeat closure of date number two, just outside my door in the hallway.

Oh my, this was fun and a little ridiculous. Two forty-somethings tongue-slapping into the wee hours of the night. Being single had definite advantages. Married people didn't do this anymore, at least not with their own spouses, and they were at home in bed hours ago with their hands folded over their gently rising and falling potbellies, keeping one ear wide awake for their teenagers to come home. We took it inside, continuing to make out on my couch until Robert left a couple hours later.

* * *

The next afternoon was game number two of five baseball games I'd be attending over the summer. Elaine's theory was simple: male fans far outnumber female fans and businessmen, i.e., eligible men, would be at day games in droves, networking or entertaining clients.

At first glance it seemed that Elaine was right. Lessie and I constituted a tiny island of femininity in an ocean of men. Three cute late-thirtyish to early-fortyish guys wearing baseball caps and no discernable wedding rings were seated directly in front of us. Two attractive similarly ringless men sat in the next section over in the same row. But I'd yet to even make eye contact with anyone but the peanut vendor.

I looked over at Lessie, who was staring off into the middle of the field, watching but not seeing the pitcher warm up on the mound. I'd told her about my date with Robert last night, but I don't think she'd heard a word I'd said.

"I had mad, passionate sex last night with three men at once," I said, testing.

"Really?" she said. "That sounds like fun."

"Then my neighbor, a sixty-year-old widow, joined in," I added.

"Good for you, Sam," she replied.

"Lessie, what is going on with you?" I asked her, grabbing hold of a muscular bicep and giving it a little shake.

"Sorry, I'm a little distracted today," she said, her blue eyes finally focusing for the first time that afternoon.

"Really? I'd hardly noticed," I said, not a little embarrassed to see that I'd acted the same way too many times in the past upon getting a crush on a new man.

"I think it's because I'm majorly in lust for the first time in years and trying desperately not to confuse it with love," she explained. "You'd think that at forty-two I'd have more control over myself."

"You could start by avoiding humidors," I said.

"Very funny. Maybe this really is love?" Lessie frowned and brushed her auburn locks off her forehead. "This thing with Eliseo is so different than it was with Steve. But I was just twenty-two when I married Steve, and I didn't know anything. How do you ever know when you're really in love, Sam?"

How do you ever know? I'd thought I was truly madly deeply in love with my ex-fiancé, David, and look what happened with us. Engaged, after three years together, and then, well, the chicken wing thing. I knew I should be over him by now, but whenever I thought about David I felt like a giant gaping wound that hadn't healed properly. At least our engagement had been memorable, not just for the usual reasons, but because we had almost gotten arrested.

David and I had been in a horse-drawn carriage going through Central Park just after he'd proposed at dinner. I'll never forget the sight of that little blue Tiffany box, David sinking to his knees to declare his love to me in a restaurant packed with voyeurs, the taste of Dom Perignon still tickling my taste buds and the two-carat marquis-cut ring flashing in the moonlight. All of these things had worked their dizzying romantic charms to temporarily disable the rational part of my brain. Without thinking, I had leaned over and unzipped his fly. When we had started, the dense foliage on that cool October night of three years ago had provided enough coverage. We were, however, so busy consummating our engagement that we didn't realize the carriage had turned back onto Museum Mile on Fifth Avenue until a taxi driver parked at the curb had thoughtfully illuminated us with his brights. As a symphony of horns erupted, another turbaned taxi driver had hung his head outside his cab and begun making lewd hand movements to the effect of wanting to know if it was going to be his turn next, which was when the mounted police officer galloped up to our carriage.

"Anyway, what about you and Javier?" Lessie said, elbowing me with a grin. "It seems like there's more going on than just salsa. Dinner tonight, free private dance lessons. Has he shown you the pelvis-grinding dance yet?"

"First of all, it's just dinner—everyone needs to eat," I said.

"If that's what you want to think, fine, but I'm sure he doesn't."

"As far as the hip-grinding dance is concerned . . ." I began.

"Pelvis-grinding dance," said Lessie with a big grin. "There's a difference."

"You're speaking, of course, of the bachata," I said. "Am I correct?"

"What else?" said Lessie, raising her arms above her head and somehow managing to gyrate her hips in a circular motion while remaining seated, a move that finally got the attention from the guys across the aisle. But a second later when Ken Griffey, Jr. came up to bat, we became invisible again as their eyes riveted back onto the field.

"Is that the most incredibly sexual dance in the world or what?" she added.

"That dance should be illegal," I said in agreement. "But Javier was a perfect gentleman when he showed it to me," I lied smoothly, and then felt myself blushing at the thought of how Javier and I had danced the bachata during my private lesson.

"Too bad for you," Lessie said, taking a sip of beer. "You're not getting off the hook. What do you think of Javier?"

"He's a really nice guy," I said. "An excellent teacher. Very patient, talented. And he's kind of cute."

"There's a 'but' here," Lessie said, raising her left eyebrow.

"He's a decade younger for one thing," I told her.

"Nine years younger, and if he doesn't care why should you?"

"Who said he's even interested? I think he's just being a nice guy," I said.

"I've seen the way he looks at you. It's obvious he likes you."

"He's smart, has a great sense of humor, and he's fun to talk to. It's just that, well, he's . . ."

"A roofer? Is that the problem?" Lessie asked defensively.

"Well, you know what my assignment is," I said, trying to tread carefully here since Eliseo did the same thing for a living.

"Samantha Jacobs, I do believe you've turned into one of those girls I hated at Brown, the full-fledged East Coast, Ivy League snob."

"Lessie, that's not true!" I protested. But, the truth was, I hadn't at all sorted out the issue of the suit versus non-suit guy in my own mind. I had never dated anyone who didn't have at least a college degree and usually one or two more degrees on top of that. I wanted "La Vie," but there was no way I was going to let my career goals or Elaine or my mother dictate who I would marry. Certainly, if I fell in love with a garbage man, I'd marry him. I'd just never had the occasion to cross that line before, until Javier, who made me feel wonderful, but who was so different than anyone I'd ever been with before.

"I think I'm really starting to like Robert Mack, the guy from the video dating service," I said, trying to change the subject.

"Oh. So there's potential with this Robert guy?"

He certainly fit the mold of the man that my mother and Elaine expected me to end up with. He was nice, smart, and fun to be with, but I wasn't 100 percent sure about him yet. As for Javier, I knew that I should ignore my intense attraction to him and move him from the romance to the just friends department. But I wasn't sure if I could.

"I guess you haven't read my last article," I said pulling the June 24 issue of *Très Chic* out of my purse and handing it to Lessie.

" 'Blind Dating in 3-D, Could Video Guy Be the One?' " said Lessie, reading the cover. "Well, could he?"

"Yeah, sure."

Lessie looked at me and shook her head.

"What?"

"You don't sound very sure."

"I am," I said firmly. But the truth was, I wasn't sure about anything.

Nine

One Simple Dinner

I opened the door and there stood Javier, looking perfectly adorable in jeans and a black linen short-sleeved shirt that had a row of embroidery running down both sides of the front. Javier put his hands on my waist and kissed me on both cheeks.

"I'm so sorry I'm late," he said. "I had a private lesson at my studio and we lost track of time."

I told him not to worry about it, he was only a couple of minutes late, but I was surprised that I felt something bordering on jealousy at the thought that he'd been alone, dancing with another woman at his studio. And why had they lost track of time?

"I love your shirt, what's it called?" I said, trying to shake off these ridiculous feelings. I'd seen quite a few Latin men wearing shirts like that at Cubana.

"It's a Guayabera or Cuban shirt," he said, looking at me intently. "Is something wrong, Sam? You seem a little, I don't know, upset or distracted."

Did Javier have mind-reading capabilities in addition to his many other talents?

"No, I'm fine. I'm just wondering if sometime I could have another private lesson?" I asked, telling myself it was just a lesson, although I might as well volunteer to be thrown into the lion pit while I was at it.

"I'd love to give you another lesson," he said, with a grin that I swear said, "I see right through you, Samantha Jacobs."

I invited him in for a tour of my apartment. When we got to my bedroom, I felt a ripple of nervousness. I trusted Javier completely. It was myself that I didn't trust, so I stayed put in the doorway.

He walked over to my nightstand and picked up a photograph of Elizabeth and me that was taken at a black-tie fundraiser for breast cancer that we'd attended last year.

"That's my best friend, Elizabeth," I said, and then gave Javier her condensed biography.

"I was looking at you, you look gorgeous," he said, staring at the photo. I just loved the way he tossed out words like *beautiful* and *gorgeous* whenever I was with him. He put the photo down and walked up to me.

"But, I don't want you to think I like you only for the way you look. It's the Sam in here that I really like," he said, pointing to my heart, which was trying to break a hole through my breastplate.

"But you know almost nothing about me," I said, wishing I had the strength to put a safer distance between us by taking a step backward.

"I know more than you think," he said.

"Such as?"

"You're smart, you laugh at my weak jokes, so you have an excellent sense of humor, you're impatient . . ."

"Wait, impatience is a bad thing," I said laughing.

"Not if you're impatient about trying to learn how to salsa. Then it's a good quality."

A momentary silence fell as we stood just kissing-distance apart, but not touching.

"And, I know that you are confused about your feelings for me," Javier said in softer, far more serious tone.

We stared into each other's eyes. I'd never been with a man who could read me so well. If he kissed me now, I would be lost—so much for Elaine, my career, my mother . . .

"Although it's difficult to understand since I am irresistible," he said with a huge dimpled grin, breaking the spell.

I laughed. If anything, Javier was too humble. He had his ego in check far more than most people I knew.

Javier took me to a Spanish tapas restaurant about a mile from my apartment. Over a bottle of red wine, and half a dozen different dishes, everything from calamari to prawns, we didn't stop talking.

I learned that Javier is a risk taker. He's tried sky diving and bungee jumping and went on a white-water rafting trip to Colorado, where he says he nearly drowned when his raft flipped and he got sucked under water for hours.

I gave him a skeptical look.

"All right, it was about thirty seconds, but it seemed like forever."

"Besides salsa dancing and risking your life, what else do you like to do?"

"Well, there's a lot of things I've tried," he said. "I like to play chess."

"You're some sort of chess champion, right?" I was learning as the evening went on that Javier excelled at understatement, especially when it came to his accomplishments.

"I was in a chess club in high school and won a couple of tournaments, but that was a long time ago," he said.

Silence. "Go on," I said, touching his arm.

"I *love* to cook."

"Really?"

"You sound so surprised, Sam."

"Sorry, I just didn't picture you spending a lot of time in the kitchen," I said. "What's your specialty?"

"I can't reveal my secret recipe to just anyone, especially a writer. How do I know this won't end up in a magazine or newspaper?" he said, leaning across the table with his hands folded together. I'd been hoping all night that he would reach across to hold my hand. "But," he said, "I could make it for you. Of course you'd have to sign a confidentiality agreement first."

"Of course."

We finally left when we realized that all of the customers were gone and the waiters were standing against the wall, giving us the universal we-are-closed-it's-time-to-leave stare.

As Javier and I rode up in the elevator to my apartment I did my best to act as though I wasn't on the verge of cardiac arrest. At the door, I turned to thank him again for dinner. He leaned forward and kissed me on the cheek, but as he moved away, I put my hand at the nape of his neck, pulling him back to my mouth. We spent the next ten minutes kissing until he gently broke away. He stroked my cheek with the back of his hand and said good night.

What the hell was I doing? I wondered as I leaned up against the inside of my door trying to catch my breath. This wasn't exactly a step in the direction of the "just friends" department. But I couldn't help how much I liked Javier.

How could one simple dinner have complicated my life so much?

Ten

Coyote Brain Dead

"You sound like you're jogging. Where are you?" my mother asked me.

"My apartment," I answered, although I thought this should be fairly obvious to her since she's the one who called me at my home number.

"Then why are you breathing like you're running a marathon?" she asked.

Talking with my mother was not just emotionally challenging, but a physical event as well—for both of us. She'd called me with her new toy, a cellular phone that she used to contact me only while she's driving, fitting her calls in between her Women's Club board meetings, an afternoon at the spa, or another black-tie cocktail reception given in honor of one of her friends' husbands who'd done something a little out of the ordinary like inventing a mechanical brain or cloning Albert Einstein. I could just picture her, totally in her element, motoring along in her black Lincoln town car, her hands-free headset over her short black bob, wearing one of her favorite designers, St. John or Miu Miu. And while she drove, I paced in whatever space I was in like a caged lion.

I hadn't spoken with her since our usual third Saturday of the month luncheon one week before I'd left New York. I was still reeling from that two-hour meal, when my mother had pulled her usual emotional outburst when I'd told her about my assignment.

"You're getting married!" she'd exclaimed. "Oh, thank goodness! I've been praying for this for twenty years!"

Tears had welled up in her hazel eyes as she'd grabbed the napkin off her lap, shook it out with a flourish, waved it up and down like a flag, and buried her face in it. Little kitten mews emerged from behind the white cloth, alternating with short bursts of full-blown blubbering. I had felt all of the customers in our section at Tavern on the Green sneaking glances in our direction, and pretended to be absorbed by the extensive wine list, resisting the impulse to shout, "Don't look at me! I'm not the one having a breakdown! I can't control her!"

After several minutes of this, the maitre d' had glided to my side and bent over to my right ear.

"Is everything all right, madame?" he'd asked me in a low velvety voice imbued with faux concern.

At his words, my mother had whipped the napkin away from her face and emerged looking fresh as a daisy. She was the only woman I knew who could cry and never get the broken blood vessels and hooded puffy lizard eyes.

"My eldest daughter is finally getting married," she'd announced, making it sound as though she'd personally arranged the marriage herself after scouring the ends of the earth in a decades-long search to find a man willing to have her daughter's hand in matrimony.

"Calm down, Mother. You haven't met him yet. I haven't met him yet," I'd recalled telling her, which was about as effective as telling a volcano to stop erupting in mid-flow.

"Well, you wouldn't need to go trotting off to a frozen wasteland like Minneapolis to scrounge up a husband if you weren't so picky," she'd told me.

My mother worshiped the institution of marriage and couldn't fathom how one of her offspring hadn't yet managed to snag a live one. Of course, she'd never had to struggle. She and my dad had had a storybook love affair, meeting at nineteen and marrying at twenty-one with eighteen wonderful years together until my father's untimely death.

"So what does my future son-in-law do for a living?" my mother demanded from her cell phone, bringing me back to the present.

During my entire adulthood, I'd done my best to keep my mother in the dark about my love life. The reason for this was simple mental self-preservation. Any inkling that I had the slightest romantic prospect in my life, and my mother would set up camp inside the nearest Vera Wang salon and begin shoving Wedgwood china patterns in my face.

Of course she'd known about my engagement to David, whom she'd met a half dozen times in the three years we were together. She'd known the salient—to her mind—facts that he'd graduated with an M.B.A. from Yale, was a partner at Ernst & Young, and most important of all, that his family had money. I'd magnanimously divulged the date of our wedding to her a full ten months in advance, but should've waited to tell her until the weekend before, like I'd really wanted to, since seven months later it was over. But hey, live and learn.

But never before had my mother been privy to accounts of my fledgling dates that were too raw and tender to predict which way they might go. That is until now, when she could read about my romantic exploits in a national magazine.

"Robert and I have only gone out a few times, Mother. I barely know him," I said, trying to sound like I didn't really like him so that we could change the subject.

But, as I knew she would, my mother pressed for details. I thought about telling her what a nice guy Robert was, about his intelligence and his quirky sense of humor. But I knew this would be pointless. Sighing, I rattled off the kind of facts I'd give if I were a soldier captured behind enemy lines.

"Hmm. University of Chicago law school," she mused. "I suppose if you're going to end up with a husband from the Midwest, that's a fairly good school. But of course Harvard or Yale would be far preferable."

"His business is very successful."

"How much does he make?" she asked, in her usual blazingly direct fashion.

"I usually wait until date number four to ask for a copy of their financial portfolios and Swiss bank account numbers."

"Hmm. I'll have to ask Martha how much her nephew makes at the recruiting agency he owns."

Martha, my mother's bridge partner and best friend, was the Martha Smith of the so vastly rich Smiths, that their servants had servants. The family owned a vast worldwide network of, for lack of a better word, stuff—oil companies, food companies, and strangely enough, dozens of miniature golf courses because their son Skip had taken a liking to this plebian pastime when he was ten, giving it up a year later for yachting or snooker or whatever super-rich kids did.

"You said he had his own law firm before that, as a solo practitioner? Well, I can't imagine he hasn't at least doubled or tripled his income. Thank God for that," she added.

My mother was well enough off financially, due to life insurance policies my father had taken out when Susan and I were kids. After he died, she'd never had to work again. But she wasn't even close to the same category as the Martha Smiths of the world, and had had to slowly ingratiate her way into their circle by hovering around the edges of their vast wealth until, finally, her years of effort had paid off and they'd let her join their club as an honorary member. If there was one thing my mother excelled at, it was being enchanting. That woman could make a pair of swans swoon—when it suited her.

I quickened my pace and could see the beginnings of a circular mashed area forming in the powder blue carpeting, like a mini running track.

"I've been in touch with Sally from your office about the details for the wedding," my mother continued. "It seems as though your magazine is only willing to pay for seventy-five guests."

She always referred to *Très Chic* as "your magazine," as if saying the name would give too much credence to my chosen profession. My mother refused to acknowledge that her daughter had to work for a living instead of being a wife and stay-at-home mother, which was, in her eyes, the only acceptable place for a woman. Not barefoot and pregnant mind you, but well-heeled and pregnant.

"I think it's too early to be focusing on details like this," I said.

"Nonsense, Samantha," she persisted. "Your wedding is just six months away."

"Just because it's scheduled doesn't mean it's going to happen."

"Seventy-five is completely unacceptable," she continued as if talking to herself, which I believe she was doing most of the time. "I'm just starting to put the list together. It looks as though we won't do with less than four hundred. Probably more like five hundred."

Then without warning, I did something that I hadn't done in probably thirty years in the presence of my mother's eyes or ears. I started crying. Not the noble, silent tears streaming down my face type of crying that I might have been able to hide. This was a cathartic-tidal-wave-wiping-out-the-village-my-life-is-over rack-ing sobs that involuntarily burst out of me like a stream of ob-scenities from a Tourette's sufferer. I was so confused after last night's dinner with Javier that I'd barely slept.

My crying fit went on until I sensed, rather than heard, si-lence on the other end of the line. For some reason this calmed me, and I was able to sputter down to a small whimper and then silence.

"Samantha," she said in a gentle voice that I hadn't heard since I was a child, "I had eighteen years with your father. They were the best years of my life. I want you to know the happiness I felt, and I know you will if you just keep trying."

I plunked down onto the couch. I'd assumed I was past the age when I could be shocked by anything or anyone, especially my mother. I was wrong. On the few occasions I can remember my mother mentioning my father after he'd died, she'd only done so when the topic had become unavoidable. But she had also zeroed in on my deepest, darkest fear, that I'd be alone for the rest of my life. Could our first actual conversation in forty years be the start of a genuine mother-daughter relationship?

But the nanosecond had passed.

"Anyway, we'll discuss the guest list next week," she said airily. "I've got to run! It's time for my volcanic clay Thai body scrub."

★　★　★

And in the quest to find the perfect man in Milwaukee, it was time for me to make an utter fool out of myself. An hour later at high noon, I stood behind a volleyball net, barefoot and ankle deep in sand, on the shores of Lake Michigan. I was wearing a plunging V-neck one-piece swimsuit, and bouncing about—my boobs, not my body. I suppose I could have worn a sports bra like all the other women here. But that would've required me to acknowledge sand volleyball as an actual sport.

I'd warned Elaine when I saw the Over Thirty-Five Co-ed Singles Volleyball League on my schedule that I didn't think this was a good idea since I'm allergic to organized sports.

It had all started in grade school when I was humiliated every single day of my life on the playground in the game of four square—a game in name only. Chamber of horrors wouldn't come close to describing what I'd experienced. Lynette Harris, the most popular girl in grade school, was the queen of Square A. Square B was always occupied by her best friend, Tess, and Square C was reserved for her lesser subjects. But it was Square D where Lynette unleashed her own special brand of torment on the unpopular girls like me. A typical day on the playground in-volved waiting in line to play as many times as I could during our thirty-minute recess. When I'd finally step onto the hallowed four-sided figure of Square D, Lynette or one of her minions would spike me out anywhere from two to thirty seconds later.

But every so often, like a cat playing with a half-dead mouse that it had every intention of killing, she'd let me advance to Square C, giving me the faintest ray of hope that I might move on to Square B and, dare I even think it, Square A? But the impossible dreams of Squares A and B eluded me throughout my grade school career.

Although six straight years of getting spiked out had scarred me for life, I harbored no ill will toward Lynette, who I liked to imagine had grown up to become one of the nation's handful of female serial killers and was now on death row in Florida or Mississippi.

But that was all in the past, and at this very moment the volleyball was hurtling right at me. Usually this was when a man jumped in front of me, shoving me rudely out of the spot, which I've learned is called my "zone." Normally this would piss me off. But since my natural inclination when the ball comes toward me is to scream, throw my arms up protectively over my face, and then crumple into a fetal position, none of which seems to assist in getting the ball over the net, it was fine with me if some guy wanted to plow into me like a punching bag and take over.

But it was now too late for anyone else to get it. I heard a chorus of male and female voices cheering me on, "Hit it, hit it!" Closing my eyes tight, I clasped my hands together into a two-handed fist, and made a swinging motion upward. I heard a soft womp, opened my eyes and saw the ball bounce once at my feet and die.

I turned around to face my teammates. The woman behind me, a beefy, strapping mountain of a woman who frankly scared the hell out of me, mumbled a curse under her breath and glared at me.

People in nine-to-five office jobs might have envied me right then, I supposed. Getting paid for hanging out on a sunny beach playing volleyball sounded great in theory. But there were definite advantages to the office job—you bought your morning coffee, slumped into your cubicle, stared at your computer screen under the artificial glare of fluorescent lighting for eight hours, and then dragged yourself home, only to start all over again the next day. The only things to do battle with were secretary spread and the thought that one day you might wake up in a nursing home with nothing to show for your life. But on the whole, it seemed better than possibly getting strangled by my own teammate whose name I'm guessing was Brunhilda, a former member of the East German women's weight lifting team.

I whipped my head back to face the guy on the opposing team positioned opposite of me, who promptly leaned into the net and said in a low voice, "It would probably help if you didn't close your eyes when you're trying to hit the ball. Just relax, don't try so hard."

He wiped the sweat off his brow with a quick backstroke of his hand. A mass of blond curly hair escaped over the tops of his ears and out the back of the Brewers baseball cap that he wore backward. I took note of his black tank top and red swimming trunks not to mention his thick muscular thighs covered with blond hair.

"Easy for you to say," I wanted to tell him. I half expected that if I dared turn around again, I'd see my teammates stringing a noose over the lifeguard stand.

We started playing again. As the ball magically avoided me for the next ten minutes or so, I had begun to relax, although I was still too nervous to actually be having fun. It was then that my eye caught the ball coming right at me again.

"Okay, I can do this," I told myself. "I can, I can, I can!" I forced myself to keep my eye on the ball, only to misjudge its trajectory. In an attempt to dive for it, I slid face-first across the sand, my mouth open in stunned disbelief until I finally stopped moving, with my arms straight out over my head, hands still clasped together white-knuckled in a death grip. It occurred to me that if I lay there long enough, they might think I'd died. I quietly spit out as much sand as I could, making a little puddle of saliva under my chin. Then the pain hit. My forearms and knees felt like they were on fire.

I felt a pair of strong arms lift me up from behind to a standing position. I was a picture of stunning beauty—completely coated in sand, my left knee bleeding, the right a red roadmap of scrapes, and both forearms scraped raw. And to top it off, a long string of sandy drool dangled from my chin. I turned around to see that it was Mr. Cute Guy from across the net who'd rescued me. The only way this could get worse was if one of my boobs had popped out of my suit. I looked down. Mercifully, they were both still intact.

With the little dignity I had left, I gave my teammates a little wave and scuttled away like a crab. I limped over to the sidelines, bent over to grab my gym bag, and slung it over my shoulder.

"But your volleyball career was off to such a promising start," said Mr. Cute Guy, running up to my side as he slipped an arm around my back and helped me to my car.

"Hey, Joe, are you coming back?" yelled a guy on his team.

"No," said Joe. "See you next week."

I fumbled for my keys inside my gym bag. Joe took them, opened the passenger door, and helped ease me into a sitting position.

"I've got a first-aid kit in my car," he said. "I'll be right back." While he sprinted off to the north, I found a bottle of water inside the bag and rinsed the sand from my mouth, pouring the rest over my body. Joe returned a minute later with a medium-sized brown paper bag.

"I'm always banging myself up. I keep a little disinfectant and a lifetime supply of Band-Aids in here," he said, rummaging through the bag. "Here we go." He pulled out a bottle of iodine and a few bandages.

"Now this is going to sting," he said smoothly, staring at my knees.

"Ow." I flinched and looked down at the Band-Aid on my left knee. "Snoopy?"

"I'm all for equal opportunity in the world of cartoon characters. How about SpongeBob for your right arm and Scooby-Doo for your left?" he asked, holding up a bandage in each hand.

After he'd finished playing doctor, I'd expected him to leave, but he lingered as I slipped on a pair of jean shorts and a T-shirt over my swimsuit, and fifteen minutes later, he and I sat across from each other in a booth at an old-fashioned ice cream parlor called Cream City. Joe devoured a hot fudge sundae loaded with pecans while I licked my single scoop of Death by Chocolate from a sugar cone.

We talked about what brought us to a sand volleyball court on Lake Michigan and our jobs.

"I became an engineer because my father was one and his father was too," he said, shoveling a big spoonful of ice cream into his mouth. "But if I won the lottery, I'd quit and never look back."

It turned out that Joe got paid to work as a chemical engineer for a food company, tackling such problems as figuring out the exact formula needed for the latest M&M color. But Joe's job was more of a hobby than a profession since he devoted the rest of his life to all things sports and music. He was also on a men's volleyball team and played rugby on Sunday mornings and softball two nights a week. On weekends, he played guitar in a garage band at weddings and the occasional opener for has-been bands at church festivals.

Was he filling up his life because he didn't have a woman in it or because he didn't want one? These thoughts bounced around in my head until he asked for my phone number when he dropped me off and gave me a peck on the lips.

"Hey, Sam, don't forget," he said. "Next Thursday is my birthday."

He'd only mentioned his birthday four times, as though it were a national holiday. But I hoped that he wanted me to save the night so I could help him celebrate.

"I'll call you," he said with a wave and then drove off.

When I got home and checked my voice mail, I found messages from Elizabeth and the man with the voice from the newspaper personal ad, Dr. Mark, whom I called back despite the embarrassing message I'd left for him. I reached Mark on the first ring, actually half a ring, as though he'd pounced on the telephone the moment it had sounded.

At first Mark seemed normal enough. He told me he liked piano jazz bars, that his favorite authors were Salman Rushdie and Hunter Thompson, and that his favorite hobby was taking exotic action vacations, something an orthopedic surgeon probably had no problems budgeting for. His next trip was planned for Tanzania to climb Mount Kilimanjaro.

"Did you know that scientists are predicting that the snow on Kili is going to be gone in just fifteen years?" he said, and with barely a breath added, "So Sam, how would you describe your build?"

"My build?" I asked, taken aback by his bizarre segue to what was probably the deal breaker for him—no fat chicks. "What do you mean?"

"Your ad says that you're 135 pounds, but, well, you know how that goes," he said chuckling.

"No, why don't you tell me how that goes?" I said, not chuckling.

"Well women tend to ignore the actual numbers on the scale, if they weigh themselves at all," he said as if giving a lecture. "Women fudge ten, fifteen, even fifty pounds in my experience."

Right, and men suck in their guts, add three to six inches to their height, and do the comb-over on their bald spots. But I guess when you have the nerve to claim that you look like Mel Gibson, it's easy to imagine that you have a license to grill women about their vital statistics. I was tempted to tell him that I only had another one hundred pounds to lose to reach my goal weight of 135, to see how quickly he came up with a sudden orthopedic emergency to get off the phone.

"I'm 135 pounds give or take a pound or two fluctuation, if that's all right with you," I said.

"Great! Would you like to go to dinner Monday night?"

"I think I've got something going on Monday night," I hedged.

"How about Tuesday or Wednesday?"

Warning. Warning. This guy has way too much time on his hands.

"I left my calendar in my car," I told him. "Let me check my schedule and give you a call back."

He didn't seem happy about it but he agreed. As soon as I hung up, I called Elizabeth.

"He's an orthopedic surgeon who looks like Mel Gibson. He goes on exotic vacations, has a voice like God, and you're wavering about whether to call him back? Do I have the situation summarized correctly?" asked Elizabeth, as if she were addressing a courtroom.

I mumbled a "hmm," knowing it was pointless to argue with her when she was on a lawyer roll.

"On the other hand, if everything about him is true," she continued, "why in the world does a guy like that need to call a personal ad? He must have some fatal flaw."

"Exactly. I'm not calling him back."

"Aren't you at least curious to see Mel in person?"

"No," I lied. "But it would be fun to show up on a date with him wearing a fat suit."

"Sam, you're too picky," she said.

I groaned inwardly. Too picky, indeed! How could one be *too* anything when it came to the most important decision in life? Think of how hellish it was to live with a bad roommate much less a person that would require thousands of dollars and half your worldly possessions to get away from permanently.

"If you were in L.A.," Elizabeth continued, "he'd probably be asking you if you'd had a boob job and the name of the surgeon who'd done it. What's the worst that happens? He buys you dinner and you waste one evening."

"Because it's not just a wasted evening, Elizabeth," I protested. "Blind dates are torture! It's like coyote ugly plus coyote brain dead. Not only do you want to gnaw off your arm to get away because the guy is so repulsive, but you also want to rip your brain out to take away the mind-numbing conversation that always comes with that package. 'So how many brothers and sisters do you have?' 'What are your hobbies?' 'What's your favorite color?' I can't go through another one of these evenings, Elizabeth! I can't do it!" I said, my heart beating wildly in my chest.

"Okay, okay, so don't! There's just one problem," she said calmly. "Isn't this your job for the summer?"

"Why did I agree to do this?" I sighed, plopping down on my sofa.

"Think of this summer as a challenge, as the most exciting time of your life," she said, in her infuriating way of sounding like a TV commercial urging wayward teenagers to sign up for technical college or to join the armed forces.

"You'll be fine. Just don't let anyone, especially Elaine Daniels or your mother, push you into anything that isn't right," she added.

"No need to worry about that," I said. No one tells me what to do. I'm my own woman. "So what's going on with you and the judge?"

She and Doug were going away that weekend to the Hamptons to his beach house. His divorce was going to be final by Labor Day and she was getting less concerned about being the transition woman. Things were going very well for Elizabeth. And maybe, if I played my cards right, things would turn out for Robert and me as well? And as for Javier, well, all I could do was try to resist him as best as I could. Step number one should be to cancel any future private lessons. Well, one more wouldn't hurt. Would it?

*   *   *

We'd met at an Indian restaurant, the kind that mysteriously stays in business despite the fact that five waiters in black suits stand idle most nights to wait on three customers. Indian classical sitar and flute music softly whined in the background.

"So how many brothers and sisters do you have?" asked Dr. Mark, a minute into our date. I stared longingly at one of the waiters leaning against the wall in the elegant dining room, doing nothing. Maybe if I looked pathetic enough, he'd take pity on me and slit my jugular on his next trip to the kitchen, which by the looks of things might not be until next month.

Mark looked about as much like Mel Gibson as I looked like a broom handle. Actually, Mark looked like a broom handle. No wonder the man was obsessed with fat; he didn't have an ounce of it. I'd seen healthier looking famine victims on CNN. So naturally, I ordered the most fattening dish on the menu. Mark winced and exhaled audibly as the waiter took my order: malai kofta, rich cheese balls in tomato cream sauce, two orders of garlic naan, and a Kingfisher beer. He ordered plain chicken tikka, no bread, no rice, and mineral water.

"Do you have any knee or ankle problems?" was question number two. Mark, the orthopedic surgeon, then bent under the table to examine my extremities. Apparently he was searching for scars, deformities, or a lack of vitamin D that had led to rare case of childhood rickets.

"I feel like a horse," I told him when his cue-ball-sized head had popped back up. "Would you like to look at my teeth while you're at it?"

"Do you have teeth problems as well?" he asked me.

"Well, this is very embarrassing, Mark. But I feel I can confide in you as a doctor. I have a recurring case of trench mouth. I brush my teeth once a month. I don't understand what the problem is." This is what I'd wanted to say. Instead, I smiled politely and lapsed into unconsciousness as Mark continued jabbering on about his favorite subject, himself.

How is it that men like Mark, egomaniacs who weigh less than one of my thighs, are considered prizes, while single women like me are practically objects of pity? Even worse, men seem to upgrade to better and younger women as they get older, but as women age, we get stuck with the bottom-of-the-barrel leftovers.

The next day at the grocery store, a sudden image of emaciated Dr. Mark popped into my brain. I've never had to worry about my weight, one of the few genetic blessings I had inherited from my mother, but suddenly I had an urge to load my cart full of the most fattening items I could find: ice cream, avocados, crackers, peanut butter, macadamia nuts, Oreos, cream cheese, and bagels. While I was waiting in line, I glanced at the candy bars, thinking about adding some to my cart, when I glimpsed a copy of the *National Enquirer.* My mouth fell open. I ripped one off the stand.

On the cover was a full-page grainy black and white photograph of an enormously fat woman with her face obscured by pixels. She had her arms around the pencil thin neck of a bubble-headed alien, a quarter of her size. A flying saucer hovered several feet off the ground in the background, in case anyone had mistakenly confused the alien with a really ugly human being.

The headline read, "Extra-Terrestrial Impregnates Mystery Woman: Celestial Wedding Bells to Ring!"

"I knew it would be tough for that Mystery Woman being over forty and all, but I didn't think she'd settle for an alien," I heard a raspy smoker's voice say over my right shoulder.

I whirled around to face a rotund, middle-aged woman in line behind me. She wore pink polyester pants and a shapeless top with an orange-and-blue flower print and had shoulder-length brown hair, which hung from her head like an overturned bowl of cooked spaghetti.

"You don't actually believe the stuff you read in here, do you?" I asked, as I rattled the paper in the poor woman's alarmed face. Why was everyone assuming your life was over at forty if you were a woman and still single?

"I sure do," she told me as she gestured with her doughy white arms. "My cousin was abducted by an alien and she said he was not an attractive man at all. Slimy and green with those big eyes, she didn't want to get near him. But you know, you don't have a choice 'cause they have those mental powers of telepathacity that hold you down against your will."

I tried to stop listening, realizing that, as outrageous as it was that I was being slandered by a national publication, there wasn't a thing I could do about it.

"What happened to my cousin on that space ship would curl the toes of a dead man!" she added with a shudder.

Maybe by the time I'm sixty-five I'll be able to laugh about this with my grandchildren.

"Grandma Samantha, did you really look like *that*?" they would ask, pointing to a yellowed copy of the tabloid. "No," I'd say to them. "But that's exactly how your grandfather looked when I met him."

I bought five copies of the paper.

★ ★ ★

Date number four with Robert was quickly revving up to the red zone of my dating tachometer. I leaned my back against the outside of a brick building as he gently pressed his body against mine, deliciously invading my personal space. I could feel my hipbones pushing into his abdomen. A momentary knot of concern swept his face as he brushed aside a hair that had foolishly fallen out of place.

"What is Samantha Jacobs thinking right now?" he asked.

Just then the movie let out at the theater next door.

"I'm thinking all these people don't need to see us acting like a couple of teenagers," I said, gently pushing him away.

I didn't want to be on display for the streams of nighttime moviegoers hurrying back to their cars. I remember seeing a couple the age Robert and I are now making out in a car parked under a streetlight when I was eighteen. I had been appalled, assuming that when I got to my forties, which at the time seemed about as old as the pyramids, I'd be mature enough to confine all such foolishness to the bedroom. What I didn't know was that at forty-one, I'd feel like I was twenty-five and still be single and dating.

"Now for the next stop on our agenda," Robert said, disengaging, "there's a little-known but strictly enforced local ordinance on the books. While living in Milwaukee, you must try bowling at least once."

"Is this attorney Robert Mack speaking?" I asked him.

Robert stopped in mid-step and took a deep breath. "I'm not a lawyer anymore, Sam, remember?" he said in a hyper-calm voice.

"You sound annoyed," I said. I felt like I'd swallowed a vat of hot grease.

"Of course I'm not," he said smiling, and the moment passed, at least for him. This was the second time I'd seen an abrupt mood shift with Robert that made me feel very uncomfortable.

"So, have you ever gone bowling before?" he asked. "Basically, if you can walk and throw a ball at the same time, you'll be fine." Grabbing my hand, he led me inside the East Side Lanes bowling alley.

We ordered a pitcher of beer and took over lane number five of a six-lane alley. Robert hammed it up, acting like a professional bowler one minute, squatting down on one knee to line up his shot, while in the next moment he posed with the big blue ball and pretended to do an instant replay in slow motion. I bowled a 72 the first game, skyrocketed to an 80, and then dropped to a 63. Robert bowled all three games in the 150 to 180 range.

"For your first time you did great," said Robert, as we walked back to my apartment hand in hand. A lone shirtless jogger ambled by without a glance in our direction, and an old man with a cane shuffled along the opposite side of the street, but I felt as if Robert and I were alone in this city of over half a million people.

"It was a lot more fun than I thought it would be," I told him. "I'm joining a bowling league first thing when I get back to New York."

"I don't want you to go back to New York, Sam, at least not alone." Robert stopped. "Sam, I think I'm falling in love with you."

Love? Where did that come from? It would seem only fair that a woman should receive some sort of warning before an announcement like that, one that could change the course of history, was made.

"Can I come inside?" he asked. He took me into his arms and bent down to nuzzle my neck. I stiffened at his touch. He stopped kissing me.

"I need more time," I said simply as I watched him walk away.

★ ★ ★

The next day I woke up feeling like the inside of a death shroud. I had that foggy, dull headache that comes with having gotten about five minutes of sleep in between hours of fitful tossing and turning. Three cups of strong coffee did nothing to lift my mood. I sat at my kitchen table looking at Lake Michigan and the beautiful, sunny day beyond. The weather gods were mocking me. There should be some way to make the weather match our moods.

The problem with going slow was how to do it without having the guy assume you were rejecting him. I really liked Robert. But I had to admit, it wasn't love at first sight. It sounds sappy, but with David my ex-fiancé it really had seemed magical, as though it had been meant to be.

David and I had met in an elevator in the Flatiron Building in Manhattan, where I'd been visiting my friend Vicky. Our eyes had caught and held for a few seconds as he stepped on, until he politely assumed the proper elevator position. I kept hoping it would get stuck, that the two of us would be trapped in there for hours, and after pouring our hearts out to each other, we'd fall madly in love before being rescued. I even lingered briefly outside the building, hoping we'd bump into each other or that he'd run up to me and say something like, "You're the love of my life, I can't let you get away." But instead, I'd watched him and his briefcase disappear down Broadway before I grabbed a cab and headed back to work.

Five hours later, I'd met Elizabeth in SoHo at a little neighborhood bar that neither of us had ever been to before. Just as I was telling her about the mysterious tall, dark, handsome stranger on the elevator, David walked in. We gaped at each other for a long moment before laughter broke the spell. He'd told me that the entire ride down in the elevator he kept wondering what he should say to me. But he'd been so nervous, the only thing that kept coming to his mind were bad pick-up lines. The rest was history, until he told me he'd never loved me.

How do you ever know whether a guy was the right one? Robert was bright, articulate, and fun to be with and was certainly very attractive. So what was wrong? I guess the problem was that I could no longer trust how I felt. The only thing I knew for sure was that I didn't want to make another mistake like I'd made with David.

That afternoon, I took a nap and then got ready for Javier, who'd called me the day before to ask if I wanted to go to Summerfest, Milwaukee's biggest summer music festival, held at Lake Michigan. It was hot and humid and still in the nineties at five P.M. I toweled off after a quick, cool shower and put on a pair of white shorts and a red cotton tank top. I looked in the mirror and saw my after-nap hair, all rough and wild like an overgrown polar bear pelt. But the dark circles under my eyes were gone, so I no longer resembled a walk-on for a horror movie. A touch of Pizzazz Pink lipstick, brown mascara, and spray gel for my hair and I was almost good as new. I heard the downstairs buzzer sound.

"Sam, wow, you look fantastic!" said Javier. He took my right hand, lifted it up over my head and led me into a twirl and a dip. I'd never been greeted like this before! Javier smelled wonderful. He had a clean, fresh scent like soap and wore a pair of khaki shorts and a light blue knit top that made his swarthy dark looks all the darker.

Pulling me close, he extended my right arm out in front of me and led me into a fox trot down the length of the hallway and back. We laughed as I pulled him inside my apartment. When we left the air-conditioned comfort of my apartment to step out onto my balcony, the hot air hit us like the blast of a furnace.

"It looks like a big sleepy ocean," he said, as we stood at the railing looking out at Lake Michigan. And it did. It was utterly calm, as if the heavy, humid air had put it into a deep slumber.

"Is that live music?" I asked him.

"Yeah, it's coming from Summerfest."

"I didn't know I lived that close."

"The water helps carry the sound. You're about a mile away."

We walked out of my building to Javier's rusted pickup truck. He opened my door and I hopped in.

"No air-conditioning, sorry about that." His arm worked the crank on my window as he rolled it down. I couldn't help but admire his swelling biceps and the fact that Javier was a true gentleman.

"We're so close, I don't mind walking," I said, and he agreed. We slowly strolled down Prospect Avenue toward the festival grounds.

"Did you work today?"

"Yeah. We're roofing a four-family apartment building."

"How do you work outside in the sun with this heat?" I asked, wondering if he'd be happier with an office job, not that being walled inside a cubicle under florescent lights while staring at a computer screen all day was superior to manual labor.

"You get used to it, sort of. In heat like this you have to take a lot of breaks." We were silent for a few minutes. "We spent most of dinner the other night talking about what I like to do. Now it's your turn. What are your passions besides dancing, Sam?"

"I love to travel. I went to Peru in May and climbed Machu Picchu," I told him, realizing that this was the first person I'd talked to about my recent trip to Peru since arriving in Milwaukee. I told Javier about my five-day trek along the Inca trail to the ruins, the waterfalls, the cloud forests, the high mountain passes, and the incredible beauty of seeing the lost city in the mist.

"Have you done any traveling outside the U.S.?" I asked.

Javier said he'd gone to the Dominican Republic last year for the first time since he'd left with his family when he was three years old, staying with his grandparents and meeting most of his cousins for the first time.

"I was there during the Latin Music Festival," he said. He stopped momentarily to pet a golden retriever that had eagerly bounded to him, but then we continued on, much to the dog's apparent distress. "I danced every night until dawn. For the first time in my life, I felt really connected to my roots. I decided after that trip that I wanted to open my own dance studio."

Summerfest was packed with wall-to-wall people. The body heat coupled with the heat index put me into something close to a drug-induced state as we slowly drifted from one music stage to another—a twelve-piece big band here, an R&B band there, and even an Elvis impersonator whose sideburns had flipped up at the ends and were peeling off from the sweat pouring down his face.

"Do you remember anything about living in the Dominican Republic?" I asked Javier a while later as we sat on the rocks on the shore of the lake, drinking beer.

"I remember Eliseo and me playing in the dirt, barefoot, chasing one other. I have another memory of my mother baking bread in the kitchen and of going to the outdoor market with her. The old women sitting on the ground selling fruit would cut off pieces of mango and pineapple and feed me. And they always pinched me," he said, pointing to his left cheek.

"I'm sure that with that dimple you were too cute to resist."

"What is it with my dimple?" he wondered. "I've gotten more attention from women because of that than anything else. Women don't love me for me, it's only for my dimple."

I had an urge to reach over and caress his face, but I restrained myself. Javier was so different than any man I'd ever gone out with before. In the past, my relationships with men had typically felt like a high-wire act; one wrong move or word and boom, it was over. But being with Javier was effortless—not that this was a date, although admittedly it had quasi-date qualities to it.

"Tell me about your family, Sam," he asked.

"There's not much to tell," I said, as I readjusted myself on the hard rocks and looked out at the lake. "My father died when I was sixteen. Cancer. I have a younger sister, Susan. She and her husband have a daughter who's five months old. Unfortunately, I don't have much in common with my sister. We get along, but I can't really confide in her or relate to her life. But I don't think she can relate to mine either."

"And your mother?"

"She talks at me, I listen. We don't get along at all." I went on to explain that I'd always felt separated at birth from my real family, but at the same time, I feel guilty for not making more of an effort to be close to the one I was stuck with.

"I respect my father," Javier told me, "but he's distant, and never shows his emotions. It's my mother and sister that I'm really close to. You know, my mother never made it past the sixth grade, but she's the smartest woman I know. When I have a problem it's her I go to."

"What about Eliseo?"

"We live together, and Eliseo works with my father and me a few days a week, but we're not close," he said, and I could tell it was a subject that bothered him. "We're very different."

"Well, you know what they say, you choose your friends, not your relatives," I suggested, as much for myself as for Javier.

"Yeah, I guess so," he said. "I know I'm lucky, but sometimes I get lonely and think about how nice it would be to share my life with the right woman."

Was he thinking about his ex-girlfriend Isabella, I wondered?

I knew I could've asked him, as a friend, but I didn't want another woman to intrude on our conversation.

"Have you ever been married, Sam?" he asked.

"Almost, a few years ago," I said, and then told him about David and about the incident that had ended our relationship after I'd brought up wanting to get pregnant. It was the first time I'd talked about it with anyone but a close girlfriend.

"So you'd like to have children?" he asked.

"Yes, with the right guy. How about you?"

"Definitely," he said. "I love kids. I've got some friends I visit in Miami whenever I get the chance. The last time I was there, their one-year-old son fell asleep on my chest. It was the most wonderful feeling."

A wave of emotions washed through me. Whenever men talked about wanting to be fathers, my insides turned to mush and the maternal lightbulb in my brain snapped on. Humans were just animals, but it was annoying all the same that I couldn't control these feelings.

It was close to midnight when we wandered back toward my apartment. We took the path near the Milwaukee Art Museum. The moon was full, reflected into the inky black water of the lake, and it had finally cooled off to a comfortable temperature.

When Javier unexpectedly grabbed my hand and twirled me quickly three times, I lost my balance and fell into him. Instead of letting go he took me into his arms and we began to slow dance. The music from all of the stages coming from Summerfest joined together sounding a bit like a symphony warming up before a concert. I clung to him, remembering high school dances where I'd once moved like this to "Color My World."

Javier stopped moving and pulled apart from me, keeping his hands on my waist.

"Sam, it's so easy to be with you," he said. "I feel like I've known you forever."

He leaned in to kiss me and before I knew it our arms were around each other and we were pulling and tugging, trying to get closer and closer although our bodies were already smashed together. This went on, for how long I wasn't sure, but then a million thoughts entered my brain at once, my assignment, my mother's expectations, Robert, and the possibility that Javier was still in love with Isabella and just biding his time with me.

I pulled away from him. "Javier, hey, I better get home, I've got a big day tomorrow."

He walked me home and I said good-bye to him outside of my building with a brief kiss to his lips. I needed to straighten out everything that was going on in my brain before things got too carried away.

*

Eleven

Love Resume

A married friend in her early forties who isn't completely happy with her spouse told me that if she had to do it all over again, she'd go about looking for a husband as if she were searching for a job. When a man decides to get married he pursues finding a wife just like a job search. He asks all of his friends and relatives to set him up. He may place a personal ad or even join a dating service. In other words, he takes action. Women, on the other hand, tend to remain passive.

This gave me the idea for the love resume.

Think of the emotional traumas, the endless pussyfooting about past romances and future objectives that could be avoided with this streamlined approach. Everything would be there in black and white. Candidates for potential romance would submit a cover letter, photograph, and love resume to you in advance. You could peruse these documents in your leisure over a glass of merlot, share them with family and friends, and then summon the promising applicants in for a face-to-face interview, based on carefully selected questions such as:

"Describe a typical first date."

"I see from your resume that you and Cindy dated for four years. What were your greatest strengths and weaknesses during that relationship?"

"I'm concerned about the eighteen-month gap between Rachel and Susan. Were you involved in any extracurricular activities during that time period?"

"Describe a romantic situation in which you lost your temper and how you handled it?"

"How would you be an asset to my life if I selected you as my romantic partner?"

"Where do you see yourself in five years? Ten years?" (If he doesn't say married with a couple of kids and madly in love with you, you can stop wasting your time and terminate the interview right then and there.)

"How confident are you that you can successfully perform the duties of this position and why?"

"With all of your experience, how do you feel about taking an entry-level position with me?"

This is a loaded question and things could get a little dicey here. If he's a gentleman, he'll gently deflect the question with humor. But he could take the lecherous approach and reduce his answer to a blatant sexual come-on like, "Entry? I prefer the rear myself." However, this question should weed out the perverts.

If and only if the interview is going extremely well would you ask the all-important gonad-shriveling question: "What are your views on monogamy?" If at this point he should start to fidget or suddenly seem engrossed in trying to determine if your walls are painted ecru or eggshell, this is a bad sign. If he says, "I think it's

*great!" you know he's lying since there's not a man on the planet
who is going to tell you his honest views on this question because
there's not a man on the planet that thinks monogamy is a good
thing. Most men view monogamy with the same grim determina-
tion with which one faces the prospect of months of painful dental
procedures to correct receding gum lines. It's not that it's impossible for him, it's just that he doesn't like it. After all, even Jimmy
Carter lusted in his heart.*

*So what is the purpose of this question? Not to find out his
views, but to tell him yours. This is your opportunity to make it
clear that any transgressions in this area are grounds for immediate
dismissal.*

*Finally, no matter how promising the candidate, NEVER offer
him a position on the spot. Always ask for at least three references.*

I walked into the Chinese restaurant and looked across tables
laden with bowls of sweet and sour soup and plates of moo goo
gai pan and egg rolls, searching for my group. The low hum of
pleasant conversation bubbled up from the dining room, which
was filled with happy couples, families with children, and, oh
God, there they were, my group, three women and three men.
This was going to be much worse than I'd thought.

Should I yell "fire"? No, people get arrested for things like
that, and I hated to see everyone's dinner getting cold until the
fire department and police figured out it was only a hoax and led
me away in handcuffs.

Should I just leave? Yes! I turned toward the door, stopping
just as my hand touched the handle. The years of etiquette lessons my mother had forced me to attend in high school had finally paid off. I never could tell the dessert from the salad fork,
but it had seeped into my consciousness that it was generally not

considered polite to make a dinner engagement and leave before you've at least said hello, and then faked an emergency. I turned back and, steeling myself, marched over to them.

"Oh, you must be Samantha Jacobs," said a pretty blond woman in her mid-thirties, who looked nine months pregnant. "I'm so glad you found us!"

We shook hands, but I couldn't tear my eyes away from the middle of the table. As I sat down across from the woman heavy with child, she completely disappeared behind the centerpiece, a frighteningly realistic two-foot-high stuffed owl, with yellow eyes that drilled into my own.

"Does anyone ever ask why you have an owl on the table?" I asked no one in particular.

"Strangely enough, many people do," chirped a brunette with a pageboy haircut and big gold hoop earrings. "We put it on the table for our get-togethers so new Mensa members like you can find us."

When Sally told me that I had to take an IQ test before leaving New York, I wondered if Elaine was trying to gather some independent proof that I was smart enough to find a man. Since even plants were able to reproduce and, in my experience, being smart was usually not a plus given the fragile egos of men, at first I couldn't understand why, until Sally had explained that Elaine wanted me to join Mensa. For years, Elaine Daniels has been a member of this international society for people with IQs in the top 2 percent of the population. But the critical factor was Mensa's official website, which claimed that many marriages have been made among Mensans.

Patty, the pregnant woman, poked her head around the owl and smoothly began the round of introductions, as if talking around a great horned stuffed owl centerpiece was something she did every day of her life. She explained that she was a Montessori schoolteacher, and then gestured to the empty chair next to her, saying that her husband would be a little late. She had no sooner finished speaking than he appeared.

"This is my husband, Zack," Patty said, with a proud grin as she patted her bulging belly. "Zack, meet our newest member, Samantha Jacobs."

"Zack?" I couldn't believe it. I felt my mouth hanging open.

"It's nice to meet you, what is your name again?" Zack asked, casting me a desperate look as if to say, "I'll give you my first-born child if you will just keep your mouth shut."

Well if it wasn't Mr. Gorgeous-No-I'm-Not-Married-Midwest-Express-Pilot who picks up women on Bradford Beach, flirts with them madly, tells them he's single, and then turns out to be married. Shades of my mini-affair in Peru with Wayne the entomologist resurfaced. I felt sick at the thought that it had almost happened again. What was with these assholes who apparently thought nothing of cheating on their pregnant wives?

"Do you guys know each other?" asked his wife, Patty, her smile fading as she looked from one of us to the other.

I paused. A bead of sweat broke out on Zack's forehead.

"No, no," I protested. "For a moment I thought Zack was someone I'd met recently . . . *on Bradford Beach*."

"Zack is an airplane steward," said Patty, who grabbed on to his arm and beamed at him like a lovesick teenager, at which he wiped his forehead and sat down.

"Samantha, what would you like to know about our little group?" Patty continued with her hands securely fastened to Zack's arm, after the rest of the introductions were over. If only she knew what I knew, she'd have him surgically attached to her body or have the words *I'm married* tattooed across his forehead.

"Is this everyone in the Milwaukee chapter of Mensa?" I asked, doing a quick check by which I could see that all of the members here, except a guy seated next to me, were married.

"There are about one hundred Mensans," Patty said, "but we're the only active members in the Milwaukee chapter."

Mensans. If you say it over and over again it begins to sound like the kind of disease that no one discusses in polite company, like having gonorrhea or scabies. "Did you hear? Samantha has mensans." "Oh, God no! She didn't seem like the type to me."

"We meet at a different restaurant once a month," Patty continued. "Then two weeks later we have our official get-togethers. We usually have a guest speaker who talks on various subjects. Last month it was chaos theory. But pretty much we Mensans get together as an excuse to eat."

"Speaking of food, can I get the recipe for that artichoke dip you made, Selma?" asked a woman for whom the expressions *granola* and *New Age* must have been coined. She had mousy brown hair down to her waist, no makeup, and wore a loose conglomeration of gauzy robes in drab olives and browns. And I was willing to bet my next paycheck there was a pair of Birkenstocks on her feet.

So much for chaos theory. This question prompted a lively debate of the pros and cons of using low-fat versus regular sour cream for the artichoke dip.

I turned to the lone single man in the chair next to me, John Krest, a thin, dark-haired man with features so sharp that they might have been carved out of granite.

"So, John, you're a writer?" I began, hoping the two of us might plunge into a matter a bit weightier than sour cream dip.

"If I had my way, people wouldn't have jobs," he responded, as his left eye wandered over my shoulder. There was a lost look about him, as if he were searching for his keys or had to be somewhere but couldn't quite remember where.

"Our society should promote people's innate talents and passions," he continued, as though poised behind a podium. "If they like to quilt, then they should become quilters and give their quilts away to people who need them. If they like to sing, they should become singers and perform free concerts for whoever wants to attend."

"What if they just like to smoke pot and get stoned?" I asked him.

"I haven't worked out all the kinks yet," he said, looking a bit alarmed and rubbing the bridge of his nose with his finger as the table discussion moved on to favorite barbeque recipes.

"Are you working on any particular projects, John?"

"I'm writing a book. It's about a leaf."

Had he said Leif, as in Eriksson, leaf, as in attached to a tree, or leaf, as in leave me alone?

"The leaf falls from the tree into the river," he said dramatically, "and as the leaf is floating down the river it asks the birds and the fishes, 'Who am I? What am I?' And every creature the leaf encounters tells the leaf that they don't know what it is."

"And then what happens?"

"Finally, when the leaf reaches the ocean, it realizes it is just a leaf and it is okay with that, and then it floats out to sea and a seagull eats it."

I'd just taken a swallow of green tea. It took every scintilla of willpower I possessed to not spit it directly into the owl's beak.

"How long is your book going to be?" I asked him, unable to resist yet another question. I assumed his answer would be in the neighborhood of, oh, perhaps two pages, if he'd really stretched it.

"So far it's about fifty thousand words."

"Wow! You must have studied a lot of philosophy," I said.

"No, actually I think Aristotle and Plato are stupid."

* * *

The next afternoon I was home lounging on my balcony, reading a book about bachata, when Lessie called me.

"Turn on the TV now!" she said excitedly. "Channel twelve."

Fifteen seconds later I was looking at Oprah Winfrey holding up a copy of the May 27 issue of *Très Chic* magazine with the cover story: "Will Our Mystery Woman Defy the Statistics and Find Mr. Right?"

"Oh no," I said as I sank into the couch. "I'll call you back, Lessie."

"With us today is Harvard-educated sociologist Dr. Victoria Huber, author of *The Single Professional Woman Over Forty: The Hopeless Search for Happily Ever After*," Oprah continued. "Dr. Huber, it's your assertion based upon your extensive studies of the demographics of the single population in our country, that a never-married professional woman over forty has a better chance of winning a seven-figure lottery jackpot than of ever getting married. Are things really that bleak?"

"I could have just as easily said she has a better chance of giving birth to a set of identical quadruplets or being the first person to walk on Mars," said the unsmiling Dr. Huber, who looked like a man in drag. "Yes, things are that bleak."

"So does the Mystery Woman have any hope at all, Doctor?" asked Oprah.

"I don't know about hope," Dr. Huber said grimly, "but I do know about numbers. I'm afraid the statistics would say no."

"I don't want to accept that!" said Oprah. The audience clapped and cheered. "Let's ask the audience, does anyone here know a never-married, professional woman who got married after the age of forty?"

The camera panned to the right and left, and then to left and right again.

"Anyone at all?" asked Oprah, her smile beginning to droop.

One woman in the last row timidly raised her hand. Oprah invited her to come up on stage. She introduced herself as Mary Louise, a plain, eerily serene woman who was a biotech engineer from Tulsa, Oklahoma.

"Who do you know who got married?" Oprah asked her.

"Well, me, actually," she said.

The audience burst into applause. Mary Louise blushed, and nervously stuffed her hands in the pockets of a red gingham-checked jumper that she wore over a long-sleeved white blouse. The gold cross around her neck gleamed under the studio lights.

"That's fantastic!" Oprah exclaimed. "How old were you when you got married?"

"Forty-four." More cheers rose up from the audience.

"Are you happy?"

"Yes, very," she said with a faint smile.

"How old was your husband when you married him?"

"Thirty."

The audience went wild, rising to their feet to give her a standing ovation. A couple of women yelled out, "You go, girl!"

Apparently, at least for talk show devotees, there was no squeamishness at the thought of a woman robbing the cradle.

"A younger man! Well that's fabulous!" said Oprah. "Okay, here's the question that I'm sure all our single ladies would like to know the answer to. How did you meet each other?"

"Well, I'm very active in the prison ministry. We met on one of my visits . . ."

"Your husband is a prisoner?" asked a stricken Oprah.

"Technically, yes. But he's not guilty! When they agree to do the DNA testing then they'll have to let him go . . ."

Oprah mumbled a congratulations and then cut to commercial.

I was beginning to understand the sickly lure of public hangings. My apartment building could become engulfed in flames and I'd still be sitting here, glued to the screen. The commercial minutes couldn't tick by fast enough until the show resumed.

"We are very lucky to have with us today Elaine Daniels," Oprah said smoothly, having regained her composure. "She is the CEO and editorial director of *Très Chic* magazine."

It was a shock to see Elaine, who looked her usual blond femme fatale self, dressed in a perfectly tailored beige suit, probably Prada. In the past month I'd conveniently erased her visage from my memory.

"Thank you, Oprah, it's a pleasure to be here," said Elaine in a voice dripping with honey.

"Elaine, tell us, how did you come up with this incredible idea of the Mystery Woman?" asked Oprah.

"Well," said Elaine fluttering her eyelashes and trying her best to look modest, "I have Dr. Huber to thank for that." Elaine flashed a smile at Dr. Huber, whose face was as emotionless as an android. "Without Dr. Huber's book, I never would've come up with the plan to prove that a professional woman over forty can *easily* find a wonderful husband, if that's what she chooses to do."

The audience applauded politely.

"Easily?" said Oprah. "So you don't agree with Dr. Huber's statistics?"

"I can't imagine that an *intelligent* woman would let some

silly little book convince her that she can't do whatever she wants to do with her life."

The audience clapped louder, mixed with a few cheers.

"Silly?" interjected Dr. Huber, who looked like she wanted to ask Elaine to meet her in the alley after the show. "Excuse me, but I can't imagine that someone who runs a superfluous *women's magazine* is qualified to intelligently comment on scientifically compiled data."

For a split second Elaine's true feelings flashed across her face. It was a look that could have dropped a herd of buffalo. But she smoothly covered it up with tinkling laughter that sounded like fingernails down a chalkboard. And then, to accentuate her femininity in contrast to Dr. Huber's severe lack of it, deliberately uncrossed and crossed her perfectly toned legs.

"Dr. Huber," said Elaine sweetly with her white-knuckled hands folded in her lap, "a *real* woman would never let a few meaningless numbers stand in her way."

The audience went wild. The camera flashed to Dr. Huber, who sat looking like a prune with her arms crossed over her nonexistent chest.

"Elaine," said Oprah, who looked nervous, "tell us what you can about the Mystery Woman. Does she have some special qualities that will help her find a husband in such a short time?"

"Special?" Elaine tittered. "She's a darling woman, but if anything, she's actually a little too ordinary. Average looks, average intelligence, and an average personality. I deliberately selected her for those reasons, because I want the single women of this country to know that they don't need to be supermodels or wealthy or need to take any extraordinary measures to find a great husband. They just need to be themselves."

That was my wonderfully supportive boss. If I'm ever contemplating suicide I'll just expedite things by getting a pep talk from Elaine first.

"We're out of time for today," Oprah said. "I'd just like to close by saying a few words to the Mystery Woman. Wherever you are, whoever you are, I wish you all the luck in the world. And I want an invitation to your wedding!"

A round of applause followed by a few hoots and shouts of approval could be heard. The camera panned over the audience. Several members held up signs saying, "YOU CAN DO IT MYSTERY WOMAN!" and "WE LOVE YOU MYSTERY WOMAN!"

I turned off the TV. I sat there stunned, and then realized I had tears in my eyes. After I'd composed myself, I called Lessie back.

"I can't believe the attention this is getting," I said.

"Are you kidding?" she said. "Do you know how many single women in their thirties and forties want to fall in love and get married? Millions. They're depending on you, Sam. You've got to do this."

"Thanks for the added pressure," I said. "You know, any single woman could do what I'm doing if she wanted to spend the time and energy on video dating, the volleyball league, personals ads, all of it."

"And money."

"True," I admitted. "I'm not paying for this, but I think treating this like a job search is the answer for women who really want to meet someone."

That's it! It should be like a job. What we needed were love resumes and love interviews, I thought. I said good-bye to Lessie and grabbed my journal. I had to get this idea down before I forgot it.

Later, having arranged to meet Javier, who'd called me yesterday, I drove over to his duplex. As I pulled up, he was standing outside his pickup truck, loading two bikes into the back.

"Sam, it's great to see you!" he said, kissing me on the cheek. "I hope you're ready for some serious riding. I'm thinking we could easily do a hundred miles today."

"A hundred what?"

"I'm kidding," he said, grinning. "Don't worry, I've picked an easy trail for us."

"You mean you picked an easy trail for me. I can see you're in very good biking shape," I said, staring at his thick, muscular thighs while he'd turned and bent over the truck to adjust the bikes.

Most of the time when I see biking shorts on a man I get embarrassed for them, like men in Speedos. It's like trying to not look at the giant pimple on someone's face. The more you try to avoid looking at it, the more you end up staring at it. But Javier's tight black shorts fit him perfectly and his royal blue biking shirt fit snugly across his muscular chest.

We drove west beyond the outskirts of Milwaukee, passing a few old farms that had survived the onslaught of urban sprawl, until we reached a turn-off about thirty minutes beyond the city. The narrow two-lane road we turned onto was hilly. We drove by pastures with grazing horses and cows, thick forests, and the occasional three-story mansion tucked next to a stream.

Javier parked on the side of the road and unloaded our bikes. We rode single file for almost an hour with him turning around every minute or so to make sure I was still following him, until we came to a little cafe, tucked away in the middle of nowhere, next to a grove of pine trees. I wondered how it stayed in business until I saw a dozen bikes in a rack outside the restaurant. Nearly everyone inside was dressed in biking gear. A few of them nodded at Javier and said, "Hello."

"These must be all the people who zoomed past us at the speed of light," I said, looking around while we waited in the doorway to be seated. "I'm sorry you had to go slow for me."

Javier grinned broadly and very deliberately crossed his arms.

"What?" I asked him.

"Sam, first of all, these guys are some of the best bikers in southern Wisconsin. *I* have to struggle to keep up with them. Second, it doesn't matter, I just love spending time with you."

The waitress seated us at a table on the patio, and I noticed that Javier hadn't even broken a sweat even though it must be close to eighty degrees.

"I do some long rides and races on the weekends when I get a chance," he told me and went on to explain that he'd decided to try bike racing a few years ago after watching Lance Armstrong win the Tour de France after surviving cancer, and had promptly joined a local bicycle club that trained for racing.

"And have you won many races?"

"A few," he said, and I could tell he was purposely being ultra modest. As with salsa, all it seemed to take for Javier to excel was to watch and then do.

"That was really fun, Javier, thank you," I told him later that afternoon, as we stood next to his truck outside his duplex.

"I'm glad you enjoyed it," he said, not making any moves in my direction.

I stood there for a moment, waiting for the moment that didn't happen. Okay, Javier, take me into your arms and kiss me, you fool! I don't have the strength to resist you but I know I should.

"Well, I'll see you," he said.

"Soon, I hope," I said, giving him a little wave and then driving away. I was disappointed at our nonphysical good-bye, but I supposed it was partially my fault since I had been giving him pretty definite don't-kiss-me vibes.

Since it was only four o'clock, I decided I had just enough time to drive over to Single No More and pick out a couple more prospective dates before they closed for the day. Twenty minutes later, I braced myself and pushed open the glass door to the office. Nothing had changed since my last visit except a slender Asian woman wearing a T-shirt and cut-off blue jean shorts was sitting in the stuffy waiting room flipping through a tattered copy of *People*. A fan in the corner blew hot air around. A chip of paint fell from the wall to the carpeting. A couple of flies buzzed around the room. God, this place was depressing.

"Can you believe this issue is two years old?" she said, tossing the magazine onto the wood veneer coffee table in front of her and brushing her inky black bangs aside from her forehead. "For the money I paid you'd think they'd subscribe to some current magazines. *And* get air-conditioning. Have you been here before?"

"This is my second time back after I signed up," I said. "How about you?"

"I've been a member for five and a half months," she said in a monotone. "I've only got two weeks left, so I want to get a few more profiles out before my membership expires. You know, get my money's worth."

"How much luck have you had?" I asked her.

"I've gone on a bunch of first dates, two or three second dates, um, maybe a third date, and one disastrous fourth. The pickings are mighty slim."

Just then Bunny Woods opened the door to the waiting room. "Well, my two favorite clients, Jane and Samantha!"

Bunny's blond bouffant was seriously wilting under the heat, but she managed to act cool and breezy.

"I don't normally do this, but since we're pressed for time today, do you two mind doing your selections together?"

Jane and I looked at each other and shrugged.

"Excellent! Come with me," Bunny said, leading the way into the video room. "I'll be in my office if you need anything," she said, patting the top of the vault.

"Do *not* go out with him," Jane said, pointing at an attractive guy named Dennis. "At the end of our first and last date, this loser winks at me and tells me he only picks up the check if he knows he's going to get lucky."

"Have you ever gone out with this guy?" I asked her, pointing to a photo of a man named Etienne, who reminded me of an older version of Pierre, my first love from Paris.

Jane drew her index finger across her throat, and went on to also nix Tom, whose breath could "melt steel"; Sean, who couldn't stop talking about his soul mate who dumped him seven years ago; and Jason, who had told her that while he liked her and personally had nothing against her race, he couldn't see things ever getting serious because his parents didn't like "Chinamen."

"I'm Japanese," Jane said. "I guess we all look alike to him."

"Maybe to save time you should point to the ones you haven't gone out with and we'll just split them up," I suggested with a smile. Looking at my watch, I could see that we only had fifteen minutes until the office closed.

Turning to the next page, she picked up the album for a closer look. "Wow, either this is a new addition or somehow I've missed him before. Look at those eyelashes!"

"You mean that one?" I said, pointing my finger at the very first photograph I'd selected at Single No More. I had a weird feeling that I couldn't begin to describe. She was looking at the man who told me on our last date that he thought he was falling in love with me. What should I do?

"Is something wrong?" Jane asked. "Do you want to go out with him?"

"No, no that's okay. You saw him first," I said, but I suddenly felt as though I'd swallowed a tennis ball. Was Robert dating other women from Single No More? I was dating other men, but after all, it was for my job. I had an excuse.

"I'll bet he's your type," Jane suggested. I smiled inwardly. Women were always naturally thinking of others' feelings. Men would handle this situation a bit differently, no doubt working out an equitable and sensitive sharing arrangement, something like, "I've got more money than you and drive a better car, so I get the first poke at her. When I get sick of her, you can have her."

We each chose two photographs. I breathed an inward sigh of relief that Jane hadn't chosen Robert after all. We gave our selections to Bunny, who then offered to pull their videotapes. But I told her I was in a hurry, which I was, in a hurry to avoid lapsing into severe depression if I spent five more minutes in there. The place gave me the creeps. I filled out my two postcards, wished Jane luck, and quickly left.

As I walked outside to my car, a brown sedan parked almost directly across the street caught my eye for some reason and I took a second look at the driver wearing dark sunglasses and a hat. I turned to put my key in the car door lock, and immediately whipped my head back around. Was that Sebastian Diaz? It definitely looked like him. What was he doing here? Before I could even think about whether I should wave, the sedan suddenly sped off. Weird. But then again, everything about that man was weird.

When I got home, I called Elizabeth to discuss the issue that had been bothering me since that first night at Club Cubana. I hadn't realized how much it would bother me that Javier hadn't kissed me good-bye earlier that afternoon. I needed to resolve what I should do about him, and I knew Elizabeth was the best person to talk to.

"Elizabeth, if you met a guy who was younger than you, let's say hypothetically nine years younger, and he'd never been to college—let's say hypothetically he's a roofer—and you found him smart and incredibly nice, would you go out with him?"

"This isn't the guy you met from the video dating service," she said. "Who are you talking about?"

"No one," I said quickly.

"You're under a lot of stress, Sam, so for now, I'll spare you my exceptional cross-examination skills and let you slide," she said. "The real issue is, who cares about the age difference? Men date and marry much younger women all the time and no one blinks an eye," she said, making it sound so logical. "If your hypothetical roofer is mature and doesn't care that you're older, why should you?"

"Yes, but a decade? He wasn't even alive when Martin Luther King was killed."

"Do you want a lover and a friend or someone you can discuss historical events with?" said Elizabeth.

It was true that Javier didn't seem to care about the age difference. I'd warned him. I'd given him a fair chance to run away from me. But he kept coming back for more.

"Well, there's a bit of a height difference," I said, "He's an inch or two shorter."

"Sam, I know you well enough to know you don't care about things like that. What's the real issue?"

"Okay, what do you think about a professional college-educated woman dating a blue-collar guy?"

"Well, I've never gone out with a guy without a college degree," she said, "but I guess if I met one I really liked, and I thought he was smart, I might go for it. But you've got a bigger problem."

"I know. My job," I said. Elaine had made it very clear whom I was supposed to end up with. Fifty percent of the 900,000 readers of *Très Chic* had college degrees. Thirty percent had master's degrees and 7 percent had Ph.D.s. Blue-collar men only appeared on their radar screens when they needed their cars or plumbing fixed or when they stayed late at work and bumped into them mopping the hallways.

We caught up on Elizabeth's life. Her weekend in the Hamptons with Judge Doug had gone great. They were now seeing each other about three times a week.

"So is Doug the . . . ?"

"Stop," she interrupted. "I don't want to go there and break the spell. I'm taking this slowly, one step at a time. I haven't even met his kids yet. And his divorce won't be final for another couple months."

"Okay, I understand. Don't ask, don't tell."

"Look who's talking. But Sam, I have a very strong feeling everything will work out for you."

"I hope you're right."

"I know I'm right," she said. "By the way, I saw your picture on the cover of *The National Enquirer*. I've got to say it wasn't your most photogenic angle."

"Very funny, Elizabeth."

"So will the wedding be in New York or on Planet Zuron?"

"Enough," I said, to her uncontrollable laughter. And I

would have laughed with her if I hadn't been so consumed by my mixed feelings about Javier.

I sat down at my computer to type my weekly report for Elaine, which I knew was not the news she would want.

Week Six Status Report:

Had date with the only man who answered my personals ad from the newspaper, Mark, an orthopedic surgeon. He might have a bedside manner at work but he'd obviously left it at the hospital. Date was, in a word, awful!

As for the Singles Sand Volleyball league, it is highly recommended that only women who know how to play volleyball or who are willing to make contact with the ball be encouraged to join. I will not be finishing out the series. However, after game number one, I met Joe, a chemical engineer who took me out for ice cream and said he would call. Still waiting.

Attended my first and last gathering of the local Milwaukee chapter of Mensa. While it may be true that many marriages have been made among Mensans, it appears that this is a fait accompli in Milwaukee. The Milwaukee chapter has only one active single male member, a would-be novelist, whom I would not consider dating if he were the last available man on earth. I do NOT recommend Mensa as a way for single women to meet men.

Returned to Single No More and selected two more potential dates.

Had fourth date with Robert Mack, things are fine.

I pressed SEND. I had been tempted to add a snide comment about what could she possibly expect with me being so utterly average, but I restrained myself, knowing that it would just be wasted energy with megalomaniac Elaine.

Although I was giving Elaine the cold hard facts about the Milwaukee dating scene, when the next issue of *Très Chic* came out, I realized that truth was a concept that Elaine preferred to ignore or hadn't quite yet grasped.

"Lessie, have you seen this yet?" I asked her, handing her a copy of the July 8 issue of *Très Chic*. We were downtown having drinks at Ilsa's, a chic restaurant overflowing with the beautiful people of Milwaukee.

Lessie picked it up and began reading the cover article titled, "Sexy Jock, Manly Mensan or Charming Surgeon—Which Would You Choose?"

"Did you write this?"

"Let's just say it was heavily edited by my wonderful boss," I said. Thanks to Elaine's *Oprah* appearance, every day there were dozens of new articles and radio spots about the Mystery Woman and single professional women over forty wanting to get married. I had become a national sensation.

I took a sip of my chocolate martini as Lessie continued to read.

"The volleyball guy is the Sexy Jock, right? And the Charming Surgeon? Isn't that the guy who was under the delusion that he looked like Mel Gibson?"

"Right," I told her. "And, Joe, Mr. Volleyball, never called, but that little fact didn't stop Elaine from making it sound like the guy is practically chasing me to the ends of the earth."

Lessie looked back down at the magazine. Her blue eyes scrunched up as she continued reading.

"The article says that Mensa is a haven of single sexy studs. She's calling them 'geniuses with penises.'" Lessie looked at me and raised a quizzical eyebrow.

"More like dorks with forks," I said shaking my head. "And Elaine had the nerve to steal that line from the book about that schizophrenic math genius. What was that called?"

"*A Beautiful Mind*," said Lessie. "This article makes it sound like you can't step outside to take out the garbage without running into a mob of gorgeous eligible men sweeping to their knees and pulling engagement rings out of their pockets."

Lessie put the magazine down on the booth next to her and reached for her glass of wine. "Eliseo is great, but I wish I lived there."

"You do live there! I mean here, remember?"

"Oh, yeah," she said.

☆ ☆ ☆

The next night was date number five with Robert for the Fourth of July. Robert picked me up around six, bringing along a picnic dinner for us—cashew chicken salad, roasted red pepper potato salad, and brownies. He hadn't made any of it, but the effort was sweet. He'd packed it in an old-fashioned wicker picnic basket, the kind with a big handle and a cover that flips open on either end. While he'd unpacked our dinner, he'd pulled out a mini American flag on a stick and handed it to me.

"And these are for later, after dark." he said, pulling out a package of sparklers.

"Sparklers! I haven't played with those since I was a kid," I said, smiling.

Next he pulled out a bottle of chilled Perrier Jouet champagne and two crystal flutes. He popped the cork. I looked at the bubbles flowing upward in my glass as he poured his own.

"A toast to Uncle Sam, bowling, and France," he said. Our

glasses clinked. I took a sip, perfectly chilled and dry. Ah champagne, nectar of the gods, my favorite.

"Do you think we should toast to another country on the Fourth of July?" I asked.

"Why not? We have a lot to thank the French for: French fries, French champagne," he said holding up his glass, "and . . ." he leaned over and kissed me.

"Sam," he said, "I know I've been a little moody lately. It's not an excuse, but I've been under a lot of pressure with my business. Will you forgive me?"

"Yes, of course." He scooted over to me and took a sip of champagne. Then he caught me staring at him.

"What are you thinking?" he asked.

"I want to talk to you about my job," I said.

"What about it?"

How would he handle learning that he's the "video guy" from the last issue of *Très Chic,* the "live one"? I opened my mouth to speak and was silenced by a loud boom. The fireworks had started.

Twelve

Safe Sex

Could salsa dancing be the meaning of life?

I pondered this weighty philosophical issue as I put on Marc Anthony's *Contra La Corriente*, one of a dozen salsa CDs I'd bought over the past couple weeks. Lying on my couch, unmoving, listening to song number three, "Si Te Vas," I felt my chest swell, thinking of dancing with Javier.

What was it about salsa dancing that made me feel like I was having the best sex of my life, starring in a major Hollywood movie, and stuffing myself with calorie-free Godiva chocolates, all rolled into one incredible feeling?

Salsa, the ultimate in safe sex—no risk of disease, pregnancy, or emotional devastation. You get the physical closeness, the emotional thrills, and the surging hormones without any of the messy stuff that came with a real relationship—arguing about whose turn it was to take out the garbage or whether to go with vinyl or steel siding? Just show up at a club, dance the night away with a few handsome strangers, and then go home. Alone.

I used to look at people with passions—things such as gardening, taxidermy, collecting thimbles from around the world—without ever really understanding their enthusiasm. But now I was living it and the CDs were just the start. I'd spent $385 plus tax on three pairs of salsa dance shoes, which together weigh less than a cream puff and amount to little more than a few strands of dental floss attached to plastic soles. As for the clothes, I don't even want to add up how much I've spent on a bolero jacket, a couple of tango shirts with ruffles and lace, two pairs of lace-up-the-back matador pants, and a bustier—the kind of practical clothes that a slutty bullfighter might invest in.

And then a few nights ago, I had gone to Cubana. Alone. It wasn't my usual night. I didn't call Lessie. I just snuck into the club the way someone might slip into a crack house to get their fix. Javier was dancing with a very young, mousy brown–haired woman when I'd walked in, and a few minutes later when he'd begun another lesson, that same mousy girl, named Nicole, chose the empty stool next to me and sat down.

Although this was only Nicole's second time at Cubana, she'd already fallen under the Javier spell. The signs were unmistakable: the dazed look, the wistful stare at Javier while he danced with another woman, and the nonstop chatter, all about him. Nicole told me that she'd arrived at Cubana at seven, and had talked with "the instructor" (she didn't even know his name for God's sake!) for an hour straight.

I looked at my watch. This meant that Javier had not only talked to her for an hour, he'd danced with her for an hour too.

The little salsa whore! Nicole was obviously just after Javier, ready to ruin everything for people like me who were here for purely wholesome reasons like getting exercise and expanding my awareness of new cultures—learning that bachata dance, for example, from that foreign country, wherever it was, when I got to, I mean was forced to, grind my pelvis into his and press my sweaty body against his and his oh-so-kissable lips were mere millimeters from mine.

Later that night, after all of the customers who'd wanted lessons had gone, Javier and I, the only ones left upstairs besides the bartender, were dancing bachata. We started dancing and soon our pelvises were very much together as we moved in smooth precision to the music. I don't know how he did it, but somehow he slipped my knee between his legs and moved me up and down as my thigh pressed up against his crotch.

"Javier, do you dance like this with everyone?" I'd asked him casually, although my heart was in my esophagus.

"No. The bachata is very passionate," he'd told me.

Really? I'd barely noticed.

"I only dance this way with very special women," he'd added a moment later, softly into my left ear.

I nearly fell off my couch remembering how Javier had made me feel that night. Dancing bachata with Javier had been an experience like none other for me. It was the sexiest, most intense ninety vertical minutes I think I've ever spent with a man. If only I could get paid to do Latin dancing. I looked at my watch and saw that it was time to go and grabbed a salsa CD and my new pair of Harley Davidson shades for the drive to Lessie's house.

Glancing into the rearview mirror at my big, dark sunglasses, I couldn't help but be painfully reminded of the last forty-eight hours. I'd had three of the worst dates of my life. Not the usual kind of bad dates. These were the sort that suck the marrow from your bones and make you think that there are worse things than living another fifty years and never having sex again, although I couldn't think of any at the moment.

"I'll bet you that some of my dates were worse. Much worse," said Lessie, as I sat slumped into one of her patio chairs while she poured me another margarita.

"Are you challenging me to a bad-date duel?" I asked her, and then made a motion with my right hand as if to fire a pistol.

She fired back with her index finger and thumb saying, "You're on. I'll even let you go first."

"Okay, Friday lunch with Todd from Brunches or Lunches. Nice-looking, financial planner, seemed perfectly normal. The first words he uttered to me as we sat down at the restaurant were not 'hi,' 'nice to meet you,' or 'what do you?' No, his very first words to me were—drum roll please—'The world is about to end, are you ready for the rapture?'"

Lessie folded her arms across her narrow chest as if to say she wasn't the least bit impressed.

"I spent the entire meal listening to him lecture me about how I was doomed to battle the forces of evil on earth after the rapture because I'm not a believer," I said.

"You call that a bad date?" Lessie taunted me. "That's a match made in heaven compared to my blind date with Roger, forty-eight, stockbroker, divorced, attractive, jazz lover, drove a convertible Porsche, and took me to a fancy French restaurant."

"This was your first date?"

"First and only. Dinner was lovely. Naturally, the delusions started around the escargot appetizer, and by the time the crème caramel was served, I'd had us married with two kids, a boy and a girl."

I nodded. Been there, done that, too many times to count. It all started when we were little girls and wrote our first names with the last name of the boy in our class who we had a crush on.

"After dinner he planned to take me to his favorite jazz bar. We walked out to the parking lot and were just twenty steps away from the restaurant when he let go of my hand, walked over to the bushes and took a piss right in front of me! Then he shook, zipped up like nothing had happened and reached for my hand." Lessie pursed her lips and gave me a smug, try-and-beat-that-look.

"Biological destiny," I said. "It's too easy for them. No squatting while trying to avoid pissing on their pants, no need for toilet paper. They love the fact that they can write their names in the snow. For some men, the world is just one big toilet."

"Roger was a misogynist," Lessie protested. "Obviously he had no respect for women."

"So?" I teased. "My turn. Larry was yesterday's lunch date. The conversation was okay, but he kept looking at me in a weird way. Not normal polite conversation looking, but actual staring. After a while I couldn't take it anymore, so I asked Larry why he was looking at me like that. He told me that he usually doesn't date women my age but made an exception for me because I looked so young in what he called my 'visuals,'" I said, holding up my fingers to make quotation marks in the air as Larry had done.

"Then," I continued, "he wondered if Single No More put a special lens or Vaseline over the camera to 'help' certain clients, like they do for aging Hollywood actresses," I said, my voice cracking. "I took a good look in the mirror today, Lessie. I think he's right, my face is sagging off my skull!"

"Sam, Larry is an asshole."

"The skin is melting off my head like wax off a candle!" I repeated.

"You don't look a day over thirty," Lessie said, putting her hand on my arm. "You're gorgeous!"

"So did I win?" I asked with a laugh.

"No! My turn," she said with a pout. "Okay, let me see, there was Barry, another blind date. First, he picks me up in a Chevy pickup truck that has a big white Playboy Bunny painted smack dab in the middle of the back window of his studmobile. Needless to say I was really impressed with that."

"That's all?"

"Hold on, sister, there's plenty more. Barry, a chiropractor by day and nutcase by night, chose to wear an eye patch for our first date. He told me he'd lost his eye in a car accident when he was twenty-five and owned a glass eye, but preferred to wear 'the patch' when he wasn't at work. But that still wasn't the worst of it. He'd just gotten a yellow lab puppy. Guess what he named him?"

I shrugged.

"Satan! He named an eight-week-old yellow lab Satan! 'Satan, come here Satan.'"

"I went out with a guy once who had a small dick and flaming carrot-red pubic hair," I said. "I think I could've gotten used to one of them, but both? No way."

"What does that have to do with anything?" asked Lessie, shaking her pretty head.

"Maybe the eye patch or the dog named Satan, but not both? Just a thought."

Lessie rolled her huckleberry-blue eyes and flipped her hand to indicate it was my turn.

"Last but not least," I began, "there was Ken. I found his profile on MilwaukeeDates.com. Where do I begin with the yin and yang of Ken? A date so horrible it will go down in the annals of dating legend and lore, a date so awful . . ."

"Sam, enough with the melodramatics," she said.

"Okay, Ken, if that's his real name," I said, "claimed to be a pharmaceutical salesman. But if he was, he's peddling hallucinogenics and imbibing most of his own samples. First, he tells me that when he was in his twenties, he was in the French Foreign Legion in the jungles of the Congo."

"The French Foreign Legion? Does it really exist?"

"That was my reaction. This being the first legionnaire I'd ever met, naturally I was curious. I asked him what it was like." I leaned forward across the patio table and lowered my voice "Ken tells me, 'You wouldn't believe it if I told you. You don't want to know.'"

Lessie laughed. "French Foreign Legion my ass. What kind of nom de guerre is Ken? Ken is the name of my plumber."

"Exactly. Then I asked him why he'd joined. He said, 'The money is good. That is, if you can stay alive long enough to enjoy it.' Then he chuckled in a danger-is-my-middle-name sort of way and took a deep drag from his cigarette. I felt like I was in a really bad movie."

"And then," I said slowly, and with as much dramatic flair as possible, removing my new sunglasses. Lessie gasped as she saw my black eye.

"I told you I could top anything you could possibly come up with," I said smugly. "So after dinner, Mr. Legionnaire and I get in his car so he can drive me home. He turns to me and says, 'I hope I don't kill you. Tonight is the first night I've driven in a year and a half. The last time I drove I was dodging mortar shells in Rwanda and I used to be a race car driver in South Africa.' I didn't have time to put on my seat belt. He zoomed out of the parking lot and slammed on the brakes, my head hit the dashboard, and bang, my black eye."

"That is a bad date," Lessie said, nodding. "A really bad date. I give up, Sam, you win."

"I can't do this anymore Lessie!"

"Calm down," she told me, rubbing her thin fingers through her auburn locks. "I have a solution. From now on just meet them for a drink, and when desperate, use the cat funeral excuse."

"The what?"

"True story. My friend Tiffany's fifteen-year-old Persian died. She loved that cat more than she's ever loved her husband, but that's another story. Anyway, she scheduled Muffy's funeral for a night that I had a blind date, so I couldn't go. My date, if you can picture this, was wearing a cowboy hat and a white-fringed cowboy shirt open to his nipples. Picture Roy Rogers gussied up as a lounge lizard."

I moaned.

"But then I remembered dear-departed Muffy," she continued. "I took a sip of my drink and told him I had to go to my friend's cat's funeral and left. As they say, all is fair in love and dating."

★ ★ ★

Robert had been out of town all week on business in California and Florida, but had called every day, sometimes a few times a day.

Exhibit A, Robert's call from Los Angeles five days ago:

"Sammie, it's so hard to get any work done when I'm thinking about you," he'd said with a hint of sadness.

He'd taken to calling me "Sammie" on day number two. Unexpectedly, I'd found this new mushy, amorous tone of his as infectious as laughter. I still had reservations about Robert, but that didn't stop me from acting like a complete fool. Exhibit B:

"How often do you think about me?" I'd asked him, day three, in a Marilyn Monroe voice, all breathless and girlish, hardly recognizing myself.

"Constantly," he'd said. "I can't even sleep."

Could it be true that I'd been relieved at the end of our Fourth of July date when he'd left me at my apartment without any heavy duty "I love you" or "I want to make love to you" declarations?

Day five had been, by far, the worst. Exhibit C:

"I can't stop thinking about you," he'd said. "Look out the window. Do you see the full moon?"

"Yes," I'd said all tremulous, as I had walked to my balcony doors to stare wistfully into the lonely evening.

WARNING! WARNING! The next sentence may induce projectile vomiting: "It makes me feel closer to you to know that we're looking at it, together," he'd said.

And so it went. It was enough to turn the stomach of the most loyal Harlequin Romance fan. This wasn't phone sex. It was something far more dangerous—phone romance. Pet names, soft voices, the hint of deep-running emotions—he'd said he thought about me constantly. Wow! All of it was calculated to make the most chaste woman fling off her clothes and jump into bed at the blink of one of his amazing eyelashes. And I certainly wasn't starting from chaste.

"Do you miss me?" he'd asked tenderly at the end of each call, giving me the definite impression that his entire emotional well-being was perched on a cliff, waiting for my answer.

"Of course I do, Bobby."

And when that first "Bobby" had come out of my mouth yesterday, I knew it was all over. Hence, tonight's date with Robert had all the makings of The Night.

The buzzer rang. My stomach lurched, but in that good nervous sort of way. I walked over to the door to press the button to the locked entrance downstairs. If I had my timing right, it would take him two minutes to get up to the eighteenth floor.

I sprinted to the bathroom and saw that my All Day Kiss-Proof lipstick had dissolved into thin air. *Très Chic* had published an article last year about the true ingredients of makeup. Lipstick was mostly animal fat. Funny how fat didn't disappear from your thighs and butt without seventy-five hours in the gym each week, plus liposuction and/or starvation. But smear some on your lips and it was gone in five minutes. I reapplied more fat to my lips, brushed some powder lightly over my face, and ran a comb through my hair one more time.

Robert stood in the doorway with his hands clasped behind his back, wearing the beguiling grin you'd find on a little boy who wanted to surprise his mother with some dandelions he'd picked for her birthday.

"I brought you a souvenir," he said, handing me a tacky snow globe with a few pink flamingos, a fat guy lying on a beach, a palm tree, and a little sign reading MIAMI HEAT.

"I love it! How did you know I needed one?" I said, shaking it as I watched the gold glitter fall over the beached whale of a sunbather.

Robert always looked good, but tonight he was particularly handsome. He wore a white cotton shirt tucked into a pair of faded blue jeans—my favorite casual look for a guy. The white creases of his crow's feet gently streamed out from his eyes against his lightly bronzed face.

Over dinner at the Thai Palace restaurant, he made me laugh, a lot—a drug far more intoxicating than all the sweet-nothings whispered over the telephone cables during the past week. But the undercurrent of sex surged through our every shy glance and when the tips of his fingers brushed against mine, I felt a direct current shoot to my loins.

At the end of the night when Robert took me home, I invited him inside. We walked out onto my balcony, looking at the lake, holding hands, and somehow ended up on my lawn chair. A minute later, the metal frame collapsed like a bent twig, and we landed in a tangle on the floor.

While Robert got to his feet, I sat up cross-legged, laughing so hard I didn't have the strength to get up.

"I didn't cause any internal bleeding did I?" he asked, pulling me up by the hand.

"Just a little brain damage," I said, and suddenly our mood shifted back to serious.

"I love you, Sam," Robert said when we reached the doorway of the bedroom, as he cupped my face with his hands. "I want to make love to you."

He took me into his arms and gave me a kiss that could win a medal, if they had award ceremonies for that sort of thing.

"I love you, Sam," he said again.

Then a second that seemed like an hour passed.

"I can't do this," I said, pulling away from him and walking over to the couch. He sat on the arm and I sat hugging my knees to my chest facing him. How had I let myself get into the very position I'd vowed not to at the start of this summer? And why did I lead him on all week? Robert deserved an explanation.

"When I was engaged to David, I thought I'd found the right person," I told him. "I was so sure he loved me and that we'd be married for the rest of our lives. And then, I found out he didn't really love me after all. I don't want to make that mistake again. Sex just seems to mess things up."

"Are you saying you're never going to sleep with me?" he asked, sadly.

There was something about the way he'd asked that made me think of a boy who has just realized that he was not going to grow up to have a career as a professional athlete after all.

"No, I'm just saying I'm not sure how I feel yet. I need some more time."

"I haven't been with anyone since my wife," he said. "I was never ready before this, before meeting you. This is a big step for me too."

I responded with silence that sapped all the good feelings and fun of the night into oblivion, as if the evening had never happened.

Looking hurt, he stood up abruptly and turned to leave.

"Please try to understand, Robert," I said, grabbing on to his arm. "It's not you, it's me."

The line was out of my mouth before I'd realized it. A line so lame and transparent that everyone knows it means exactly the opposite. It was you. Otherwise we'd be horizontal faster than a pair of rabbits.

"I'll call you," he said abruptly, and was out the door before I could say anything else.

Had he really just said the three most fateful words a man can utter? *I'll call you.* The words reverberated over and over again inside my brain. Okay, so maybe I was scared of falling in love again, of making another mistake like I had with David. Or maybe it was something else? But why couldn't Robert seem to accept my explanation and be more patient, I thought, as I cried myself to sleep.

★ ★ ★

"Nice to see you, Sam," Javier said, grinning broadly, as I arrived at his duplex for a private lesson the next afternoon. "New dance shoes?"

I'd bought another pair over the Internet, silver, with two-inch heels and special cushioned soles. He seemed to notice everything.

"How's my favorite salsa instructor?" I asked him, giving him a kiss on the cheek.

"Favorite? You mean I'm just one of many? You're cheating on me, Sam?" he said in a teasing voice.

"Yes, but you're the best."

"Well, thank you. We're going to do something a little different today. If you want to become a *salsera,* you need to understand the music. So the first thing we're going to do is listen to it."

"Haven't we been doing that?" I asked him.

"I mean really listen," he said, selecting a CD from his case. "Okay, now, what can you hear?"

For a moment I couldn't isolate the myriad of different sounds I heard. I knew nothing about the technicalities of music and had never tried to analyze or dissect it before. But then one of the sounds grabbed me.

"I can hear the really fast drumbeat," I said, moving my hand in time with the beat.

"Those are the timbales, played by the drummer. That's good that you can hear that. Now, see if you can clap to the rhythm."

"It's almost like you can't hear the first beat, you have to feel it," I said, clapping.

"That's it!" said Javier excitedly. "This isn't easy. There are lots of people who never get it. Some people can teach themselves to hear the beat, but believe me, natural rhythm is a gift. I think salsa is in your blood, Sam."

I felt a thrill go through me. Samantha Jacobs: world traveler, famous humor columnist, and salsa goddess.

Until this moment, the only analysis I'd given to music was to decide if it moved me or it didn't. Discovering that salsa didn't just move, it transported me to cloud nine, had come as a shock. Up until two months ago, I wouldn't have thought it possible to find a type of music I loved more than the blues.

While we practiced dancing, I concentrated on timing my steps with the first beat of the music. It made a big difference. I felt smoother, more confident. After a few songs, Javier turned up the tempo of the music. The faster we moved the better it felt. After a while, the brassy horns and repetitive rhythms seduced me into an altered state. It felt as though Javier and I were alone in the world.

Javier bent me backward into a dip that practically went down to China. He swept me across the floor in an arc and pulled me back up to face him at the precise moment the last note of the song played. I felt like my soul had dropped out of the bottom of my salsa shoes.

"Can we do that again, like maybe a million times?" I asked him. I was breathing hard and my heart was pounding, as much from the physical exertion as the intense feelings evoked by being with Javier, the dancing, and the music.

Javier laughed. His brow was covered with sweat and the back of his blue silk shirt clung to him. "Can we take a break first?"

"What's the problem, can't keep up with me?" I asked. A breeze from the fan a few feet away cooled the moisture at the back of my neck and I felt a chill at the small of my back.

"I have no doubt I could keep up with you," Javier said in a low voice as his eyes traveled down my body. "If you'd let me."

Danger! Danger! What was I doing here? Why don't I just

slather my body with honey and leap into a hornet's nest? If he decides to put on a bachata, I'll have to do something drastic like fake a heart attack or amputate a limb. My new motto after the other night at Cubana was, "Just Say No to Bachata." From now on it was strictly salsa for me. Salsa was fun, technically challenging, and best of all, perfectly safe because to do it right, one must maintain a pelvises-several-inches-apart platonic distance.

"How's it going with getting the loan to remodel the studio?" I asked him, as I purposely steered the conversation to a neutral subject. We both looked around the room at the broken and bent blinds hanging limp from two small windows and at the linoleum floor with bald patches that Javier had expertly led me away from while we danced.

"I just got turned down by another bank," he said. "But I've got a meeting with a lender who specializes in loans to small minority-operated businesses."

I wanted the best for him, but part of me wanted things to stay exactly the same. I didn't want to picture a sleek modern studio filled with beautiful women who would be getting the one-on-one lessons with Javier.

"With salsa it seems as though women get all the good parts, the twirls, the dips. The man does all the work," I said.

"You see that painting on the wall behind you?" said Javier, pointing above my head.

I turned around to look at a framed picture of a ship sailing toward a sunset.

"Yeah, but what does that have to do with salsa?" I asked, turning back to face him.

"The man is the frame, the woman is the picture. In other words, it's the man's job to make the woman look good."

It all made perfect sense. Well, not really. But did it matter? It was enough that dancing made me feel alive and wonderful in a way that nothing else ever had.

"How does dancing make you feel, Javier?"

He was quiet for a few moments.

"When I'm dancing with a woman who I can really dance with, it's like we're floating, like there's no one else in the world," he said, echoing my own thoughts. "It's like heaven."

Heaven! I had no idea a man could feel that way about dancing.

"How does it make you feel, Sam?"

"I can't really describe it," I said slowly, "but when I dance with you it makes me feel like melted butter."

Javier broke into a huge one-dimpled grin, which shouldn't have come as a surprise. I suppose a line like that would make any red-blooded man happy.

"Let's practice some more." He walked over to the boom box and selected a new CD, as I waited for the first beat of the angst-ridden plunk of the bachata guitar.

"Oh, salsa," I said, trying to keep the disappointment out of my voice.

We began practicing. Suddenly, he twirled me three times and swooped me into a new dip that left me breathless and teetering on my new salsa shoes. As he held me, face bent over mine, he leaned in and kissed me. His mouth tasted sweet.

"Let me put on some different music," he said hoarsely.

Yeah, sure, salsa is safe, as safe as eating broken glass. I stood frozen in the same spot, my breath heavy, as he changed the music to bachata and came back to me.

We danced and kissed and kissed and danced, our bodies fused together and moving in perfect rhythm. When the last note of the last song played, Javier picked me up and laid me down on the couch. Our clothes came off so quickly it was as if they'd dissolved; I wasn't sure who had pulled off what. But then, everything went into slow motion.

Javier kissed my mouth and neck and then slowly moved down my body, igniting every inch of my skin until I was on the verge of exploding. And then he made love to me so tenderly, so gently, I felt a tidal wave of emotions swell inside of me.

I knew Javier was holding back, patiently waiting for me. When I came I cried out and he came a moment later. We lay there in each other arms breathing heavily. Everything felt so right, so wonderful, so . . . wait! My brain synapses, which had suffered a near nuclear meltdown, came back to life.

"I have to go," I said, standing up. I pulled on my clothes so quickly I forgot to put my panties on. I grabbed them and stuffed them inside my gym bag.

Javier just sat there, his wavy brown bangs tousled over his forehead.

"Don't go, Sam," he said, not making a move to stop me. "Stay with me tonight."

"I have to go . . . I'll see you," I said.

"I'll call you tomorrow," said Javier.

I rushed out into the dusk to my parked car. During the fifteen-minute drive back to my apartment, I kept my mind as blank as possible. Like Scarlett O'Hara, I decided I would think about this tomorrow. The only thing I was sure of was that I was going to take a hot bath and go right to sleep.

When the elevator doors opened, I saw a woman sitting on the floor, slumped against my apartment door. Her hands covered her face and her shoulders moved up and down.

"Lessie?"

She pulled her hands away from her face. Mascara had smeared down her cheeks.

"You're looking at the stupidest woman in the world," she said between sobs. "I'm so dumb I don't deserve to live! I'm going to weaken the gene pool."

"Lessie, what are you talking about?" I crouched down to her level and put my hand on her knee.

"I'm pregnant!" Lessie wailed. "What am I going to do, Sam?"

Thirteen

The Palm Polygraph

MARY
Tom, I had so much fun tonight. Thank you for a wonderful evening.

TOM
Mary, I had a fantastic time too. You're very special to me you know. (Tom leans over and kisses Mary passionately). I'll call you.

Three months later
Mary is sitting in her apartment in a chair next to the telephone. She is gaunt, has dark circles under her eyes and a crazed look about her. A thick cloud of cobwebs is attached from the telephone to her head.

FEMALE ANNOUNCER *(Voice-over)*
Ladies, I think you can guess by the looks of Mary that Tom never called.

(Announcer in studio replaces shot of Mary.)

Has this ever happened to you? (Pause.) A ridiculous question. Of course it has. There's not a woman on the planet, including our sisters living among the fourth-world Stone Age tribes in the remote jungles of Papua, New Guinea, where telephones don't even exist, who hasn't heard a man say those three fateful words, "I'll call you." While women can take a small measure of comfort in this, our common universal bond, one that crosses all language, cultural, religious, and socioeconomic barriers, at the same time we do recognize that this sucks. But thankfully, there's an old product with a revolutionary new design that will help you avoid Mary's plight in your future romantic dealings.

(Announcer holds up an object that looks like a Palm Pilot.)

The new Palm Polygraph Machine! Don't be fooled by its size. Although it fits conveniently into the palm of your hand, it is a fully operational, CIA-approved polygraph machine that will give you instantaneous and accurate results. The Palm Polygraph is easy to use and takes just seconds.

(Flashback to Tom and Mary in the car at the end of their date. Mary pulls out a Palm Polygraph and puts the cup on Tom's ring finger.)

ANNOUNCER *(Voice-over)*
The next time a man says, "I'll call you," just pull out your handy Palm Polygraph, slip the finger-sized cup to the end of his left ring finger, and ask your question. The built-in digital screen will give

you an easy-to-read response that will let you know exactly where you stand.

MARY

You're going to call, Tom? (She pauses as she consults the screen.) Are you sure about that? Well, this was nice while it lasted. Thanks for everything. Good luck to you, Tom, and have a nice life. (Mary shakes Tom's hand good-bye.)

One week later

(Mary is on a date with a different man. They are laughing as they clink their wine glasses together.)

ANNOUNCER *(Voice-over)*

Mary is now a smart, sophisticated dater, who with the help of the Palm Polygraph has immediately moved on to greener pastures. Imagine, no more waiting by the phone. No more wondering. Never again be a needless victim of "I'll call you." Buy now, ladies. Don't delay, and remember, there are a lot of fish in the sea!

"It's been five days since Robert said he'd call, and nothing," I said to Elizabeth. I stretched out onto my new patio chair. An enormous white ship silently floated across the lake, dwarfing a handful of sailboats that were sprinkled over the sapphire blue water. The ship looked like it was barely moving. But less than a minute later, when I looked for it again, it was gone.

"He's lapsed into a coma. It's the only possible explanation," Elizabeth said. "Have you checked the hospitals?"

The lawn chair creaked and I experienced a momentary stab

of fright as I remembered how the last chair had snapped in two when Robert and I were lying on top of it together, five nights ago.

"So that's why men say they're going to call and don't. You've finally given me the answer to one of the greatest mysteries of the universe. Thank you, Elizabeth."

"Sarcasm does not become you," said Elizabeth.

"I think I blew it with both of them."

"Both of them? Are you talking about the hypothetical roofer too? What's going on with him?"

"Well, during my last salsa lesson we made love. It was great, fantastic actually. But then I freaked out."

"Why?" she demanded.

"I don't know." I told her. "The dancing can get pretty hot and it's easy to mix things . . . It's hard to think when I'm with him. It might be one of those mini crushes that don't even count."

I had to admit this sounded plausible, but truthfully, even I didn't believe what I'd just told her. Javier had also said he'd call me and hadn't, which had upset me far more than I'd expected.

"But I thought you liked Robert?" asked Elizabeth.

"I don't know," I confessed. "Sometimes, Robert feels like the right guy for me. But I think I'm afraid to let myself fall for him. The whole thing reminds me too much of David," I said. I stood up and started pacing the balcony.

"Have you slept with Robert?"

"No.

"So, you made love with the roofer and not with Robert. Doesn't that tell you something about your true feelings?" said Elizabeth.

"I wish someone would just tell me what to do," I said.

"Oh no," she said in the tone of a surgeon unexpectedly finding cancer during a routine appendectomy.

"Oh no, what?" I asked.

"You're going to do it again," she said. "You're going to agree to marry the wrong man."

"What?" I cried, but I knew in my heart that I couldn't laugh off whatever Elizabeth was about to tell me. Over the years, she had demonstrated time and again an uncanny, practically paranormal ability to give dead-on accurate advice. Even more disconcerting was her ability to figure out for me what I was thinking when I couldn't do it for myself.

"Sam, I'm going to be brutally honest with you," Elizabeth said. "I don't think you ever really loved David. He wasn't right for you and on some level you knew that. But you agreed to marry him anyway because it was easier to give in to the pressure your mother has put on you your whole life to marry the so-called perfect guy, than to go on being single and wait for the right person."

"You're wrong, I loved David," I said defiantly.

But in that instant I realized that I had never before looked at my relationship with him from that angle. I'd always focused on the fact that he was the one who hadn't loved me. Was it possible I hadn't loved him either?

Time had done its usual trick of erasing the bad memories and replacing them with only the good. But there had been warning signs. We'd had a lot of arguments during our last few months together, and had stopped having the long talks we'd had when we'd first started going out. Suddenly he was busy all the time at work, even busier than usual. And there were certain things he refused to talk about, ever. Like his ex-fiancée who'd broken his heart two years before we'd met and something that had happened to him at summer camp when he was thirteen. But I'd thought it was just my own wedding jitters instead of admitting to myself what I knew in my heart of hearts, that he really hadn't been the right man for me all along.

"Don't you remember how you complained that he was a workaholic?" Elizabeth continued. "That he was too selfish with himself and his time? That he didn't really listen to you or understand you?"

While I tended to take a forget-and-forget-again attitude toward the low points of my life, I could always depend on Elizabeth to remember all of them in excruciating detail, which she conveniently dredged up from her encyclopedic memory under the file: Samantha Jacobs's Bloopers and Blunders.

"And you haven't forgotten the pre-nup, have you?" asked Elizabeth.

When David had first sprung the big P on me a couple weeks after our engagement, I couldn't believe it. I was hurt and insulted. He had tried to appease me by telling me that it was really his parents, from whom he stood to inherit millions, who wanted it, not him. But I had known it was really his mother who was behind the whole thing. She'd never liked me and thought I wasn't good enough for him. I'd balked. We'd argued. I'd accused him of being a momma's boy. But a month later, I had given in and signed it, feeling like our life together was over before it had even started.

"With David you took the easy way out, you settled," Elizabeth said.

"Settled? You're always saying I'm too picky."

"You're that too," said Elizabeth.

"How can I be both?" I asked in a haughty tone as if to say, Surely you must be discussing some other totally screwed-up human being.

"Okay, what's wrong with the roofer?" she asked.

"His name is Javier Lora and there's nothing wrong with him," I said quickly. "He's kind and gentle and smart and wonderful. Except he's . . . well my assignment . . ."

"Fuck your assignment! What do you want?"

There was nothing quite as shocking as hearing someone you have never heard swear before, say, out of the multitude of choices available, the F-word in particular. More than anything, this told me quite clearly how upset Elizabeth was, and how much she cared about me.

What *did* I want? I had no idea what I wanted, but at least I was insightful enough to recognize that I didn't know. I should get some credit from the universe for that, at least, shouldn't I? Actually, what I wanted was for the higher being who ruled the universe to hand me a schedule of exactly what I should do with the rest of my life, every second of it mapped out, no room for choice, freedom, or any of that other crap that people fought wars and died for.

"I want more time to think," I told her. "I've got Elaine breathing down my neck. I've got my mother calling me every other day and asking me questions like should we go with chocolate cosmos or calla lilies for the guys' boutonnieres. Am I the only one who sees that there is no guy?"

"Sam, calm down. You have all the time in the world," said Elizabeth serenely.

"All the time in the world?" I exploded. "What are you talking about? It's only six weeks until Labor Day."

"That's an artificial deadline," she said.

Just then my Call Waiting beeped.

"Sam, stop letting other people and events decide your life for you. Please don't do anything that you don't want to do. Promise?"

"I promise," I told her, and then switched to the other call. "Hello?"

"I want to know what's going on with your widower from the video dating service, what's his name, Richard? Ralph?"

"Robert. Robert Mack," I said to Elaine, who was apparently unfamiliar with customary telephone greetings.

"Yes, Robert. How are things going with him?"

"Fabulous. Things couldn't be better."

I was getting really good at lying—too good. Of course I was doing it over the phone. Lying was nothing I'd ever had any success at before this summer. I've been told my entire life that I have one of those faces that is so expressive and easy to read that I might as well have a digital tickertape affixed to my forehead giving a running readout of my every thought and emotion.

"Why hasn't he proposed yet?" she snapped, and then without waiting for an answer asked another question. "How many dates do you have lined up for the next week?" she asked.

"A few," I said. "At least two. I'd have to check my calendar. But I also have the singles cooking class and Three-Minute Dating."

"What happened to the guy you met playing volleyball?" asked Elaine.

Joe, the M&M engineer/sports/music fanatic, was probably in the hospital bed next to Robert, another tragic coma victim.

"He never called."

It felt good to tell the truth, even about something trivial.

"My dear, why is this so difficult for you?" she asked, her voice dripping with saintly understanding and concern, as if to say, tell me about your troubles, bare your soul to me, trust me. And in that moment I wanted to believe I was seeing a new side of Elaine. I wanted to break down and tell her everything, that I didn't know if I'd ever see Robert again, and that I thought Javier could be the right guy for me, and mostly that I felt lost and alone and confused. But of course, I couldn't trust her.

"Could your problem, my dear, be . . ." she paused, "men?"

"I don't have a problem with men," I said with a carefree chuckle, knowing that this was precisely the single most troublesome area of my life.

"I'm afraid you do, my dear," Elaine said, "and if I'd known that, I would've found someone else for this assignment."

A chill ran down my spine. She'd said it casually, as if we were discussing something insignificant like a three-cent postage stamp price hike, instead of something very near and dear to my heart, the continuation of a steady paycheck and finally getting my column, "La Vie."

"But there was no one else," I protested. "I'm the only single woman over . . ."

Elaine cut off my words with a snort. Of course there were other never-married women over forty. Not at *Très Chic*. But there were freelance writers, hundreds, maybe even thousands across the country who fit the over-forty, reasonably attractive, and never-married status needed for this assignment. And at that moment, a cold fear gripped me, as I realized just how precarious my situation was. Maybe it wasn't too late to get a freelancer to take over this assignment? No one knew that the Mystery Woman was I. Elaine wouldn't stoop that low, would she? Of course she would. She'd sell her own mother for a buck.

"You're not going to pull this off, are you?" she said in a hyper-calm tone that instantly turned my bowels to jelly. "I want results, Samantha, and I want them yesterday or don't bother coming back to clean out your desk."

Click!

I'd completely forgotten about Joe the M&M engineer until Elaine had asked about him. That made three men who'd told me they were going to call and hadn't.

It seemed about the only absolute positive in my life was salsa. While dancing, my worries, my fears, and all of my thoughts—except trying to follow the man I was dancing with and doing the proper footwork—just fell away. Salsa was keeping me sane, but was so much more than that. Nothing I'd ever experienced before had made me feel so shockingly alive and utterly joyful.

Javier and Robert hadn't called, and I could be on the verge of losing my job. I needed a heavy dose of the best antidepressant on the market. I jumped up and got ready to go out. An hour later I walked into Club Cubana.

I didn't see Javier when I walked in, but didn't have time to look for him since an older man in his late fifties immediately took my hand and led me to the dance floor. Although the tempo of the salsa song was fast, we were moving much slower than the other couples on the dance floor. His style was fluid and so smooth it felt more like ice-skating than dancing. Although I preferred a faster pace, I was thrilled that I'd been able to follow his lead.

After we'd finished dancing, I saw Javier coming toward me. My heart leapt at the sight of him.

"Sam, I'm sorry I didn't call you," he said, taking hold of my hands. "I want to talk to you. Let's go out to the balcony."

The air was chilled and the balcony was empty. We leaned against the railing, facing each other. It felt so good to be with him.

"I'm so happy you're here tonight," Javier said. "I was worried you might have regretted what happened when we were together the other day."

"Javier, I . . ."

"I know I'm not the kind of guy you usually date, Sam," he continued. "But to tell you the truth, you're not the kind of woman I've ever been with before. But when I'm with you everything seems right. I feel like we were . . ."

"Javier . . ."

"Sam, please let me finish." Javier moved closer and clasped my hand to his chest. "Well, I guess I'll just say it. I love you, Sam."

"You do?"

"Yes, I do," he said, and then he broke out into a huge grin, flashing his dimple.

As Javier brought my hand up to his lips, I sensed someone watching us, and turning, saw Sebastian Diaz staring at us. But I felt an unmistakable, intense gaze coming from the person behind him, whom I couldn't quite see because Sebastian's massive body partially blocked him. Then he stepped out of the shadows.

I felt faint, although I've never fainted before so I'm just guessing this was how it felt, like someone had drilled a hole in my head and filled it with formaldehyde. In slow motion my brain processed what my eyes were claiming they saw. But it didn't seem possible. I'd never told Robert about Cubana, and what were the chances that the very man I'd been thinking about for five days would magically appear? Had he followed me here?

My heart dropped to my stomach, did several back flips, and

then ended up in two different places, half of it on the northern side of the balcony with Javier, the other half on the southern side with Robert. I had never before felt so torn between two men. There was every logical reason in the world for me to join Robert. He was everything Elaine and my mother had in mind for me. But . . .

"Let's dance, Sam. We haven't danced all night," Javier said, grabbing my hand and leading me out to the dance floor. When I looked back over my shoulder, Robert hadn't moved.

I heard the music playing, and oh shit! It was the dance that dare not speak its name—bachata.

Javier pulled me close, much closer than he'd ever danced with me before in public. Maybe he was caught up in the emotions of what he'd just told me and didn't care that he'd temporarily abandoned his usual professionalism. He moved his hands up to my head, cradling it as if he were holding an expensive piece of crystal. Then he bent me back in a dip that induced temporary amnesia.

I felt my leg slipping between Javier's as he squeezed it tight between his thighs. Of course I was upset about Robert, but weirdly, all I could think about as our cheeks pressed together was how good it felt to be with Javier. And normally he didn't wear cologne, but tonight he was wearing a scent that was musky and animal sexy.

At the exact moment the middle of my naked right thigh was pressed up against Javier's nether regions and we moved up and down in rhythm to the music, I glimpsed Robert and Sebastian skirting along the edge of the dance floor. At least a half dozen dancing couples blocked a solid view of them. I caught them only in pieces—a shoulder, a strong chin, a set of distressed eyes. But then the sea parted long enough for me to catch a full view of Robert, who stared at me, looking more shocked than any-thing else. Then the two of them disappeared down the stairs.

Easing my way back into a semi-lucid state, I told Javier I had to run to the bathroom. I darted downstairs to catch Robert. I had to explain. But he was gone.

I walked back inside Cubana, standing at the door for a mo-ment wondering what I should do.

"Looking for someone?" asked a voice suddenly at my side, and I saw Sebastian towering over me.

"Yes, a friend of mine," I said.

"Who? Maybe I can help."

"Robert, Robert Mack."

"Who?" Sebastian asked again, in a silky-smooth voice.

"The man you were talking to on the balcony. The one you just walked downstairs with," I said. Why did I always feel, while talking to Sebastian, like a trout that was trying valiantly to pad-dle upstream to spawn, but kept swimming into the rocks?

"Oh, he's just somebody I bumped into at the bar. Actually, he asked me a few questions about you and Javier, and seemed to get quite edgy. Is he a close friend of yours?"

"How would that be any of your business?" I said a little too sharply.

"I didn't mean to pry," he said, and then, with an almost im-perceptible nod, like an obsequious butler, he walked away, leaving me feeling guilty for being rude to him, which was all the more infuriating since I had never liked the man to begin with.

I walked back upstairs. Javier was dancing, but stopped in mid-dance, something he'd never done before, and came directly over to me. He pulled me back out to the balcony, which was once again empty.

"Sam, is everything okay?" He slipped his arms around my waist.

"Well, I need to tell you something, Javier, something I should've told you before the other day happened," I said. What I had to say was hard enough, but was made all the more difficult by our close physical proximity. I didn't want to do this but I had no choice.

"Javier, I've been dating quite a bit this summer and there is . . . there's a man that I started seeing before you, and I got involved and I need, I mean I want to see where things go with him."

Javier stepped back from me. He looked upset and surprised. I felt terrible. I shouldn't have let things go so far with him. The last thing I wanted to do was to hurt him.

He just stood there. I wished he would say something, anything.

"I need to get back to work," he said finally, and then walked back inside.

I knew that this was the right thing to do. I liked Robert and wanted to see where things could go with him. So why did I feel like I'd just made one of the biggest mistakes of my life?

Fourteen

Cheer Up, Listen to the Blues

—If it wasn't for bad luck, I wouldn't have no luck at all,
hard luck and trouble is my only friend
—Booker T. Jones and William Bell

"Okay, we've got The Cowboy Junkies, The Smiths, *The Way We Were*, *Love Story* and *The Yearling*," I said, fanning out the videotapes and CDs toward Lessie. "Choose your weapon."

"*The Yearling*?"

"It always makes me cry when the fawn . . . you know, at the end when Gregory Peck . . ." Lessie's blue eyes, rimmed by puffy red lids, grew big and watery. "Have you ever seen it?"

"No," said Lessie.

"I don't want to give the plot away. Trust me, it will make you bawl."

"Just what I need, more crying," Lessie mumbled. "Do you have any blues?"

Some people like to listen to the blues when they're depressed, but I prefer The Smiths, music to blow your brains out by. This may sound odd, but for me, the blues is a surefire cure for depression. Let country music have their dead dogs and broken down pickup trucks, but I'd take the blues any day. Until I'd discovered salsa, I loved the blues more than anything, the way a bee loves honey, thoroughly and completely. But I could still appreciate and enjoy its anguish, its brazen indifference to political correctness, and its blatant sexism. When B.B. King sings about his woman who can't see the doctor when he's away and should "just suffer" until he gets home, I always feel better realizing that, hey, I don't have it so bad after all.

"The blues," I said, patting her on the arm, "an excellent choice. Maybe it will even cheer you up?"

Lessie looked at me for a long moment. "You know something, Sam, you're really weird sometimes."

"I'll take that as a compliment," I quipped, putting on a B.B. King CD while Lessie raided my freezer and cupboards.

We settled ourselves on the couch with a smorgasbord of misery foods on the coffee table in front of us. She picked up the Chubby Hubby and I chose the Cherry Garcia. After a while, Lessie grabbed the bowl of sour cream and onion potato chips and I reached for the cashews. Then we switched, and switched again, crunching and slurping in the silent company of our own thoughts.

When I was younger, I'd assumed that by the time I got to the age I was at now, I'd know what I wanted and would always make the wise choice. In fact, things had only gotten worse. I felt most of the time like a lumberjack backpedaling on a log, trying desperately to stay afloat to avoid the murky water of error below. But somehow, I was constantly losing my balance, falling in, and like a half-drowned cat, getting back on the log, only to fall off again, just after my clothes had dried.

I couldn't stop picturing Robert with that shocked, sad look on his face when he saw me with Javier on the balcony and then the two of us dancing together. Assuming Robert would ever speak to me again, maybe things could work out with him? That, of course, would be the perfect scenario. And then would we live happily ever after? Could Robert make me happy?

But I couldn't stop thinking about Javier either. I'd never let myself picture or consider the possibility of having a serious relationship with him. I just couldn't let myself go there, as much as I wanted to. I'd purposely prevented myself from caring too much about Javier and had conveniently convinced myself that my feelings for him were just a silly crush, which I realized wasn't the truth.

But my problems were nothing compared to Lessie's. I was very worried about her. When she had come over this afternoon and taken off her sunglasses to reveal eyes so bloodshot and swollen that I barely recognized her, I'd assumed the worst. So when I finally got up the nerve to ask, I wasn't expecting her response.

"I haven't told him yet," she said, and then sobbed loudly, adding to the ocean of tears she'd already cried over the past few days.

It seemed a shame that Lessie had wasted such an awful surfeit of valuable energy on crying, energy that could've been put to better use say, single-handedly building a bridge from Los Angeles to Honolulu.

That women are able to cry at absolutely nothing and everything was certainly nothing new. We've been doing it from the dawn of time, ever since our cavemen husbands grunted that they'd rather go on a dangerous saber-tooth tiger hunting mission with the guys than snuggle with their women under the antelope skins next to the fire. Even worse, human beings (all right, men) have not evolved a wit in the tens of thousands of years that have elapsed since that so-called primitive point in our history.

A few months ago Elizabeth and I had been at our usual Friday night hangout in Manhattan when we'd overheard a group of fifty-ish businessmen at the bar swilling their scotches and bourbons and talking about how they'd rather play golf than make love with their wives. I sometimes wonder, why do I even bother?

I glanced at Lessie as she drizzled a teaspoonful of Cherry Garcia ice cream onto a sour cream and onion potato chip and popped it into her mouth.

Then again, perhaps her pregnancy hormones were wreaking more havoc than usual on her emotional equilibrium. When my sister, Susan, was pregnant last year, she'd told me she'd cried more in those nine months than she had in the previous thirty-five years of her life—and she has a happy marriage and a great job as a architect designing new art museums. One day, seven months into her pregnancy, Susan had burst into tears at the sight of an empty ketchup bottle that her husband had returned to the refrigerator. It was at that moment that she claimed to finally understand what existentialism was all about—the utter absurdity of life, the cry in the wilderness that was never heard. I don't know why she didn't just throw out the empty bottle and buy another.

"Lessie, are you sure you want to have this baby?"

"I'm forty-two. This might be my last chance to be a mother."

It was a reason, but not necessarily a good one. Single motherhood was nothing to enter into lightly, although for most single mothers, I suppose, that was exactly how it happened. You're having carefree, fun sex with your boyfriend, and then one day the condom breaks or you forget to take a pill. Then the guy who was so cute, so attentive, and so wonderful suddenly vaporized and you were on your own.

"Lessie, this might be a bit personal, but how did you, I mean were you guys using . . . ?"

"Not the first time," she said, and then gave me a shame-faced sideways glance like a dog that's just been caught nipping a sirloin steak off the counter. "I know, I know, I'm worse than a teenager," she went on in a rush. "It was really stupid. But who would've thought a forty-two-year-old woman could get pregnant for the first time in her life, the first and only time in her life she didn't use birth control?"

I knew what she meant. After being technically able to have a child since I'd turned thirteen, but never having been pregnant, birth control and sex seemed completely unrelated. At this stage in my life, using contraception had become an unnecessary hassle, like having to fiddle with the burglar alarm code every time you left your house, but never getting burglarized. Of course, the day you didn't bother was the day it happened.

"When was the last time you ate?" I asked Lessie, noting that she had devoured a full pint of ice cream and nearly all of the chips. But I was really thinking, What the hell was she waiting for? Why didn't she just tell Eliseo and get it over with?

"Yesterday. I've been really nauseous, but today I'm starving," she said. The food and the music seemed to be doing her some good. She had color coming back to her cheeks.

"Have you talked to Eliseo at all?" I asked, brushing close to the subject, but not quite hitting it full on.

"I've talked to him, but I haven't seen him," she said. "I told him I have the flu. Not too far from the truth. I've lost three pounds."

"Do you want to order a pizza?" I asked her, changing the subject temporarily because now I was really concerned. I've never been pregnant, but I understand that traditionally, pregnant women gained, rather than lost weight, and Lessie didn't have much to lose to begin with.

I called a place called Pizza Man that Lessie said was the best in town and that guaranteed delivery in twenty minutes, and ordered a large cream cheese, Canadian bacon, and pineapple.

Sitting back down next to the human vacuum cleaner, I asked her a few necessary questions.

"Are you sleeping?"

"A little. Enough," she said, nibbling a handful of cashews like a squirrel.

"Exercising?"

"Well, I've cut back on my usual workout, but I'm still doing pilates."

"Have you set up an appointment with your OB-GYN?"

"Yes, for next week. And I appreciate your concern, I really do, Sam. I might be a little emotional right now, but really I'm fine."

Fine! Fine? When the hell was she going to tell Eliseo?

"I'm going to tell Eliseo tomorrow night. I just wanted to be sure that I was ready to have this baby no matter what, in case he . . . Well, I'm finally ready for any reaction from him."

I breathed a sigh of relief.

★　★　★

"Sam, Sam." I felt someone shaking my arm. "Wake up, Sam."

I woke up and looked at my watch. It was midnight. We'd put on *Love Story* after finishing the pizza, and apparently I'd fallen into a food coma. It was just before the end of the movie, during the hospital scene where Ali MacGraw was moments away from dying, but managed to look breathtakingly beautiful, and healthy as Hercules on steroids.

"I'm ready to tell Eliseo now," said Lessie.

"Now? Well, okay, I'm sure everything will be fine. Good luck."

"No, I need you to come with me," she said.

"Isn't it a little late or early or something?"

"I don't want to wait until tomorrow night, I want to tell him now. And I want you to stay in the car in case he throws me out."

"That's not going to happen, Lessie," I told her. "But of course I'll go with you."

I got up, brushed my teeth, and threw on a sweater. As soon as we got downstairs to the underground parking garage, the cool summer night air woke me up.

"How are you going to tell him?" I asked her, as I turned onto the freeway.

"Well, I won't be using the 'Hi, honey, guess what, I've got great news' approach. I really don't know what I'm going to say."

Fifteen minutes later we pulled up across the street from Javier's duplex. The downstairs dance studio was dark.

"Okay, give me twenty minutes," she said. "If I don't come out by then you can leave."

I grabbed her hand. "Lessie, it's going to be okay," I said, hoping that I was right.

She leaned into the window and smiled. "Thanks, Sam."

For ten minutes I listened to the radio. Then I reached over to the glove compartment and pulled out a salsa CD. I looked at the digital clock on the dash. Javier was going to be home any minute from Cubana. My heart started pounding at the thought of seeing him. As much as I tried to push him out of my life, it wasn't working.

Just then I saw Javier pull up in his pickup truck, followed by someone in a small red car that parked directly behind his. My pulse quickened. I wanted to catch him before he went inside. Who knew what was going on upstairs with Lessie and Eliseo?

I'd just put my hand on the door handle and was about to get out of my car when I saw Javier's ex, Isabella. She looked even more flawless and beautiful than the last time I'd seen her. Her dark chestnut hair shone under the streetlights and flounced perfectly about her shoulders. She looked like a Breck girl running to catch the subway. When she reached his side, Javier put his arm around her shoulder, and as the door closed behind them, my favorite song on the salsa CD ended on an upbeat note as a sharp pain stabbed through my heart.

Fifteen

Mission Possible

Week Nine Status Report:

Attended Singles Cooking Class. Got sick in the bathroom on undercooked chicken. Left early. Met no one.

Attended Three-Minute Dating event. Met forty men. Chose zero.

Went on blind date with pharmacist from Single No More. By end of our date, I was begging him to open his pharmacy at two A.M. on pretense I was interested to see where he worked. Actually was hoping that if I threw my arms around his ankles and begged, he'd give me a couple thousand prescription-free Valium. He refused and for some reason didn't ask me out again.

Ophthalmologist from Brunches or Lunches cancelled our date, claiming to have suffered a sudden bout of situational blindness caused by extreme job stress. (Does this

malady really exist? Sounds suspiciously like he was worried
I'd turn out to be fat.)

    Continue to have wonderful dates with Robert Mack.

I pressed SEND. Okay, the last line of my report was a bit of a stretch, but that sounded better than calling it what it really was, a bald-faced lie. I was now so deep into pathological liar territory that when I died, they were going to dissect my brain and put it in a jar next to Charles Manson's and other assorted sociopaths and serial killers.

Why do relationships have to be so difficult? Maybe our great-great-great-grandparents had the right idea with arranged marriages. You met your fiancé five minutes before you said "I do," had eleven children, worked your twenty-acre plot of land, and died at forty-five. Think of the simple beauty of such a life—no choices, no decisions to make. You were stuck with whomever your relatives picked out for you and since everyone you knew was in the same boat, there was no resentment, no room for comparison, no coveting thy neighbor's hot studly husband.

I was about to make myself a smoothie when the "You've got mail" voice boomed from my computer loud enough to cause an avalanche in Switzerland. I walked back into my office and clicked on the new message.

An e-mail from Sally:

"Hi Sam, sounds like you're a little depressed. This is on the Q-T. Elaine thinks you're lying about still seeing Robert Mack, and she's madder than a bull charging at a red cape. My advice is to make your reports sound a little more upbeat—lie if you have to, for goodness sake. And be prepared to produce Robert or a suitable fiancé in the flesh for a possible surprise visit from your fairy godmother. No details yet, but if I get wind of anything I'll let you know. Good luck. Sally."

A little depressed? Yes, you could say I was a little depressed. Javier makes love to me and tells me that he loves me, and twelve seconds later gets back together with his ex-girlfriend Isabella. Even taking into consideration the fact that I told him I'm dating other men, and one man in particular, how he could do this? Had it taken him all of five seconds to fall out of love with me, if he ever was in the first place? If Javier had been on the rebound from Isabella when we'd met, as Sebastian Diaz had warned me, then maybe I was just Javier's quickie crush that had lasted only until he'd gotten back together with her?

Then there was Robert. He claimed to love me too, but then why didn't he call me after I turned him down, but before he saw me with Javier that night at Cubana? He should have taken the mature, gentlemanly approach to my refusal to go to bed with him and gotten even more interested in me. Wasn't rejection the most attractive quality a woman could possess, at least for most men? But, on the one hand, maybe his fragile state of widowerhood had cancelled out this normal male gene? Maybe when I told him I wasn't ready to sleep with him, rather than feeling emboldened and spurred on by my rejection, it made him feel like an unused shoehorn gathering dust on the top shelf of a closet?

On the other hand, maybe Robert never really loved me either? The phrase "I love you" certainly doesn't mean what it used to. Today, people say it all the time because it sounds nicer than the truth, "You're okay, but I'm only hanging out with you until someone better comes along."

On the other hand (yes, I know I have only two hands, but if men weren't so ridiculously complicated, I wouldn't need more than two), did it matter who called whom if Robert was the right man for me? Elizabeth said I should stop letting other people and events decide my life for me. Perhaps it was time to take action. Bold action.

So I did. I called Robert, three times in two days, leaving three voice mail messages. And nothing. Nothing!

I'm not a person to be pressured by outside forces, you understand, but it was after I reread the e-mail from Sally that I devised Plan B, and decided to go to Robert's office or his home. I would just show up, and we'd have an adult discussion about what was going on with us. There was just one problem with Plan B. I found Robert's business listing in the phonebook, but it only had a phone number and a P.O. box listing, which was very strange indeed. There was no home listing. So I'd had no choice but to leave a fourth message yesterday with his answering service, to which I also got no response.

When I talked to my mother yesterday about my concerns regarding Robert—his lack of family and friends, all of his mysterious traveling, his erratic moods, the P.O. box—she simply dismissed them, telling me that the reason I was still single at forty-one was because I was too picky and looking for reasons to dislike rather than like a potential mate.

"Too picky." I'd heard that opinion over and over from my mother and even my best friend, Elizabeth. Maybe they were right? So today I put Plan C into action.

I strode from my car, a woman on a mission. I could get Robert to speak to me if only I could find him. I'd worry later about how I really felt about him. I shuddered as I approached the familiar two-story building, although I was ready for anything at this point, including, if absolutely necessary, holding Bunny hostage until she'd divulged his home and office addresses.

I pushed on the glass-paned door, but it didn't budge. Pressing my nose up against the glass, I peered inside, seeing darkness and dust, normal signs that a business might have gone out of business, except for Single No More. It had looked exactly this way the last time I'd been here. Maybe Bunny had gone home sick for the day?

Now what?

I turned back to my car and there he was, just there, on the sidewalk, as if he'd been standing there his whole life.

"Hi, Sam."

Club Cubana and now this—he had to be following me. He had the beginnings of a five o'clock shadow and looked tired, as if he hadn't been sleeping well for quite a while. His hands were in his pants pockets and he was leaning his back against my car, looking like a bored Calvin Klein model facing another twelve-hour photo shoot.

"How have you been?" he asked nonchalantly.

How dare he look so handsome and be so damned casual after I'd wasted valuable minutes scouring the ends of the earth for him!

"What are you doing here?" I snapped.

"I was driving to your apartment when I saw you pull out of your parking garage. I followed you here because I needed to see you," he said. "By the way, you look great, Sam."

You better believe I look great. I look awesome as a matter of fact. And what about my four phone messages?

"Have you been out of town?" I demanded.

"No, I got your messages, Sam. Sorry I haven't called but . . . Listen, we have a lot of things to talk about. Can we go somewhere?"

"There's a coffee shop across . . ."

"I meant somewhere private."

I followed him in my car. Every time we stopped at a stop-light or stop sign, I looked into his rearview mirror searching for some clue in his eyes about what he was thinking. But each time he had the same blank expression. My sweaty hands slipped on the steering wheel and I wiped them on my jeans.

Robert had suggested going to my place, but I'd insisted on going to his. I wanted to see where and how he lived. Was he a slob? A neat freak? Was he hiding a wife and five children? There were a number of strange things going on that I wanted answers to.

We pulled up to an eight-story brick building in a trendy part of the city, which is always distinguished by the number of cof-fee shops, gourmet grocery stores, and art galleries about. Tak-ing the elevator up to the fifth floor, we walked to the end of the hallway.

"I hope you'll forgive the mess," he said, as he put his key in the lock. "My cleaning lady's been sick."

Sun streamed into the room from two skylights, one over-looking a granite-covered island in the kitchen and the other over the fireplace in the living room. The floors were well-polished oak or maybe maple, and the walls, exposed cream-colored brick. Two butter-colored leather chairs so fat and plump they could almost double as small love seats were set on a red oriental rug. The mess, as far as I could see, was a couple dishes in the sink, a little dust on the tables and lamp shades, and a pile of clothes crumpled on the floor next to the queen-size bed in the corner of his efficiency apartment.

"It's gorgeous," I said.

"Thanks," he said, not looking at me. "After Sarah died, I sold our house and bought the first place I looked at. This is it. It's small but it's home."

I looked up at the cathedral ceilings and the generous expanse of floor space that could have doubled as a dance floor in a small club. This was small? It was at least four times the size of my apartment in Manhattan.

We settled ourselves in the living room area with our drinks. The coffee table was the DMZ zone, with a Corona on my side of the table and a Miller on his.

We drank in silence for several minutes. I kept hoping he'd say something, set the tone, since I had no idea what he was thinking or feeling. But I had a strange feeling that my entire future depended on what was going to happen here this afternoon. One wrong move could mean the difference between a future with two well-worn rocking chairs and visiting grandchildren, or a singular hell in a cramped apartment with a baker's dozen of cats as my entire source of joy and meaning in life.

I looked up and caught Robert staring at me.

"It killed me to see you with that guy at the club, Sam," he blurted out suddenly.

"I looked for you downstairs to explain, but you'd left," I said. "Why haven't you returned my calls?"

"I needed time to think, sort things out," he said, and then took a swig of his beer. I kept forgetting that it took men at least nine times as long to think about things as it did women.

"I know I probably don't have a right to ask," he said, "but what's going on with you and the salsa instructor?"

Robert looked hurt and upset, but I reminded myself that this wasn't the time to let my emotions cloud my judgment with a man, yet again.

"Actually, I have a question for you first. What were you doing at Club Cubana?"

"I had a meeting with a client," he said.

"A client?"

"Yes, Roberto Lopez. He's a lawyer who wants to relocate to Chicago. I wanted to set up a meeting at his office, but he suggested Club Cubana so I agreed to meet him there."

"Roberto Lopez, who's he?"

"That tall, built guy I was on the balcony with. You know, the guy I was with when I saw you with the salsa instructor."

The hairs on the back of my neck stood up.

"He's a lawyer?" I asked. And if he was, why in the hell did they meet at a salsa club instead of Robert's office?

"Yes, he does personal injury," said Robert.

"And his name is Roberto Lopez?"

"Yes, why? What's wrong, Sam? Do you know him?"

"No. Yes. Well, I've met him at the club, but I don't really know him," I said.

Why would Sebastian Diaz, if that was his real name, lie about what he did for a living and give Robert a false name? It didn't make sense.

"Why didn't you meet him at your office?" I continued. "And where is your office anyway? There's only a P.O. box listed in the phone book. I must say that seems a little strange for a business."

"It's downtown. My associates and I share a small space with three closet-sized offices, three desks, three computers, and no view. We don't meet with clients at our office. That's why I didn't have the address listed. I'll take you there if you want to—"

"No, no that's okay," I said, suddenly ashamed at my suspicions about Robert, who seemed genuinely upset and who was clearly waiting for me to give him some answers about Javier.

"About the salsa instructor," I said. "He was giving me private dance lessons. He has . . . had a crush on me, and well, the truth is, I liked him too, only I didn't realize it until a few days ago."

"I want you to know, I understand," he said. "I don't like it but I understand."

"Anyway, he's got a girlfriend," I said.

"Sam, I've done a lot of thinking," Robert said, as he began peeling the label off his beer bottle. "I've behaved like a spoiled kid. I had no right to act the way I did when you said you weren't ready to make love. I want you to know I respect your decision and we can wait as long as you want. Will you forgive me and give me another chance?"

I'd been doing a lot of forgiving when it came to Robert. But he seemed so vulnerable this afternoon, as though he might break in two if I said the wrong thing. Before I could answer, Robert came over to me and put his arms around me and then Plan D, which wasn't planned at all, happened.

☆ ☆ ☆

The fire in the fireplace crackled and tiny flames from candles around the apartment flickered and danced. A ghostly stream of light from the moon came in through the skylight in the kitchen.

"This arrow is pointed directly away from me," Robert said, tracing the Cupid tattoo on my stomach.

His clothes did a good job of hiding his pudgy stomach. He didn't have a beer belly exactly, more like the stomach of a reasonably fit middle-aged guy who hadn't done a sit-up since high school. But the extra pudge hadn't lessened Robert's lovemaking abilities. He was far more passionate and skilled than my ex-fiancé, David, had ever been. Then again, Robert was older, and had been married before.

"You don't seem like the tattoo kind of woman."

"You don't like it?"

"I do," he assured me, bending down to kiss it. "It looks good on you."

"Can I ask you something?"

"Of course."

"Do you salsa?"

He laughed. "Salsa? Only with chips."

"I'm serious, I don't know what it is but I love it, I can't get enough of it. Are you at least willing to try it, for me?"

"I don't think dancing is my thing, Sam," he said.

"What is your thing?"

"You," he said, kissing my collarbone and breast before propping his head back on his hand with his elbow jammed into a pillow.

"The other one is getting jealous," I said playfully.

"We can't have that," he said, bending down to kiss my right breast. It tickled and felt sensuous at the same time.

"So maybe dancing is out, but don't you have a passion, something you love to do?"

"Besides making love to a beautiful woman who I'm crazy about?"

"Yes, besides that."

"My job, I guess. I'm proud that my business is a success," he said. He leaned over and we kissed for a while, but I couldn't fully enjoy the moment because his last statement made me wonder if he was a workaholic like David had been.

I told Robert I was starving and he offered to cook for me. In his kitchen, the Spanish tiles felt cool on my feet. I stood on the other side of the island in one of his long-sleeved button-down shirts that just covered my behind. As I watched him cook, we talked about one of my favorite topics, traveling, and about going to Hong Kong together some day, a city both of us had always wanted to visit.

"So what are you doing for the rest of your life?" he asked me as he handed me a plate of steaming fettuccine Alfredo. "Are you busy?"

I smiled at him, not knowing what to say. Was he the right man for me? I certainly hoped so.

Sixteen

Double Dipped

I'd like to say it ended happily ever after, but that only happens to a few select women, the ones for whom the grass really is greener. And not just during the summer months. You know this type of woman. We hate her.

She floats through life and every good thing the universe has to offer comes to her effortlessly, as if she were a giant walking sponge—great jobs, her parents and siblings for best friends, oodles of cash netted through every investment she makes. She was the kind of woman who, if she hadn't marry her soul mate at twenty-one, was having the time of her life being single. She's turned down five marriage proposals by the time she's twenty-nine and hasn't spent a single Christmas, birthday, or Valentine's Day without a man since puberty. Usually, in fact, she's dating three or four men at once, juggling them with the ease of a short-order cook at Denny's. All of them, of course, are madly in love with her and jostling for her attention. But, if she does choose serial monogamy, then she's doing "The Amazing Overlap." Before giving the current guy his pink slip, she's already met and cultivated the new one, who drops off the vine plump and juicy into her welcoming hands, at just the right moment.

I didn't have any female friends like this, thank goodness. Otherwise I'd have to have her assassinated. But I'd certainly hoped for the best for Lessie. When we had driven over to Javier and Eliseo's after our movie marathon, I'd left in a flood of tears after seeing Javier with Isabella. But I had assumed Lessie and Eliseo had worked things out since she hadn't come out in twenty minutes. But Lessie had finally called me this evening to tell me that Eliseo was not going to take any role in the raising of his child, much less ending up with Lessie as she'd hoped.

I'm not in the habit of kidnapping people, especially when they happen to be dear friends of mine, but I didn't have much of a choice given the emotional state Lessie was in. After talking to Lessie, I drove straight over to her house.

"We're going out dancing," I said to Lessie, who was sitting on her couch staring zombielike at a sitcom on TV. A string of canned laughter erupted from the television.

"I don't want to salsa dance ever again," she said. She was capable of holding a conversation, but it was like she wasn't really there.

"You love salsa," I said during another burst of canned laughter. It sounded like a bad joke that had fallen flat at a funeral.

"I don't want to run into Eliseo," she told me, eyes still focused on the screen.

"We won't, we're going to a new club." I turned off the TV and Lessie finally looked at me.

"You let the pony come out of the corral for a ride," she said in a flat voice.

"What?" Had she really gone off the deep end? What did horses have to do with anything?

"You had sex. It's as plain as the nose on your face."

I was startled. I'd assumed she was too deep in the fog of her own problems to notice.

"But you'd better be careful, Sam. Did you know that sex can lead to pregnancy?" Her attempt at humor nearly broke my heart. I felt so bad for her, but what else could I do?

I helped her pick out her sexiest short black dress from her closet and told her to take a shower. While Lessie got ready, I went outside to her patio and sat down. The night was perfect. I could see stars—not many, but more than I'd ever seen in Manhattan. I sat there for a moment, just basking in the feeling that my life had changed, hopefully, for the better.

Lessie tapped me on my shoulder and I jumped.

"Do you want to talk about him?" I asked Lessie as I drove us to the club.

"There's nothing to talk about," she said, staring straight ahead through the windshield.

"Is Eliseo going to be involved at all?"

"Sure, once a month when the check arrives," she said. "But at least I know that decent men still exist. Javier was wonderful about the whole thing."

"He was?" I said, momentarily jolted to hear his name.

"Two days after I told Eliseo, Javier called me at home," Lessie explained. "He told me he was ashamed of the way his brother was behaving and wanted to know if I needed anything," she said. "Javier will definitely make some woman very happy some day," she added, and once again I felt a stab of regret that it was not going to be me. Javier's heart had been with Isabella all along. I was with Robert now, and he'd be back in just a few days.

Lessie and I walked into Babalus. It had a tropical feel, totally different from Cubana. Well-dressed couples and foursomes sat around white tables, potted palm trees were here and there, a tropical wall mural was splashed behind the bar, and the walls were covered with the warm oranges, yellows, and reds of a sunset scene. Babalus reminded me of Latin nightclubs that had flourished in the 1950s when couples went out for a night of cocktailing, dinner, and dancing. I half expected that at any moment I might bump into the white-tuxedoed Ricky Ricardo.

A twelve-piece band was playing on a small raised platform in the corner of the club. A disc jockey was one thing, but a live salsa band was absolutely mesmerizing. Each member of the band moved in unison, playing with the kind of contagious energy that could raise the dead. The lead singer, a plump Latina woman, wore an outfit that showed off every curve, a low-cut silver sequined midriff top with cleavage to her navel, and a short black skirt that skimmed the top of her chubby thighs, which were encased in black fishnet nylons. She belted out lyrics in Spanish while gyrating her hips and swinging her plump arms in time to the brassy, pumping rhythms.

"Is that the Lone Salsero over there?" Lessie asked me.

I'd never seen the man stationary before. With his back against the bar, he stood watching everyone coming in while sipping a glass of white wine. As Lessie and I walked by him, he winked and smiled at me. Yikes!

The first person I saw after Lessie and I had grabbed a table near the band was the woman who had been fixated on Javier's "package" at Cubana about a month ago. Whenever she passed under the overhead lights, the red and blond streaks in her hair lit up like they were on fire. At the time I talked to her, I remembered her saying that Javier could make your spine melt, a comment I could finally begin to appreciate as I'd become more and more passionate about salsa.

And then I saw the Lone Salsero approaching and prayed to the powers that be that he wasn't coming for me. But a moment later, he was at my side.

"You are very beautiful," he said in a thick accent. "Will you dance with me?" He stood there patiently, twirling one end of his mustache as he waited for my answer.

"Go on, Sam, I'll be fine," said Lessie, who lightly elbowed me and flashed me a wicked glad-its-not-me smirk. Seeing that smirk made all the difference. At least she was feeling better. I let the Lone Salsero lead me to the center of the dance floor and a minute later saw Lessie dancing with a man who came up to her chin. I made sure I caught her eye over the Lone Salsero's shoulder. She rolled her eyes, but was smiling.

The Lone Salsero was an incredible dancer, not to mention astonishingly athletic. He twirled and dipped me a dozen times and by the end of just one salsa song, I was suffering from near hypoxia. Back at our table, as I tried to catch my breath, I looked for Lessie and saw her standing on the other side of the club at the bar talking to someone I didn't recognize. I was just about to take a sip of water when I saw something that made me stop breathing once again.

Like royalty, the crowd parted when Javier and Isabella walked in. They went straight to the dance floor and the crowd circled around them. Short bursts of applause broke out when Javier flipped Isabella over in a one-hundred-eighty-degree turn, and again when Isabella dipped Javier, a move I'd never seen before. When they were through, I heard an enthusiastic round of clapping.

I sat there wishing I could make myself disappear. It was bad enough that he got back together with her, but to flaunt it in my face like this was just outrageous! I could feel the tears welling up in my eyes. I crossed my arms and stared dismally at the band, hoping somehow he would leave me alone for the night.

"Hi, Sam," said Javier, and then a moment later, "I think we have some things to talk about," he said.

How dare this man who said he loved me and then forgot me a nanosecond later have the nerve to even speak to me.

"I don't want to talk," I said.

Javier looked genuinely puzzled. "Have *I* done something wrong?" he asked. But before I had a chance to say anything, he grabbed my hand and pulled me to the dance floor.

We started dancing, but halfway through the song I couldn't stand it anymore, and I unleashed all my pent-up feelings.

"Alright, Javier, I am—"

Twirl.

"angry. Extremely—"

Twirl.

"angry. You told—"

Double twirl.

"me you—"

Triple twirl.

"loved me and—"

Twirl.

"then a minute—"

Twirl and dip.

"later you—"

Twirl and dip.

"got back—"

Quadruple twirl.

"together—"

Dip.

". . . with her," I said, jerking my head in Isabella's direction as best I could from a forty-five-degree angle. Just add some bolts to my neck and I'd look like Frankenstein. I looked over and caught Isabella's eye. She gave me a sweet smile, which seemed genuine enough and made me wonder if Javier had told her anything about me.

"What about her?" he asked as he brought me up into a vertical position.

"I saw you with her at one in the morning going into your house just a few days after you told me you loved . . ."

"Sam, come with me," he said, starting to lead me in her direction, while I pulled back like a small child who is about to be dragged into the dentist's office. But when he said please and flashed that damn adorable dimple of his, I let him take me over to Isabella, who looked devastatingly beautiful in a black spaghetti-strap dress and three-inch heels. She was standing by herself, sipping what looked like an orange juice.

"I'd like you to meet Isabella," said Javier. She looked at me with an open, friendly face and smiled, which was when I noticed that she also had a single dimple on her left cheek. "Sam, Isabella is my sister," Javier said simply.

Now would've been the perfect time for the dramatic refrain of a daytime soap opera orchestra to swell, signaling a shocking turn of events. I felt like a fool. But then again, why should I? I had believed Sebastian when he had lied to me and told me that Isabella was Javier's ex-girlfriend.

"I've heard a lot about you, Sam. It's nice to finally meet you," Isabella said, and held out her tiny hand.

"It's nice to meet you too, Isabella," I stammered.

"I'll be back in a minute," said Javier to his sister, as he guided me to the back of the club, away from the band and the dance floor.

"Now, why were you so angry with me?" he asked.

"I thought Isabella was your girlfriend. When I dropped Lessie off the other night, I saw the two of you walk inside together and well, I just assumed . . ." I hung my head. "Javier, can I ask you a question?"

"You can ask me anything, Sam."

"Sebastian Diaz is a friend of yours, right?"

"My best friend," said Javier.

"Do you trust him?"

"Of course I do."

"What does Sebastian do for a living?"

For a moment, Javier assumed a guarded expression. "I think you should ask Sebastian that question. I'm sure he'll be at Cubana next week."

If Sebastian had lied about who Isabella was, then I'm certain he'd also lied to Robert when he had told him he was a lawyer. But why? Well, one thing was obvious: Javier, who seemed a little overprotective of his friend, wasn't going to tell me anything. I'd just have to find out for myself why Sebastian had lied. Then again, did it matter anymore?

"By the way, how is Lessie doing?" Javier asked.

"Better than expected, under the circumstances," I said.

He nodded stiffly. "I love my brother, but I can't respect a man who never seems to grow up and keeps running away from his responsibilities."

"What do you mean 'keeps running away'?"

"This is going to be his second illegitimate child," said Javier, who then caught the look of surprise on my face. "I thought Lessie would've told you."

Oh God, I wonder how she'd felt when she'd found out. I looked over at her dancing. She was so wonderful, smart, and beautiful. What the hell was wrong with Eliseo?

"Javier, I feel terrible about everything," I began, but then found that I didn't know how to go on.

What do I tell him, I think I could've fallen in love with you but you were all wrong for my assignment? I needed to give Robert a chance because he's the perfect great-on-paper guy I've been ordered to find this summer?

"Sam, I'd be lying if I told you that I wasn't hurt," he said while looking directly into my eyes. "I fell in love with you. I'm *still* in love with you."

He searched my face and waited for a response. The upbeat salsa music pulsing in the background suddenly sounded like a sick joke.

"Javier, you are a wonderful man," I said, feeling hot tears spring to my eyes. "I don't regret a moment we've spent together. But you deserve someone better than me," I said, which was all true but hardly expressed the depth of my feelings for him. I wanted to tell him everything, that if only I'd known that Isabella was his sister, then . . . Well, then what? Would I have slept with Robert?

A moment later, as Javier slowly turned and walked away, my heart cleaved in two and the tears started spilling down my cheeks.

Seventeen

Que Sera Sera

"We need to choose the motif for the wedding by the end of this week, Samantha," my mother told me. It had to be another call from her car since she sounded like she was zooming through a wind tunnel. "Alfredo really can't do a thing without it."

Alfredo was the wedding planner my mother hired last month. I wondered exactly what he was planning since, yet again, I couldn't help but observe the conspicuous lack of a groom. Was I the only sane person who'd noticed what should be blazingly obvious to everyone around me?

"Weddings have motifs, like theme parks?"

"Really, Samantha, sometimes I can't believe you sprang from my loins," she scolded me, as if I'd had a choice in the matter. "But, as Alfredo has pointed out, and he's quite right, you don't choose the motif, the motif chooses you."

"What is that supposed to mean?"

"The motif is based on something you share with your fiancé, a symbol that embraces your oneness, your special bond. Don't you remember Susan's shovels?"

"Those were shovels? I thought they were some weird fertility symbol," I said. Here it was two years after my sister Susan's wedding and I'd finally gotten it. Susan had met her husband on an archeological dig. Aha! Shovels. They had been everywhere at her reception: chocolate shovel-shaped candies on every plate, shovel-shaped tea light holders, and shovel place card holders.

"But we don't want something too whimsical," my mother added.

Had my mother actually said the word *whimsical*? Apparently, along with his other wedding planning duties, Alfredo had brainwashed my mother. It was either that or New York had been invaded by pod people and she'd been one of their first victims.

"Are you there, Samantha?" she said through the jet stream of air that sounded through my telephone.

"Yes," I said, "whimsical would be tragic."

I couldn't deal with my mother under the best of circumstances, but I'd cried myself to sleep two nights ago after finding out that Isabella was Javier's sister. I knew that things could never work out for Javier and me, but I couldn't help but think that everything might have been different if I'd found out sooner.

"Susan was fitted for her matron of honor dress on Saturday," continued my mother without skipping a beat. "She likes the crepe and chiffon in silver. I agree. It's better for her line."

"Susan? Mother, assuming I do get married I'm not sure that I would choose Susan as my . . ."

"Don't be ridiculous. Who would you choose other than your own sister?"

"Well, Elizabeth. Remember, she was going to be my maid of honor for me, when I was going to marry . . ."

When I'd planned my wedding to David, this issue had been decided for me. My sister had taken a year off after earning her master's degree in architecture, and was in the middle of a one-year dig in a remote part of Nepal. That's where she'd met Stan, her husband. Susan doesn't have an actual degree in archeology or any formal training, but when we were kids, she was always digging up animal bones and calling them fossils. Growing up, I had dolls in my bedroom. Susan had bones.

"Speaking of your prior engagement, funny little coincidence, Alfredo is also planning David's wedding."

"David? My David? He's getting married?" I said, beginning to hyperventilate.

"Well, Samantha dear, I know you cared for him, but he's hardly *your* David anymore, is he?"

"Who is he marrying?" I asked and swallowed hard, but there was no saliva in my mouth. I sprinted over to the kitchen faucet, turned on the cold water and lapped some up with my free hand.

". . . No one I know. Alfredo says she's a lovely girl but I must admit, I'm a bit surprised. He didn't seem the type to plunge into a ready-made family."

"What?"

"Her husband died, poor thing. She has identical twin boys, just three years old."

David was getting married to a woman with my twin sons! *My* dream family.

"Samantha, I thought you were over David."

"I am. I'm fine, just surprised, that's all," I said, forcing my voice to sound breezy.

Of course I wasn't fine. It was the slap heard round the

world, the call you never wanted to get. Everyone liked to imagine that, after a breakup, your ex has spent countless months and many anguished nights regretting that the relationship had ever ended. You wanted to imagine that he was still pining away for you and wishing he could find the strength to call and beg you to come back to him. It didn't matter who dumped whom, or how abysmal your relationship had been, the second you heard he'd chosen someone else, anyone else, you'd been rejected, and it hurt like hell.

"Oh dear, I shouldn't have broken the news to you like this," she said, in a rare moment of insight.

"I'm fine, but, um, I need to ask you something, okay Mom? How do you know when you're really in love?"

"What has gotten into you, Samantha?"

"Well I . . ." and then I heard a sound like a needle scraping across an old-fashioned LP.

". . . all very simple. When you're in love, you just know it," she said. "Now, I've got to run. Think about your motif. I'll call you tomorrow."

Well, that was a big help. Anyway, looking at my watch, I saw that I had just enough time to get ready. An hour later I opened the door. Robert stood there in a black double-breasted suit and a white collarless shirt without a tie.

"These are for you," he said, handing me a dozen of the most gorgeous white long-stemmed roses I'd ever seen in my life. I didn't want to cut a millimeter off those lovely long stems.

"Oh, they're beautiful! Come in."

He gave me a sweet kiss on the lips and then I sprinted to the kitchen, where I scoured the cupboards for a vase.

As we drove to the restaurant, Robert kept glancing at me.

"You seem nervous," I said.

"No, no nothing to worry about," he said mysteriously. "I've done this before."

What did that mean? Driving? Going on dates? I decided that this momentary awkwardness was probably just the temporary phase that often happened after that first intense intimate physical encounter with a new lover, particularly if it was followed by a couple days of breathing space, which gave your mind plenty of time to start playing tricks and making you wonder if you'd imagined how wonderful it had all been.

"How was your business trip?"

"Very productive," he said. "I was able to place another client in an accounting firm in Houston. They've hired me to fill another opening."

"That's great. So you'll be taking another trip there?"

"Probably in a few weeks," he said, with another glance and smile in my direction. "Traveling for business is very tiring. But I knew that's what I was getting into when I bought this business. And," he added, frowning, "I'm going out of town again. Tomorrow morning, I'm afraid. I've got a flight at nine."

Leaving again, already? David had never traveled much, but he'd spent so much time at the office that he might as well have. Was Robert planning on traveling this much for the rest of his life? Our life, if we ended up together?

The restaurant was beautiful. The walls had murals of gondoliers floating in moonlit canals, the coliseum, and another of a couple kissing in front of the leaning Tower of Pisa. The hostess, a girl of twenty dressed all in black, led us to the best table in the restaurant, next to the windows that looked out onto the street.

I could see we were in for the kind of long leisurely dinner during which the wait staff was only too happy to let you dine for hours and make you feel as though they were born to serve only you. Our waiter, Todd, brought a loaf of crusty bread and a plate with a pool of olive oil and capers for dipping and then handed Robert the wine list.

"Don't you love dinners like this?" I said, taking a bite of French bread that I'd dipped into the olive oil. "The Europeans really know how to live; eating, sleeping, making love, and more eating."

"I love to watch you eat," Robert said, smiling for the first time that night. "You look so sexy."

When Todd returned to take our orders, I chose the pasta with asparagus and anchovies, while Robert ordered ravioli filled with artichokes and mushrooms in a creamy vodka sauce.

"Anchovies?" Robert said, with a grin, after Todd was out of earshot.

"Anchovies are an aphrodisiac as you know," I said, trying on a sexy smile.

"I hope you're not trying to tell me you need them to get into the mood for me?" he said.

"Definitely not. I'm in the mood right now," I said quietly. I wanted to slip my stocking-covered foot out of my shoe and rub it against Robert's crotch, but glancing at the side of our table, I could see it was too dangerous. Not enough tablecloth to cover the maneuver. I forced myself to stifle the urge to do something that people could only get away with in the movies.

After dinner, feeling comfortably full, I leaned back in my chair and sighed. For a moment we were silent, as I listened to the tinkling of forks against the china, murmured conversations, and soft laughter.

"Sam," Robert said, "do you remember when I told you I had to decide whether to hire another associate or merge with another recruiting firm?"

"Yes."

"Well, I've been thinking about maybe selling my business. I could get a job with a firm in New York? What do you think?"

"But how would you feel about not being the boss anymore?" I said, suddenly realizing that Robert had clearly been doing a lot more concrete thinking about the future of our relationship than I had.

"It would just be temporary. After a while, I could start my own firm in Manhattan, if that's what we decided to do. Unless, you don't want me to move there?" he asked, with a hopeful look in his eyes.

"Of course I do," I assured him. "But are you sure you want to leave Milwaukee? You've spent a lot of time building up your business here."

"When you leave, Sam, there will be nothing here for me other than my business. I don't want to live without you in my life," he said, lifting my hand to his lips and kissing it.

Now, Sam, I told myself. Now was the time to tell Robert what you were really doing in Milwaukee. But before I could say anything, our waiter brought a bottle of champagne to our table.

"When did you order that?"

"I don't know, maybe Todd just read my mind?" said Robert, who was acting very odd. Todd handed us dessert menus and then opened the bottle of champagne with a loud pop.

"What can I get you for dessert, miss?" the waiter asked.

"Oh, no, I couldn't. I'm stuffed," I said, holding the menu out for Todd to take back.

"Sam, choose something," Robert urged me. "I'll eat most of it."

"You're acting very strange, you know."

"Just humor me, Sam."

Crepes, homemade gelatos, sorbets, tiramisu . . .

And then I came to the last item: *Samantha Jacobs, will you marry me?*

Robert stood up walked over to my side of the table and got down on one knee. Somewhere, part of my mind realized that all of the conversation in the restaurant had stopped. I sensed that all eyes were on us. Robert reached into his breast pocket and pulled out a tiny black box and handed it to me. I opened it. A round solitaire diamond ring set in silver sparkled in the light from the candle centerpiece.

"Sam, will you marry me?" he said, and I noticed tears in his eyes.

I looked at him, this man who was handsome, smart, successful, and so clearly in love with me. I would be crazy to say no. With a simple "yes," the deck of cards that was my life would magically fall into place. Elaine and our readers would be happy. I'd get "La Vie." My mother would be thrilled. And me, yes, finally answering a question that had been lingering in my brain unanswered for most of the summer, yes I think Robert could make me happy.

"Yes, I will," I said. Robert threw his arms around me, holding me close. We kissed.

I heard a spark of applause. We broke apart and I looked up to see everyone in the restaurant standing and smiling.

Robert took the ring from the box and slipped it onto my finger. He stood up and then handed my champagne flute to me. He clinked his glass to mine and then turned. Silence descended again.

"A toast to my beautiful bride-to-be."

Eighteen

Escape to New York

Was it just twenty-four hours ago that my fiancé left my queen-sized bed, which now felt like a vast empty wilderness without him? I hadn't stopped staring at my ring since Robert slipped it on my finger at the restaurant the night before last. I held it under a ray of sun coming in from my bedroom window. It was beautiful, and sparkled like an ice crystal. I grabbed his pillow and brought it to my face and caught a faint whiff of his cologne, something with eucalyptus and very outdoorsy.

Robert had left the day before at seven in the morning. But throughout the day he had called me a half dozen times, from the airport, the taxi, or while snatching a few minutes in between his client meetings. Last night when he'd returned to his hotel room, we'd talked for hours. In between Robert's calls, I'd made so many to my family and friends that the phone had practically fused to my head.

First I had called Elaine. "Congratulations on a job well done," she'd said cheerily, immediately followed by, "It's about time, Samantha." Now that was more like it, the warm and fuzzy Elaine we all knew and loved.

When I called Elizabeth at work, she screamed into the phone loud enough to puncture my eardrum. "Oh, Sam, I'm so happy for you!' she cried. "I knew you could do it!" Elizabeth was always there for me. She was the most unselfish person I knew. I was very lucky to have her as a friend.

My sister, Susan, was next. I wanted to get to her before my mother did since they have each other on warp-speed dial. My six-month-old niece, Matilda, was crying in the background, so it wasn't the best time to talk, but I could tell Susan was pleased for me.

"Maybe now Mother will get off my back?" I said to her.

"No, next you'll be required to produce another version of the little monster you hear screaming in the background," Susan pointed out.

I reached my mother at home. It came as no surprise when she'd breathed a heavy sigh of relief and instantly burst into tears.

"Thank God it's finally happened," she said, as though I'd been waiting my entire life for a heart transplant that had finally been scheduled. "When are you coming back to New York? We've got a million things to do before the wedding."

"Wouldn't you like to meet your future son-in-law first?"

"Yes, of course, but . . ." and then she launched into talk of motifs, flowers, engravers, and ice sculptures.

Finally, I broke off the call with my mother and phoned Lessie. I'd saved her call for last since I'd known that in so many ways it would be the most difficult one of all.

"Sam, I'm so happy for you, but this means you're going back to New York," Lessie said. "I thought we'd have another month to hang out."

"I might have to go back a week or so earlier, but I don't see why I have to rush back. I don't start my column until September, and I need some time to relax and get used to this whole thing."

"You're going to tell Javier, right?" she asked.

Javier. Of course I had to tell him. And I had to tell him much more than the news of my engagement. I hoped he could forgive me for lying to him about why I was in Milwaukee and, if there was some possible way that the two of us could stay in touch, be friends . . . But who was I kidding? There was no way I could ever think of him as just a friend.

The doorbell rang. It was only seven-thirty in the morning. I jumped out of bed, put my robe on, and answered the door.

"Good morning, are you Samantha Jacobs?" asked a squat man who came level with my chest. He stood ramrod straight as if trying to get the most mileage out of every centimeter of his height.

"Yes, I am," I said, wrapping my thigh-high purple silk bathrobe around me a little tighter. I really shouldn't answer my door when I was dressed like a woman of the night.

"I'm Mr. Sassafras, the building manager," he said with a jovial smile. "It's nice to finally meet you, Ms. Jacobs." The s on the end of my name leaked out like the hiss of a deflating tire. I got the distinct impression he was one of those kids in grade school who'd been picked on mercilessly for not being able to say his s without sounding like he had a mouthful of marbles and spit.

"I know it's very early," he said, "but there is a group of reporters and a sea of TV cameras outside the building. They want to see you."

Every *s* he pronounced slobbered over me as if a Saint Bernard had pinned me down and was licking my face.

The telephone rang.

"Excuse me for a moment, Mr. Sassafras," I said. I'd dragged the last *s* out on his name a bit longer than normal. I wasn't trying to make fun of him, but his speech impediment was as infectious as a bad rash.

"Hello?"

"Is this Samantha Jacobs?" asked a clipped voice.

"Yes, who's calling please?"

"This is Chip Simpson, a reporter with the Fox news network affiliate in Miami, Florida," he said brusquely. "Miss Jacobs, is it true that you're the Mystery Woman of *Très Chic* magazine?"

I froze.

"What makes you say that?" I wavered.

"It came over the wire this morning. The AP is reporting that an anonymous but reliable source has named you as the Mystery Woman. Would you care to comment?"

Oh God, how did this happen?

"No, I'm sorry, no comment." I slammed the phone down. A split second later it rang again. I hesitated, but had a feeling I should answer it.

"How did this happen?" Elaine demanded.

"I don't know," I said. "I was hoping you could tell me."

"We don't have time to talk about this now," she snapped. "Sally has booked you a flight back to New York. It leaves at eleven. Come straight to the office and make sure Robert is in New York by four tomorrow. We're shooting the cover shot then and moving up the release issue for August sixteenth."

This was all happening so fast. Eleven. That gave me almost

no time to pack much less say good-bye. And Javier, I was supposed to have dinner with him tonight. I didn't even have time to call him! I'd already hurt him so much and now I was doing it again. He would never forgive me.

"So far, no one has a photo of you. You need to leave without anyone seeing you. I don't want our cover issue blown," said Elaine.

"There's no way; there's a mob outside," I said.

"I don't care how you do it. Put a bag over your head if you have to. Just make sure you leave without anyone getting a photo of you. This is my story!"

Click!

★ ★ ★

An hour later, after I'd taken a forty-five-second shower and thrown my Milwaukee life into three suitcases, Mr. Sassafras returned to my apartment, having generously offered to drive me to the airport himself.

"Here," he said, handing me a large plastic bag. "I thought you might want to disguise yourself! Isn't this exciting?" he said with a small squeak. He rubbed his hands together quickly and looked around the room as if we were two spies plotting our escape from a terrorist cell in Prague.

I looked into the bag and pulled out a wig and a musty smelling leopard fur toque hat. Then I reached deeper and grabbed a pair of rimless mirrored sunglasses. I held up the wig, which was a mass of black shoulder-length braids studded with gold beads and shells attached to a beaded headdress.

"My wife was Nefretiti last Halloween," Mr. Sassafras, I mean Solly (he'd insisted that we be on a first-name basis), said by way of explanation.

"Isn't this going to look a little suspicious," I asked, holding up the fur hat. "It's seventy degrees outside."

"Oh, no you're going to look glamorous, just like Marlene Dietrich," he said.

No, I'm going to look like a lunatic.

"Sam, before we leave, can I get your autograph?" he asked me, pulling a pen from his pocket and sliding a copy of the May 27 *Très Chic* out from under his arm. "It's for my wife. She's been following your story all summer. Just wait until she gets back from visiting her mother in Tennessee and I tell her we've had the Mystery Woman living in our building. She's going to die!"

I scribbled my signature across the silhouette head. Was this going to be my first of many autographs, just for getting engaged? I'd much prefer that it would be for something I'd created, like a book of humorous essays or a choreographed dance that would win first place in a salsa competition.

"This is so thrilling," Solly went on, as we took the maintenance elevator down to the parking garage. "These kinds of things don't happen in Milwaukee, and certainly not in my building. I've never had to escape from the paparazzi before!"

That's because they're not paparazzi I wanted to tell him. But clearly he was having the time of his life. I hated to ruin it for him. We struggled off the elevator with my heavy suitcases and carry-on bag and walked over to his van. Then it hit me.

"Oh no, I need to get back upstairs. I forgot to grab my files and my journal." I looked at my watch. It was nine-thirty. I might not make this flight, but these were too important to leave behind. They were copies of my weekly factual reports, all the humor essays I'd written on the side this summer in preparation for my column, and my original articles the way I'd written them before Elaine had edited them.

"I'll be right back, Mr. Sassa . . ."

"Solly, remember?" he said with a big grin and a wink. "Hey, you'd better put on your disguise," he said, holding up the plastic bag.

"I'll put it on when I get back to the car, I promise." Looking like an escapee from a mental institution for the thirty-minute drive to the airport was a small price to pay to make one bored but extraordinarily nice man happy.

Taking the elevator back up to the eighteenth floor, I was just about to slide the key in the lock when someone shouted.

"Hey, Samantha!"

I heard a click and saw a flash.

"Got it!" said a tall man holding a camera and wearing a cheap suit and a cheap smile.

Nineteen

A Touch of Heaven

By Samantha Jacobs

I look out onto the dance floor at my favorite Latin nightclub and watch a young Latino couple. The woman, a wisp of a girl with a bare midriff, pierced navel, and waist-length black hair, is struggling to follow the lead of her handsome partner. He steps back from her occasionally to show off his fancy footwork. But it doesn't matter that her salsa dance skills don't come close to matching his. The pure bliss on their faces says it all. They are either in love, on cloud nine, or suspended somewhere in between.

Some people compare partners dancing to foreplay or take it a step further and call it the ultimate in safe sex. Not a few compare it to a drug. The less prurient and prone to addictions say dancing makes them feel like a kid again. Others even claim that it comes close to a spiritual experience.

For me, Latin dancing is all of that and much more. When I dance with a man whose touch is as light as a feather and yet communicates exactly what moves I should make. When we're flowing together gracefully as one, the feeling I get is undeniably sensuous, but nearly impossible to describe. The closest I've come is to say it makes me feel like melted butter.

I've always loved to dance, but the kind I'd done before I discovered salsa last summer was limited to fast and slow dances done at weddings and the infrequent girls' night out to discos. Salsa took me by complete surprise. Never before has anything triggered in me a gut-level emotional response so intense it completely takes over my mind and heart, evoking emotions far too complex and powerful to express with mere words.

On the one hand, it is so simple. A man and a woman move together, in rhythm, to the music. The perfect follow merely reacts to her lead's touch. Unlike in the bedroom where a woman can take charge, while dancing, she shouldn't anticipate moves or initiate any. By necessity, a woman gives up complete control to her partner. On the dance floor there are no concerns of equality or sexism, and she is free to let a man make her feel like a woman.

But what is that nebulous, enigmatic, mystical something that makes salsa so incredible?

Is it the satisfaction that comes when a man and a woman working as a team are able to successfully coordinate and execute intricate dance steps and arm movements? Is it a mere chemical reaction, a dancers' high caused by the release of endorphins? Is it a connection with the music, your partner, or both?

After months of trying to unravel the mystery of why salsa consumes my soul, I've finally come to terms with the fact that the thing I love most about it is that it makes me feel utterly alive in a way that nothing else ever has.

My friend Javier, a Dominican by birth and part-time salsa instructor, once told me that when he's dancing with a woman who smoothly follows his lead, "It's like we're floating, like there's no *one else in the room."* And then, *he'd paused and added,* "It's like *heaven."*

I remember being floored by his words. It was as if he had read my mind. And, in that instant, I realized that men and women weren't so different after all.

And maybe, it is enough to simply know this?

"What is this?" Elaine snarled, and then tossed my copy of "A Touch of Heaven" across her desk. She took off her black reading glasses and began cleaning the lenses.

"The piece I wrote for the September thirtieth 'La Vie' column," I said. She knew very well what it was, but still hadn't forgiven me for having been out-scooped by *People* magazine last month.

It turns out that the guy who'd snapped my photo in the hallway just before I'd left Milwaukee happened to live one floor below me in my apartment building. When he saw the reporters outside that morning, he'd called a friend who worked for a local television station to find out what the hullabaloo was about. He'd figured out who I was and took a chance that I was still inside my apartment. So he'd waited for me, caught me as I'd come off the elevator, and then sold the shot to the highest bidder.

"Salsa is fun," Elaine said, without a trace of warmth in her voice. "But this piece isn't going to work. 'La Vie' is a *humor* column. Ha ha, funny, make our readers laugh, remember, Samantha?"

I'd accomplished the nearly impossible task—according to the statistics of Dr. Victoria Huber—of finding the great on-paper and in-person professional educated man in the city with the worst possible chances, *and* doing it in less than the ridiculous time frame Elaine had given me. Sales of *Très Chic* had steadily increased from the first Mystery Woman issue at the end of May and skyrocketed in August when the big issue came out. "Mystery Woman Finds Her Prince Charming in Milwaukee," had featured a cover shot of Robert and me. Sales had tapered off a bit since then, but Elaine had reached her goal of the hallowed one million circulation.

And then to top it off, I'd had to pinch hit for Maya Beckett when she quit *Très Chic* without giving notice, just two days before I'd returned to New York. There was supposed to have been a transition period before Maya Beckett gave up "La Vie" and I took over. But Maya had left after ten years at *Très Chic,* eight of those writing "La Vie," without giving a single day's notice. Luckily, I'd spent a lot of time on my journal over the summer so "The Three Date Rule" and "The Mammary Mirage" were ready to go with just some minor editing. But I guess none of this was good enough for Elaine.

I remember when I first found out in May that Maya Beckett was giving up "La Vie." Elaine had said that Maya's original plan was to return to one of the regular departments. In my opinion, she'd lapsed into temporary insanity. Why would she give up the best job in the world? Even if she needed a change, as Elaine had told me then, Maya had far too much talent to make a move back to the mundane. It's not that you can't get exciting and interesting assignments in Features. It's just that there's a world of difference between creative humor writing and, say, doing an interview of Cameron Diaz to find out why she loves to belch.

But the weirdest part of all was that no one knew where Maya was. It was as if she'd disappeared into thin air. She'd never been very close to anyone on the staff and kept her personal life very private. But you'd think someone would have known what had happened to her.

I'm sure lots of offices are hotbeds when it comes to gossip, but at *Très Chic* the tittle-tattle could corrode stainless steel. You couldn't cough without someone spreading a rumor that you'd contracted a new strain of incurable tuberculosis. But wild rumors were all we had to go on—everything from Maya having joined a far-right religious sect in Mississippi to another that she'd secluded herself away to write a tell-all book about Elaine Daniels.

"Samantha, dear, when is the next time your handsome fiancé is coming to town?" Elaine asked with a sugarcoated smile. Uh-oh. She wanted something.

"He's coming in tonight," I said, grinning like a Cheshire cat, despite being wary of Elaine.

Just five hours from now, assuming his plane got in on time, I was going to meet him at my door wearing a black silk robe with nothing underneath. I hadn't seen him since last month when he left to go back to Milwaukee the day after the engagement party my mother had thrown for us at the Rainbow Room. The two weeks Robert spent here, we'd hardly had a moment alone together. Whenever we had been alone in my apartment, we'd often drop off to sleep exhausted, with barely a kiss good night. Our appearance schedule had been jam packed, taking us from photo shoots to parties to press conferences and even an appearance on *Larry King Live*. My life had been so different before that *People* magazine photo was snapped just six weeks ago. I missed it. But what exactly was it that I missed? Milwaukee, or . . . No! I'm not going to let myself think about Javier and the fact that he hadn't returned any of my calls.

"Can the two of you pop in tomorrow?" Elaine said, interrupting my thoughts. "We need some more photos. Candids. Raul will be taking you two around the city. You know, Central Park, the Statue of Liberty, all the usual landmarks."

"Tomorrow is Saturday," I said evenly. I'd planned to be horizontal with Robert for most of the weekend except for a mandatory brunch with my mother, sister, and her husband on Sunday. And these photo sessions were never a pop. I'd been photographed so much in the past six weeks since I'd returned to New York, I think my body had spontaneously produced cataracts to protect my eyesight.

"Well, I . . ."

"Excellent. On the way out, tell Sally to call Raul and let him know you'll meet him here at ten."

I knew that Robert wouldn't mind spending the day being photographed. In fact, it seemed to me that he couldn't get enough of the publicity. Me? I'll admit I loved it at first. But I was looking forward to returning to blessed anonymity after Robert and I were married and the public finally forgot about us.

I raced home, hopped off the subway, and jogged up the stairs to my usual stop at Union Square. At my favorite gourmet grocer's a couple blocks from my apartment, I picked up a mixed bouquet of flowers, champagne, Brie, and French bread.

"Special weekend planned, Miss Jacobs?" asked Mr. Wong, the owner, as I dumped my purchases on the black conveyor belt.

"You could say that," I said, feeling a smile on my face as wide as the shop.

"Did you see today's *USA Today*?" he asked me as he scanned each item.

"No." I silently groaned, no doubt another Mystery Woman story.

Mr. Wong skirted around the register, and pulled a copy of the paper off the stand. He pointed to the bottom of the front page and then handed it to me. The headline read: "Milwaukee Reports Apartment Shortage: Surge of Single Women Flock to

Mystery Woman's Mystery City to Relocate for Its Fabulous Singles Scene."

This was my fault. Elaine had altered my articles, but I'd let her do it. I could've given up "La Vie" and gone public with what I knew. Sure Milwaukee was a nice town. But wait until all these women found out the dating scene there was just like it was everywhere else, a crapshoot with choices ranging from a very few select cuts of prime sirloin to the overabundant run-of-the-mill meat loaf.

I sprinted the two blocks home and opened the door to a ringing telephone. The caller I.D. showed Robert's number.

"Are you ready for some of the hottest sex of your life?" I said in my most sultry voice.

"Sam," he said, "I can't come to New York this weekend."

"What?" My voice was shrill.

"I'm sorry. I got stuck in Denver yesterday and I have to fly to Houston tomorrow. Do you remember that firm . . . ?"

"I don't care about fucking Denver or Houston! This is the second weekend in a row you've cancelled," I shouted, and then realized, it was the first time I'd ever yelled or sworn at him.

"I need to put the time in now to get my firm in the best possible position to sell it, so I can move to New York and never have to leave you again," he said patiently.

I didn't say anything. My chest felt heavy. I was trying not to cry, but the tears started spilling down my cheeks.

"Sam, please try and understand," he said, pleading.

"What about next weekend? Am I still coming out for your birthday?"

"Are you kidding?" he said. "If I'm on my deathbed, and between now and then a shark bites off both of my legs, and I'm kidnapped by bandits and have to escape and drag myself by my knuckles fifty miles to meet you at the airport, I'll do it. Next weekend is ours. I promise."

I laughed through my tears.

"I love you, Sam," he said.

"I love you too," I said hoarsely, willing myself to push away the thought that I'd gotten engaged to another workaholic. Everything would be fine once Robert moved here. I just needed to calm down.

How could I salvage my weekend, I wondered after we hung up. I looked at my watch. I had plenty of time to get ready and try out one of the many Manhattan salsa clubs I'd been dying to sample. I hadn't been dancing since Milwaukee and was going through serious salsa withdrawal. If nothing else, at least for a few hours tonight, I could just be—having incredible fun while a salsa high temporarily made my worries disappear.

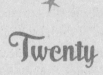

Twenty

Wedding Blues

"So, Mother, what's this big news you couldn't tell me over the phone?"

"I got Robert a job!" she said with a huge smile and a self-congratulatory, delighted gleam in her eye. If it had been possible, she would've given herself a pat on the back as well. I couldn't have been less delighted if she'd told me she was planning on moving in with Robert and me after our wedding and sharing our king-sized bed.

She stood in the corner of the dressing room looking chic as usual. Over the summer she'd changed her hairstyle, going from a straight black bob to a short, choppy cut that made her look years younger, and she was finally letting a little of the gray show through, as well. Her black blazer with silver buttons and white Palazzo pants fit her perfectly and were no doubt very expensive. But that style of designer sportswear that shouted, "I've-just-stepped-off-my-yacht" wasn't for me.

"I like this one," said Elizabeth, who stood behind me button-ing up the thousand and one silk-covered buttons on my dress.

"Hmm, I don't know," I said, looking in the mirror with my hands on my hips. I liked the draped neckline, but the skirt was a little too poofy and flouncy for my taste. It was the kind of wedding gown that would've appealed to me ten years ago, but now it seemed a little silly.

I was just about to ask Elizabeth about her weekend with Judge Doug, but could see in the mirror that my mother was practically about to burst.

"Tell me about this job you found for Robert," I said to hu-mor her. Later would be time enough to let her know that of course Robert would choose his own job.

"He'll be working for Martha's nephew at his recruiting firm," she said.

I cringed inside. My mother's best friend, Martha Smith, was the kind of woman that people didn't say no to. This wasn't go-ing to be easy to get out of.

"Martha was very impressed with Robert when she met him at the engagement party," said my mother smoothly, as if she'd barely had a hand in the matter, but still deserved all the credit, something I've always wondered how she's managed to do. "I happened to mention to her that he was in the market for a po-sition in recruiting, and she was kind enough to talk about it with her nephew."

My mother and Robert had taken to each other like two old school chums who hadn't seen each other since their wild carefree university days. As they talked about everything from Robert's ca-reer, to the stock market, to sharing the same favorite movie of all time, *North by Northwest*—and this was just in the first five min-utes after they'd met—I had stood there feeling like the uninvited party crasher, thinking how dare this perfect stranger get on better with my mother in mere minutes than I had in forty-one years. Why couldn't Robert be like all my previous boyfriends, especially David, men whose relationships with her had been perfectly normal and acceptable—in other words, abysmal.

"I like this one," Elizabeth said, lifting the train and tossing it over her arm. "I'm practicing."

"It makes me look like a giant meringue pie," I said, shaking my head. I leaned into the mirror and wiped a stray spot of mascara from under my eye.

"You mean I have to spend three days now unbuttoning you?" Elizabeth demanded, grinning broadly. "My fingers are going to fall off."

"These are just one of the many duties of the maid of honor," I said. "You get all the grueling work. I get all the glory."

I caught a short grimace from my mother. She was still upset that I'd asked Elizabeth instead of Susan. But I'd talked to my sister about it beforehand and she'd understood completely.

"Robert hasn't been able to get a job yet," my mother continued. "How is he going to support you?"

"Oh, I don't know," I said, posing for a side view in the mirror. "I suppose we'll go on welfare and start selling crack cocaine to make ends meet."

"How about this one?" Elizabeth suggested, holding an ivory satin number in front of her.

"What's that on the bottom?" I asked the sales clerk, who wisely hadn't said much since the four of us had entered the cavernous dressing room a couple hours ago. We'd been carrying on several strains of conversation at once, so it would've been quite a feat for her, a total stranger, to jump in, a little like trying to board an airplane in the usual manner, but in mid-flight.

"That's a fishtail train," the clerk told me.

"But I can't dance in that," I said, shaking my head.

"It's removable," she said. She was the quintessential sales-clerk, helpful but not too helpful, friendly but not too friendly, and didn't make me feel like if she didn't get a sale off me, she'd wind up sleeping on a street grate that night.

"Really? Can I see the back?" I asked. Elizabeth turned it over. There was a big beaded bow over the bustle area. I shook my head, saying, "I don't do bows."

"Martha says Robert will be making in the low six figures the first year," my mother continued in her typical unrelenting fashion. "And if he puts his time in, it should jump up within a few years."

Puts his time in. I knew what that meant. Working sixty to eighty hours a week and beholden to one of the richest families on the East Coast. I would rather go on welfare.

"Excuse me, Miss Jacobs," the clerk said. "I think I've got the perfect gown for you. I just remembered it came in yesterday. Let me just go get it."

"Mother, I don't want Robert to think I arranged this behind his back, that somehow I doubt him. I'm sure he'll be able to find something once he settles here. He's busy concentrating on selling his firm in Milwaukee."

"It's too late," said my mother, who'd turned away from me just enough so that I couldn't catch her eyes in the mirror.

"Too late for what?" I said evenly, but my heart was hammering.

"I already talked to Robert about this job," she said.

"What! When?" I whirled to face my mother.

"Before he went back to Milwaukee," she said smoothly. "He thinks it's a great idea. Now calm down, Samantha, what could be bad about Robert getting a great job?"

The fact that you arranged it behind my back and were interfering in my personal life, not to mention, the real problem, that Robert hadn't discussed this with me. Why?

I heard a knock at the door. The sales clerk slipped in with a dress.

"We haven't had time to press it yet, please ignore the wrinkles," she said. "I think this is the dress for you."

There's that moment in a woman's life when she stands on the pedestal in front of the three-way full-length mirror and sees herself in her wedding dress for the first time. This was it, the perfect dress. An A-line cut in Thai silk, with a low V back, a beaded tip of the shoulder neckline, and no train. It was beautiful, the most beautiful dress I'd ever seen. Elizabeth and even my mother were speechless. All of the other customers and clerks in the store had stopped what they were doing to stare at me.

I burst out crying.

☆　☆　☆

"Do you know, I think it's five months to the day that we were last here and I told you I was going to Milwaukee," I said later that afternoon.

It felt good to be with Elizabeth in our usual booth at Heavenly City bar. We'd barely seen each other since I'd come back to New York.

"Sam, what's wrong?" Elizabeth asked. I'd covered up my outburst at the bridal salon with a lot of talk about wedding jitters and not getting enough sleep. But the truth was very different.

I took a sip from the thin lip of the chilled martini glass and carefully set it back down on the table. "I'm worried that Robert is going to turn out to be a workaholic like David was," I said.

The heavenly smell of garlic wafted up from the plate of Camarones al Aljillo the waitress dropped off.

"Because he cancelled his last two visits to New York?" said Elizabeth, who was pretty—so pretty that she should be pressed inside a book like a rare delicate flower and discovered perfectly preserved in a hundred years—until she opened her mouth and went into lawyer mode.

"That and it seems like all he does is work, work, work. He doesn't have any outside interests, no family, no friends, at least none that I've met," I said, stabbing a shrimp with my fork.

Elizabeth nodded and didn't say anything. She was the best listener I knew, an incredibly valuable skill that most people think they excel at. But let's face it, when most of us are listening, we're actually just wondering how we can turn the conversation back to ourselves.

"And there are other things. Before I left Milwaukee, I hadn't told him who I really was. By the time I got a hold of him, he'd found out I was the Mystery Woman from the news like everyone else. I was sure he was going to be upset, but . . ."

"What?"

"He was thrilled. A little too thrilled with the publicity if you ask me. And you should've seen him after the Larry King show. He was acting like he was a movie star or something."

"I don't think you can blame him for that," she suggested. "It was his fifteen minutes of fame. You've had all summer to prepare for it."

Not really, I told her. I'd never experienced fame before, not even the temporary-I'll-be-forgotten-in-a few-months type that I was currently experiencing. In a word, it was bizarre. I felt like my life had taken on a life of its own, that it didn't belong to me anymore. People recognized me everywhere I went and acted as though they had the right to ask me intensely personal questions like, "So, Sam, how long did you wait before sleeping with Robert?" I don't know how anyone could prepare for this.

Although, one of the unexpected side benefits of my temporary fame was that I'd had the best salsa night of my life the evening I'd gone out after Robert cancelled his trip last weekend. I'd danced for three hours straight and had been dipped and twirled so many times I was on a salsa high for the rest of the weekend.

"Sam, I talked with Robert for a long time at the engagement party and that night the four of us went out to dinner," she said, referring to the night Elizabeth, Judge Doug, Robert, and I had gone out. It was the first double date Elizabeth and I had ever been on together. Amazing. We've known each other almost our entire lives, but we'd had to wait until we were forty-one for our romances to overlap at just the right stages to schedule a double date.

"I like Robert, a lot. I think he's great for you," said Elizabeth. "After this weekend with him everything will be fine, I'm sure of it."

I told myself that she had to be right. I'd talked to him this morning before I left for the bridal salon. Everything was set for my trip to Milwaukee tomorrow. But I couldn't shake this feeling that something was wrong.

"So, what about Javier? Did you ever call him?" asked Elizabeth.

Javier. At the sound of his name my feelings jumped from pangs of guilt to waves of regret. Lately, everywhere I turned I heard some reference to Milwaukee, salsa dancing, bike racing, or something that reminded me of him. It popped up in the most unexpected of ways. Like yesterday, I was taking a taxi home from the gym and the cabbie had NPR on his radio. I was zoned out in the back of his cab not thinking about anything when I'd heard a reference to the Dominican Republic. As I listened to the announcer, I couldn't help but remember that afternoon in Javier's studio when we had made love:

"In a country long associated primarily with the merengue, bachata, a back-country music that originated among rural peasant populations of the Dominican Republic, is attracting a growing audience of Latino and mainstream audiences in larger cities in the United States. Mainstream record stores are beginning to market bachata albums . . ."

"Yeah, but he hasn't returned my calls, not that I can blame him," I said.

I felt so terrible that I'd had to leave Milwaukee without having a chance to explain anything or say good-bye to him. Javier found out through the press that I'd lied to him all summer.

"Uh-oh, you've got that look in your eye," said Elizabeth.

"What look?"

"You know what I'm talking about," she said.

"No, I don't."

"Sam, how do you really feel about Javier?"

I didn't know what to tell Elizabeth, because I couldn't understand myself how I truly felt about Javier. I knew that Javier was good and kind and really loved me. If the timing had been different, if I'd had another job or a different mother, maybe things would've worked out with him.

Although I had doubts about Robert being a workaholic, hopefully that would all change when he moved here. It was the distance that was putting so much strain on our relationship right now. It wasn't right for people who were engaged to go weeks being apart. Once we settled down and started our lives together, Robert and I would be just fine.

Twenty-one

Disappearing Act

It didn't take us more than three seconds beyond crossing Robert's threshold to get all of our clothes off. The first time, we made love a little wildly and desperately, as if it were our last time and we both knew it. Separation will do that to you. It reminds you of how precarious everything is, that nothing is guaranteed. But by the third time, the fears I'd expressed the day before to Elizabeth had melted away.

"I don't think I can stand being apart from you, even for a couple hours," he said, as he held me in his arms the next afternoon. I had lunch plans with Lessie, and Robert had a meeting downtown.

"Good," I said with a big smile. I was still a little upset at his two cancelled trips to New York over the last month. But the previous night and that morning had almost made up for it.

"When do I get my birthday present?" he asked. He had me up against the wall of his kitchen. I started to get that tingling feeling in my loins again, even though they'd just cooled down after being on fire for the past twelve hours straight.

"I don't know," I teased, thrusting my hips against him harder. "Have you been a good boy?"

I'd spent the last week shopping for the perfect gift for Robert. What do you get for a forty-five-year-old man with no hobbies? I'd ended up buying him an abstract watercolor called "Urban Myths." I'd left the painting in New York, but had brought him a photo of it already hanging in my apartment. We'd seen the painting in a gallery on one of our only free afternoons in New York. It had bright splashes of reds, oranges, and blues and looked vaguely like a child's finger painting, but we'd both loved it on sight. I smiled at the memory of that day. It had been one of those perfect unplanned days that we'd spent meandering in and out of galleries and shops, stopping to have lunch, later a glass of wine, then dinner.

"Haven't I been?" he asked, as leaned in to nuzzle my neck. I knew he was referring to his sexual prowess, which I'll admit left me aching for more.

"I guess so. But you'll just have to wait until tonight," I said, and then gently pushed him away. If this kept up we'd never get out of here.

Robert had offered to drop me off, but it was so beautiful outside, I wanted to get a little exercise. The sun was shining and it seemed warm for October. I walked three blocks to the restaurant that Lessie had chosen.

When I reached the restaurant, there was Lessie by the doorway. I wasn't prepared for seeing Lessie pregnant—I mean really pregnant. She was finally showing and wearing maternity clothes. But she was the best-looking pregnant woman I'd ever seen in person and one of the only women I knew who could get away with wearing this outfit: a black beret, a tight white long-sleeved turtleneck that proudly showed off the curve of her belly over a three-quarter-length jean skirt and black cowboy boots. She hadn't gained any weight in her face, arms, or legs and looked radiant.

"Cute," I said and patted her hard tummy.

"I'm almost five months'," she said, "can't hide it forever."

"It's so good to see you, Lessie," I said, after the hostess had settled us into a booth next to the windows. "How have you been?"

"I'm great," she said with a smile. I could see that Lessie had changed, and not just physically. She seemed peaceful and at ease with herself. "It really helps that my mom has been great about the whole thing. I think she figures this will be her only grandchild so she's going all out. She's driving down from Minnesota next weekend with my old crib and a bunch of baby clothes."

"How did it go at work when you told them?" I asked her, after we had each ordered a salad.

"They're not thrilled. I'm supposed to be a role model, and an unwed mother is not the role model they typically have in mind for high school students. But they can't fire me, so they're handling it."

"Have you heard from him?" I asked.

"Nothing. Javier told me that he'd had to break it to their parents. His father hit the roof. The roof, get it?"

At least Lessie hadn't lost her sense of humor, but it made me sad all the same that Eliseo had turned out to be a cad.

"I found out more," Lessie continued. "The other woman Eliseo got pregnant has taken him to court a bunch of times and he owes her thousands in back child support. I'll be lucky to get a dollar from him."

"Are you going to be able to make it, financially I mean?" I asked her, knowing that teachers weren't particularly well paid.

"I'm bringing in extra money with the freelance photography I'm doing and I have some saved. You know, Sam, I just can't believe I was so stupid to fall for someone like Eliseo," said Lessie.

"Don't be so hard on yourself," I said. "I've never been able to make my heart and brain work together."

"Well that's what I'm trying to do from now on. There's another teacher at school, Marty, and . . ." she paused, looking a little flustered.

"And?"

"And, he's just a friend for now, but he's been really good to me. He'd marry me tomorrow if I'd said yes. But I'm taking this one slow, not jumping into anything with a man anymore. You know, Sam, I think I've finally grown up. I'd never had to before. I let my ex-husband, Steve, take care of me, and then after we got divorced it was like being let out of jail."

I filled her in on my life, giving her all the details I hadn't had time to go into in the few phone conversations we'd had since I'd left Milwaukee.

"Are you coming to the wedding?" I asked her.

"No," she said seriously, as a smile snuck out of the left side of her mouth. "An invitation to the Mystery Woman's wedding? This is the hottest ticket in the country. I'm going to auction it off on eBay and retire off the proceeds."

"Very funny," I said with a laugh. But I'd much rather have a normal wedding, outside of the prying eyes of the public. Elaine was planning a special *Très Chic* wedding issue, and trying to squeeze as much free publicity out of this as she could.

"Of course I'll be there. But I might need two seats. In two months I'll be as big as a house," she said, patting her stomach.

"I doubt that. So, how is Javier?" I asked her, forcing my voice to sound light and carefree as if this question had just popped into my brain even though I'd been dying to ask her for the past hour.

Lessie looked down and didn't say anything. My heart fluttered.

"I don't know how to tell you this," she said, finally looking up at me. My throat went dry. "He's been seeing someone. It's that Latina woman that we saw that night at Babalus, the tall one with the red and blond streaks in her hair."

The one who'd had her eyes on Javier's package, and by now probably her hands and mouth on it too.

"Are they just dating or . . . ?"

"I hear that it's pretty serious," she said carefully.

I forced a smile, but inside I was devastated. That would explain, at least partly, why he hadn't returned my calls. "I'm happy he's found someone. He deserves it."

Lessie looked at me pointedly. "Sam, he only mentioned it to me once. I think he felt uncomfortable talking to me about you because he knows we're friends. But Javier really loved you."

Loved. Past tense.

"Are you okay, Sam?" asked Lessie. "You look really upset."

"Of course, I'm great," I said, and began to tell her about my birthday plans for Robert. I'd spent countless hours thinking that if only I'd known then what I know now things might've turned out very differently. I guess that until this moment, a part of me kept hoping for a miracle, that somehow Javier and I . . . But now it really was too late.

★ ★ ★

An hour later I let myself into Robert's apartment. It was strange to be in his condo alone. The skylights let in the last of the late afternoon rays that fell over the wood floors. I took a shower and then sat at his tiny kitchen table and polished my finger- and toenails. I was taking Robert to the Italian restaurant where we'd become engaged. I'd even called up ahead of time to see if our waiter, Todd, was working tonight and had arranged for us to be seated in his section.

As I got dressed, slipping on a pale green strapless raw silk cocktail dress and matching long-sleeved bolero jacket, I wondered where Robert was, mildly annoyed that his meeting was going longer than expected. By the time our scheduled dinner reservation had come and gone, I was furious, thinking that once again he was letting his job take priority over our relationship. But an hour after that I was completely panicked. I called the police.

"He's an adult," said the kind but clearly bored desk officer assigned to answer what to him was merely a routine call. "I'm sorry, miss, we can't do anything until he's been missing for twenty-four hours."

I paced back and forth across his apartment wondering what I should do. I wanted to call Elizabeth or Lessie, but I didn't know if Robert had Call Waiting so I didn't want to tie up the phone in case he called. Sometime just before dawn, I changed into my sweatpants and one of Robert's T-shirts, crawled into his bed, and cried myself to sleep.

When I woke up it was mid-morning, and I felt ashamed for having slept, but didn't have much time to dwell on my guilt since a moment later, the doorbell rang. I flew across the room. Robert had probably lost his key, but the important thing was, he was all right!

I flung the door open.

"Can I come in?" he asked. I'd forgotten how tall he was. He seemed to tower over me. I stood there speechless until the lenses of my brain came back into sharp focus.

"No, you can't come in. What are *you* doing here?" I demanded.

"That's what I'd like to discuss with you, inside, so we don't disturb the neighbors," he said in his silky smooth voice. Then he tipped his head toward the hallway as if I'd forgotten we were in a building with multiple condominiums.

And then my brain suddenly took a detour.

"Is this about Javier?" I asked, my stomach suddenly in knots. "Is he okay? He's not hurt, is he?"

He got a strange look on his face and then quickly recovered his mask of indifference.

"Javier is fine," he assured me. "But I would think your first concern would be for your fiancé."

"Never mind what my concerns are. And how do you know Robert is missing?"

His massive hands hung at his sides until he slowly reached into his breast pocket, handing me a flat black leather case that looked like a cardholder. When I opened it, I saw a badge for Special Agent Sebastian Diaz of the F.B.I.

Twenty-two

Bar None

I'd fully expected, given what Sebastian had told me about everything Robert had done, to be led through three or four solid steel and barred doors and then into one of those rooms with the two-way mirrors, where I'd find a frightened and disheveled Robert, fastened to a metal chair by leg chains, with the wild desperate look of a trapped animal.

Instead, Sebastian took me to his office, which had a desk, a couple of metal filing cabinets, two chairs, and a partially obstructed view of Lake Michigan. This was what watching too many cop shows and reading too many legal thrillers did for the ordinary person. Mass media completely warped your expectations. If I'd still had my sense of humor I would've been able to laugh at my momentary disappointment at the too-ordinary surroundings.

"Can I get you anything?" Sebastian asked. "Some coffee or soda?"

I shook my head no. I was too shocked by everything Sebastian had told me at Robert's condo to think about eating or drinking. I looked out at the lake. It was another warm, gorgeous day. But I couldn't appreciate it. Without any warning my life had completely fallen apart.

"There's something you should know before you talk to Robert," said Sebastian.

"There's more? I don't think I can handle anything else."

"I don't think Robert would tell you this himself, so that's why I'm going to tell you, for what it's worth. He insisted that I bring you here before he agreed to cooperate with us. He wanted to talk to you in person. Girlfriends are not normally our concern, unless they can screw up or help an investigation, but . . ."

There was a soft knock at the door, and when Sebastian opened it, Robert walked in, un-handcuffed and looking exactly as he had yesterday when I'd kissed him good-bye. Obviously, he had gotten a full night's sleep. I couldn't look at him, but I felt him staring at me as he sat down in the chair across from me.

Sebastian nodded to the other agent who'd escorted Robert here.

"I'll be back in twenty minutes," said Sebastian. "Knock if you need one of us. There will be an agent right outside the door."

The door had barely closed before Robert blurted out, "Sam, I don't know what to say. I'm sorry."

"You're sorry! How could you do this to me? You lied about everything!" I shouted. After Sebastian told me everything about his investigation and about Robert, the real Robert, whom I didn't know at all, the only thing left inside of me was anger.

"I didn't lie about the fact that I loved you," he said. "I still love you, very much."

"Love," I snorted. "That's rich. You obviously don't know the first thing about love."

"Listen, I'd never planned on going out on any Single No More dates, and certainly not falling in love. But when I found out you wanted to meet me, and I saw your photograph and video, I think I fell in love with you right then and there. I had to meet you."

I felt his eyes on me, but I refused to look at him.

"Sam, you've got to believe me," he pleaded. "I wanted to start a new life with you in New York. I was going to go clean and get a real job."

"Oh, you mean like your real job as a lawyer, before you stole all that money from your clients and went to prison?"

Robert winced. Apparently my words had landed like a slap across his face. And then it hit me.

"You used my mother to get you a job working for Martha Smith's nephew! You played her perfectly. How convenient. You'd marry me and then waltz into a job that would pay you more money than working for God. And then, by magic, your past is wiped out. Presto, you have the perfect legitimate life."

"It wasn't like that, Sam," he said. I could see more of his phony tears in his eyes. He had played me perfectly too.

"You even lied about having a dead wife. Sarah this and Sarah that. Let's all feel sorry for Robert Mack, the poor widower."

"For what it's worth, there really was a Sarah," he said softly. "She was my girlfriend when I was eighteen. She died in a car crash. She was the first . . ."

"Just stop. Stop!" I held up my hand. "I don't want to hear any more of your fucking bullshit!"

He looked shocked. I'd actually shocked myself. I'd never been so angry in my entire life. I stood up and walked over to the door and knocked on it. The agent opened it.

"Wait, Sam. You have to know, I never meant to hurt you, I love you," he pleaded, and then started crying.

For a brief moment I felt sorry for him. But it passed.

"Good-bye, Robert." I turned and walked out without looking back him.

Twenty-three

Meltdown

For several long minutes after I told her everything, Elaine sat behind her enormous teak desk saying nothing. Her face was a blank page, impossible to read. As for me, I was beyond white-knuckled. My hands had permanently bonded to the black lacquered armrests of my chair.

I wish she'd start her tirade so I could get this over with. I had steeled myself for an explosion to rival the eruption of Mount Vesuvius. I could imagine confused geologists in California noting unusual seismic activity in Manhattan after Elaine went ballistic. As I waited for her response, I heard sounds I never usually noticed. The chair I sat in squeaked every time I moved, and I heard my heart thump inside my chest.

"Samantha, dear, you must be devastated," she said finally, in a voice that bordered on a whisper. She leaned forward in her chair with her arms extended out over her desk, her hands folded together as if in prayer.

"I'm so sorry. I had no idea that Robert, that he was actually . . ."

Elaine's unexpected kindness brought another wave of tears to my eyes. I began crying. Again. I hadn't thought it possible. I know the body is 60 to 70 percent water, but I'd cried so much in the past two days that I couldn't believe I had a drop of liquid left inside of me.

"Of course you didn't. Men can be such selfish bastards. I'm just wondering, do you know when this will hit the press?"

"I'm not sure. I think in the next day or two," I said between sobs. "The investigation is done."

She rose and walked over to the windows and gazed out for a long moment. Finally, she turned back to face me.

"Samantha," she said gently, but firmly, "I think you need some time off to collect your thoughts and get your life back together."

"Yes, I do," I agreed. "But what about my column?"

It felt good to say "my column." It should. I'd worked hard to get it. For a half a second I forgot about Robert and felt proud that I'd accomplished something I'd wanted for a very long time. My first three columns had attracted hundreds of warm letters from readers with comments like, "That's exactly how I feel!" and, "You are hilarious. Please don't stop!"

"Don't worry about a thing. You just take care of yourself," said Elaine.

She escorted me out of her office like a mother taking a child who'd skinned her knees to get a bandage.

"Take all the time you need, Samantha."

"Elaine, I don't know what to say. Thank you for everything," I said. We stood there for an awkward second. Although the moment called for it, I'd sooner hug a drooling werewolf than Elaine, so we shook hands.

I went home to my apartment, but I felt like I didn't belong there. It was the middle of the day on a Monday and everyone I knew was at work. Their lives were humming along smoothly, gearing up for the rest of the week.

I sat in my favorite chair and stretched my legs out onto the ottoman. Every move I made had a surreal, slow-motion quality to it. I had the feeling that if I weren't very, very careful, I'd have the reverse–Midas touch on everything I did. Plug in a lamp and I'd short-circuit my entire building. Call for my investment account balance and I'd trigger a stock market collapse. Put on a new pair of nylons and I'd get three runs in each leg within two seconds—well, that happened anyway, even when my life was going great.

I was too tired to be angry, and the shock had worn off. The only thing I could feel at this moment was overwhelming sadness. But I tried to console myself with the thought that things couldn't possibly get any worse. Things could only improve from this point. Right?

On the bookshelf opposite me there was a framed photograph of Andre and me, snapped at the top of Machu Picchu just after we'd finished the climb. We had our arms over each other's shoulders, both of us smiling and triumphant. It had been taken six months ago, just before this whole thing had started. I couldn't imagine ever again feeling that kind of carefree happiness. It was difficult to comprehend that at this very moment there were people laughing, making love, falling in love, and having babies, when I couldn't foresee doing much of anything ever again.

My mind drifted back over the past two days since Sebastian had rung Robert's doorbell, and the perfect life I'd imagined for Robert and me had dissolved in an instant. After I met with Robert at Sebastian's office on Saturday, Sebastian had taken me back to

Robert's condo so I could get my things. Sebastian then drove me over to Lessie's house. Just before I got out of his black sedan, I finally remembered to ask him about something that had been bothering me ever since last summer.

"*Do you remember that night at Cubana when Javier and Isabella were dancing together?*"

He nodded, clearly uncomfortable at venturing into the non-work realm of our relationship.

"*Why did you lie to me and tell me that Isabella was Javier's ex-girlfriend?*" *I'd been thinking of it constantly since I'd found out about who Robert really was. How could I have chosen such a loser over Javier? I felt sick thinking about it.*

Sebastian shrugged his shoulders.

"*I love Javier like he's my brother,*" *he said.* "*But he's too nice for his own good. Sometimes he lets other people take advantage of him. I knew you were lying about why you were really in Milwaukee, so I didn't want you to get too close to him. But I can see now . . .*" *He paused.*

"*See what?*"

"*I was wrong about you, Sam, I'm sorry.*"

The doorbell rang. I jumped, and looking outside, could see that night had fallen. I must've been sitting there in the chair for six hours. I noticed that the muscles in my legs had stiffened to boards, and I wobbled to the buzzer like an old lady to open the door.

"I took a couple days off of work," announced Elizabeth, who plopped down an overnight bag. "I'm going to stay with you until the news breaks."

As much as Elizabeth didn't like her job, I'd never known her to call in for a single mental health day or ever take all of the vacation she was entitled to. I hugged her tight.

"Have you eaten?" she asked.

"I don't think so," I said.

She walked over to my telephone and called our favorite Thai restaurant.

"You're going to be okay, Sam," she said, with the receiver pressed to her ear.

"With friends like you, how could I not be okay?" I said. I felt the tightness around my mouth slightly loosen' as I attempted my first smile in days.

Two days later, I picked up my *New York Times* and took it over to the kitchen table where Elizabeth was drinking coffee and eating half a grapefruit.

"The circus begins," I said, as a dropped the paper in front of Elizabeth and we read it silently together.

INDICTMENTS HANDED DOWN AGAINST MILWAUKEE DATING SERVICE: MYSTERY WOMAN'S FIANCÉ ENTERS GUILTY PLEA

A federal grand jury in Milwaukee, Wisconsin, handed down indictments yesterday against Bunny Woods, the owner of the Milwaukee franchise of Single No More, the nation's largest video dating service, and against her husband, Dmitri Woods, a former guard at the Urbana halfway house in Milwaukee. The charges against the couple include theft, extortion, and fraud, in connection with a scheme that has left single women across the nation reeling in shock and anger.

Also implicated in the plot is Robert Mack, 45, former fiancé of Samantha Jacobs, better known as the Mystery Woman of the New York–based *Très Chic* magazine. Mack pleaded guilty on lesser charges of fraud in exchange for turning State's evidence. He faces up to three years in prison.

The indictments were handed down after a 15-month investigation, spearheaded by Special Agent Sebastian Diaz of the F.B.I., into the operations of the Milwaukee office of Single No More.

According to the indictment, Bunny Woods, 47, and her husband, Dmitri Woods, 49, devised a plan to fill the depleted ranks of Single No More by recruiting newly paroled male prisoners who had been convicted of white-collar offenses from federal minimum-security camps in Wisconsin and Minnesota. Dmitri Woods is charged with stealing master lists of names and addresses of released prisoners from the halfway house where he worked as a guard, which he then provided to Mack. Mack then contacted and recruited the convicts. In exchange for nominal sums of money, Mack lured the convicts to the office of Single No More, where they went through the process of posing as legitimate clients, having photographs taken, making videos, and preparing false profiles.

Investigation has revealed that some of these imposter clients went beyond the original plan and actually went on dates with unsuspecting female clients. In exchange for a standard $2,000 fee, the service had guaranteed its legitimate clients that it did a thorough background check, including a criminal check, on anyone applying for membership before allowing applicants to join the dating service.

"I feel sick to know I might have gone out with a sexual offender," said Jane, a former client of Single No More and a Milwaukee anesthesiologist, who refused to give her last name. "We join services like this to weed out the bad ones for us. And what did they do? They set us up to meet these creeps. They put our lives in danger."

Mack, a former attorney, who earned his law degree from John Marshall Law School in Chicago, Illinois, lost his license to practice law when he was convicted in 1996 in federal court of three felony theft offenses for embezzling over $225,000 from his clients. Mack was sentenced to three years in prison and spent the last six months of his sentence at the Urbana halfway house in Milwaukee where he originally met Dmitri Woods.

Recently, Mack had experienced a spate of publicity including an appearance on the *Larry King Live* show after he became engaged to Samantha Jacobs, 41, a native of Scarsdale, New York. Jacobs, a 15-year employee of *Très Chic,* was sent to Milwaukee during the summer in the hopes of finding a professional, well-educated husband to flout a new statistic reported earlier this year by Harvard sociologist Dr. Victoria Huber that a well-educated, never-married woman over 40 has a better chance of winning a seven-figure lottery jackpot than of ever tying the knot. Jacobs joined Single No More last May and met Mack, who had also posed as a legitimate client of the service. They dated throughout the summer and became engaged early last August.

"At least the article doesn't make you look bad," said Elizabeth when she'd finished reading.

"No, not at all. I got engaged to a three-time convicted felon. Who hasn't done that at least once in their lives?" I said. "And to top it off, I probably dated some of his jail buddies."

"You can't beat yourself up about this, Sam. You didn't know. None of us did. He fooled all of us," she said, shaking her pretty brunette head. "He seemed so nice."

"I had warnings, but I didn't listen to them, as usual," I told her. I had ignored what my gut was telling me, that Robert wasn't right for me. But I'd also ignored what else my gut had been telling me, about who was right for me. And because of that, I'd lost Javier, the sweetest, most wonderful man I'd ever known.

"Sam, you will meet a great guy someday. It will happen," she said with the confidence of a happily coupled woman. Elizabeth was sure Judge Doug was going to propose before Christmas.

Could I ever meet another man like Javier? A man whom I'd felt so comfortable with, it was as though we'd known each other forever? It was impossible to imagine.

Elizabeth left an hour later to go back to work. I flipped on the TV. I just wanted to veg in front of the idiot box and forget about my life. I had five entire minutes of blessed mind-numbing TV-land drivel until I flipped the channel one too many times and saw Elaine seated behind her desk holding a press conference.

"I was just as shocked as you were by this unfortunate turn of events," she said, reading from what looked like a prepared statement. "But what you didn't know and what I myself just found out, is that Samantha Jacobs knew almost from the beginning that her fiancé, Robert Mack, was a fraud and a convicted felon."

"What? What are you talking about?" I screamed, but no one heard me, except perhaps everyone within a three-block radius.

"After Miss Jacobs found out about Mr. Mack's true background, they devised a plan to get engaged and go through with the wedding scheduled for December thirty-first. But at some point in the future after the publicity had died down, they planned to get their marriage annulled. All of this was in exchange for securing a lucrative job in New York for Mr. Mack along with a sizable payoff to him."

"You can't be serious!" I screamed at Elaine, who was managing to ape perfectly the pained, deeply troubled and unjustly wronged victim, as she paused significantly to let her last words sink in.

"It is also with deep regret that I am forced to announce that Miss Jacobs's articles that were published in *Très Chic* this summer about the Milwaukee dating scene were exaggerated and in several instances outright fabrications. Of course, I fired Miss Jacobs as soon as I found out. I sincerely apologize to the readers of *Très Chic* and everyone across the nation who was following this story."

"Mrs. Daniels, what in your opinion was Miss Jacobs's motivation?" one of the female reporters called out.

"Well I can't be sure of course, but I believe she did it for the most selfish of motives," Elaine said smoothly. "To promote her career as the new columnist for 'La Vie' at the expense of our readers who wanted to believe in the dream that they too could defy the statistics, meet a wonderful man, and get married."

Oh God! My life was no longer in the toilet bowl. It had just been flushed far back into the bowels of the New Jersey sewer system.

Twenty-four

Missing Persons

I'd barely moved from my chair in the past twenty-four hours. Elizabeth had offered to come over again last night, but I didn't want to see anyone. My mother, my sister, Andre, and Lessie had called, all of them mouthing words of sympathy and encouragement. I'm not even sure what I'd said to them in return.

I felt as hollow as if organ thieves had scooped out my insides in the night and the only thing they'd left was skin and bones. I was completely numb. I couldn't cry. I couldn't feel. My brain was on automatic pilot.

I remember so many times over the past fifteen years of my life feeling so bored that I would have welcomed almost any jolt just to spice things up. But now I'd give anything to have that boredom back. I craved normalcy.

I stared at the television set, watching yet another tearful interview of a betrayed *Très Chic* reader. Throughout the day CNN featured clips of women picketing outside the *Très Chic* building—me, not the magazine. Several dozen well-dressed women bundled up in wool coats, gloves, and scarves moved clockwise in a semicircle on the sidewalk. Some were holding signs, others were there mingling on the sidelines out of curiosity or, I suppose, for moral support. WE HATE YOU MYSTERY WOMAN! was the most common sign. Others included BURN IN SINGLES HELL FOREVER MW. Clearly, the cold spell that had hit New York two days ago had done nothing to dampen their enthusiasm.

The phone rang. I picked it up without thinking.

"I know you didn't know Robert Mack was a fake," said an unfamiliar voice.

"Who is this?" I asked. My initial reaction was to clutch at the voice like a nicotine addict for a cigarette. It was the first positive thing I'd heard about myself in days. But then my brain remembered to be wary. It could be a reporter trying to ingratiate herself by buttering me up.

"This is Maya Beckett."

Her voice was small, as if she were calling from overseas. A hundred thoughts swept through my brain at once. Where was she? Why had she quit *Très Chic* two months ago without giving notice? And why in the world was she calling me?

"Listen, I think I can help you. Can you meet me in an hour?" she asked.

A cold drizzle fell as I exited my building and walked to the corner to hail a cab. Maybe I was imagining it, but it seemed as though everyone I passed was examining my face extra carefully. The dark sunglasses I wore on this gray dismal day were practically an invitation for passersby to give me a good ogling so they could figure out if I was someone famous who was trying to hide her identity, which of course was exactly what I was trying to do.

Maya had refused to tell me any more on the phone, and the place she had suggested for us to meet was strange, giving the whole thing a bit of a cloak-and-dagger feel to it. But at this point I had nothing to lose. Maybe she had some information that could help me? Normally I'd take the subway uptown, but it was easier to face the possibility that one cab driver might recognize me versus a mob of irate *Très Chic* readers that might take their anger to the rotten vegetable level or even worse.

Thankfully, the cab driver, a woman in her mid to late forties, had barely glanced at me during the drive. We crawled through the traffic.

"I've been married three times," she said breaking the silence, which had been interrupted only by the static of her radio and the steady scrape of the wipers back and forth across the windshield.

"The first two cheated on me. The last one, the only one I really loved, went out for a carton of cigarettes and never came back. So I decided to try being a lesbian," she said, the same way someone might say, "I decided to try that new Ben & Jerry's flavor."

I felt as though I should say something, but I don't know that I could've thought of anything to say, even if my brain had been in peak working condition.

"It's not bad, but sometimes I miss having a hairy hard body next to mine at night. Not that any of my husbands had a lot of muscle or hair, but I liked the way they felt."

Swish, swash, swish, swash went the wipers.

"Have you ever thought about trying it?" she asked with a glance at me in her rearview mirror. "Nah, by the looks of you I don't suppose you have."

I didn't know what that was supposed to mean, but I didn't

care enough to try and figure it out. We stopped at a light. She studied me in her mirror and then turned her body around to face me. "Are you all right, honey?" she asked me. "You look like you ain't got a friend in the world. I'm not coming on to you or nothing. It's just, well, you look like shit."

I smiled. It was the nicest thing anyone had said to me in days. "I'll be okay," I said.

"This one is on me," she said with a flip of her hand when we pulled up to the curb and I handed her a twenty-dollar bill. "We girls need to stick together. You just take care of yourself," she said with a smile.

Inside the white spiral building that had always looked to me like an upside-down wedding cake, I looked about for Maya. The last time I'd visited the Guggenheim, I'd come with my sister, Susan, when she was eight months' pregnant, and she'd waddled down the exhibit ramps like a rocking ship, taking lots of breaks.

"When I think of Elaine Daniels, this is what I see," said Maya when she appeared at my side five minutes later, pointing to a statue by Alberto Giacometti, aptly named "Nose." The bronze head hung from a rope suspended in a rectangular cage with an enormous pointed nose that would've made Pinocchio's look like a button in comparison.

"I didn't mean to be so mysterious," Maya said. "The Guggenheim is my favorite museum. I live just a couple blocks away. I come here at least once a week." She was much taller than I, probably six feet in her stocking feet and close to six three in the black leather boots she wore. Her thin legs stuck out of a red leather miniskirt. If she walked into a bar, heads would turn. But if you took her features apart one by one, the bump on the bridge of her nose, her shiny but too-thin straight brown hair, and her mouth, which was too wide for her narrow face, they weren't attractive. But at a glance, the total package was striking.

"I have to tell you something difficult, but promise me you'll hear me out," she said tensely, moving with the fluid grace of a dancer.

"Okay," I said. What could possibly be worse than what I'd just been through? God, could it really have been just one week ago today that I'd found out my fiancé was a lying scoundrel?

"I'm the person who told the press that you were the Mystery Woman," she said.

"Okay," I said with a shrug. I was far too shell-shocked to let anything I might hear jolt me. "How did you find out?"

Maya exhaled and looked relieved. "Elaine told me," she said. "But Elaine wanted it kept secret. The only other person who knew was Sally."

"Do you remember the day you called Elaine to tell her you'd gotten engaged?"

I nodded. How could I ever forget celebrating the day that I'd made the biggest mistake of my life, saying yes to Robert's proposal?

"Right after that call," Maya continued, "Elaine had called me upstairs and told me that I was being transferred back to Features and she'd decided to give my column to you."

I couldn't help but be amused by Maya's proprietary tone about "my column." I'd felt the same way for the short six weeks I'd had it.

"But Elaine told me you were giving it up voluntarily, that you asked to be transferred back to a regular department," I said.

"Who'd be crazy enough to do that?" Maya said. "I loved that job. I never wanted to leave it. At first, Elaine told me she was no longer happy with my work, which I didn't believe. I don't mean to brag, but I got tons of fan mail. So I confronted her and demanded to know what was really going on."

I raised my eyebrow but said nothing.

"Then she told me everything. About you, your assignment in Milwaukee, and that she'd promised 'La Vie' to you if you pulled it off. She said if I agreed to go along with everything, she was going to give the column back to me in January while you were on your honeymoon."

"That bitch!" I said. A security guard, a small thin black man wearing wire-rim glasses, raised an eyebrow in my direction and lowered his chin in disapproval.

"I quit right then and there," Maya went on. "I was so furious all I wanted to do was get back at her. So I went to a good friend of mine who works for the Associated Press and well, the next day, you were exposed."

"It's okay. I probably would've done the same thing in your shoes."

"But I've got a plan to fix everything," she said.

Twenty-five

Lottery Winner

I gazed across the table at Andre, whom I hadn't seen in nearly seven months, not since our trip to Peru. We were at the Wolfgang Puck Cafe in Los Angeles. We'd spent the day, my last in town, finally seeing the tourist highlights, including the Hollywood Bowl, the Walk of Fame on Hollywood Boulevard, and a bus tour of the stars' homes.

For the first week after my meeting with Maya, I went out to White Plains to stay with my sister, Susan. Domesticity, spending quality time with my niece, and staying away from the media had helped immensely. I'd even tried a couple of salsa clubs out in the burbs, but they couldn't compare to the clubs in Manhattan or L.A. But then my sister and I had started to get on each other's nerves and I knew it was time to leave.

Luckily, Andre had called, offering his condo to me. He told me I could stay as long as I needed. I'd been in L.A. for over a month. Andre had been out of the country for the first two weeks so I'd been alone, mostly just vegging out by his pool after salsa dancing every night until four A.M., which had been more therapeutic than anything else.

Salsa had certainly helped me to keep my sanity, but it had done far more than that. Salsa was so freeing, so liberating that I'd finally been able to discover who I really was. I wasn't the person that Elaine or my mother had expected me to be. It was too late with Javier, but in the future I would never again make the mistake of falling for a man just because he was someone that other people approved of.

"Sam, why don't you fly to Paris with me tomorrow and we'll celebrate New Year's Eve there together?" Andre asked me.

"Two weeks is a long time for you to stay in one place, isn't it?" I said, teasing him. Andre lived to travel and, luckily for him, could do so whenever he wanted to, thanks to a trust fund that he'd gotten when he was twenty-five.

"There's salsa dancing in Paris," he said with a gleam in his eye.

I couldn't explain it, but I had a feeling I needed to get back to New York. But for what I wasn't sure, other than the fact that I was finally ready to face reality.

"I appreciate the offer, but it doesn't feel like the right thing to do," I said. I would always love Andre, but only like a brother.

"You're going to find someone, Sam. You are the most interesting woman I know. And you should see how beautiful you look right now," said Andre.

"Thanks, Andre," I said, wondering if he would ever settle down.

"So here's the sixty-four-thousand-dollar question, what are you going to do when you get back to New York, Sam?"

I didn't have a clue. From the Guggenheim, Maya and I had gone straight to Maya's reporter friend at the AP. I'd given him copies of my files from the summer that showed how I'd originally drafted my articles about my Milwaukee dates. But it had been Sally, Elaine's executive assistant, who had actually saved the day. Elaine had treated Sally like her personal slave for years, so it hadn't been too difficult to convince Sally to go on the record with everything Elaine had done. She'd provided her own e-mails and computer files as proof of my own. After that, Maya's reporter friend had flown to Oxford Federal Prison in Wisconsin to interview Robert. He'd also interviewed Sebastian Diaz, who'd corroborated that I'd known nothing about Robert or his dealings with Single No More until that fateful day when Sebastian had shown up at Robert's condo to tell me everything.

According to my latest phone call from Elizabeth, who was reading my mail and paying my bills while I was in L.A., three New York publishing houses were trying to find me to sign a book deal about everything that had happened over the last seven months. *Très Chic* was in serious trouble. Sales had dropped off 40 percent and the press had crucified Elaine Daniels ever since the AP article had come out about everything five weeks ago, including what Elaine had done to Maya Beckett.

"You've got one of those faraway looks on your gorgeous face," Andre said. "You're thinking about him, aren't you?"

"I don't hate him anymore. Now I just feel sorry for him. I think he really loved me, in his own way. But I finally realize, I was never in love with him."

What I thought was love was really, as it had been with David, just being in love with the idea of getting married and having a family with a man who'd fit the qualifications of what

I'd been conditioned to look for my entire life—superficial qualities that I've finally learned, at the ripe old age of forty-one, don't matter in the least. I had to admit that it was extraordinarily painful and not a little embarrassing to see how shallow I'd been my entire adult life when it had come to men—just like the "fictional" character Mary in my essay, "The Three Date Rule."

"Maybe three more years in prison will finally change Robert and he'll go straight, maybe even marry a nice woman someday?"

"Sam, I'm not talking about Robert. What about the man you are in love with?" asked Andre.

I didn't say anything. Aside from my father's death, losing Javier was one of the most painful events of my life. I knew from past experience that someday I would get over him, but at the moment it seemed impossible.

*   *   *

My plane landed exactly on time at JFK. I took a cab to my apartment and walked in. A fresh bouquet of purple and white irises sat on my kitchen table, along with a note from Elizabeth welcoming me back and reminding me that I could meet up with her and Doug that night. But I didn't want to socialize.

I looked at my watch, seven o'clock on New Year's Eve. Right now I would have been walking down the aisle at The Plaza, in front of five hundred of my mother's closest friends and a few of my own. In another twenty minutes I would've been married, ready to fly to Europe for my three-week honeymoon the next day. And then? We would've been happy, for a while. Eventually it would've fallen apart. Being in love with the idea of a man wasn't enough to make a marriage work.

I didn't feel like unpacking and was far too restless to sit in my apartment, so I bundled up and went out. I walked the streets for hours, passing elegant couples in tuxedos and long evening gowns, street bums curled up on street grates drinking from bottles in paper bags, and groups of laughing twenty-somethings full of life and optimism. I looked into bar and hotel windows at midnight and watched champagne toasts, chaste cheek kisses, and passionate full-mouth smooches.

And as I walked, I thought about everything I'd learned over the past seven months. I'd agreed to marry Robert because it was the easy thing to do, for my job and to please my mother. It's not that I didn't like him, and I'd convinced myself that I'd loved him, but I'd fooled myself into believing that I had to end up with the great-on-paper guy or I could never be happy. I couldn't believe it took me forty-one years to finally grow up. I smiled inwardly. That was what Lessie had said the last time we'd had lunch together. Ironically, over the past summer I'd felt that between the two of us, I had been the mature one. After all, I wasn't necking in humidors or having sex without birth control. But at least Lessie hadn't held back her feelings. And because I had, I'd lost the love of my life.

At two A.M. I walked into my apartment. A moment later I heard a frantic knock on the door. Normally I'd look through my peephole, but for some reason I flung the door open only to see the one person I was certain I'd never have the joy of seeing again.

"Javier! How did you get here?" I asked, flabbergasted and elated at the same moment.

"I flew," he said, breathing heavily. His nose and cheeks were red from the cold. "Where have you been, Sam? I've been walking all over your neighborhood for hours looking for you."

"Really?" I restrained myself from throwing my arms around him.

"Lessie told me you were getting back from L.A. tonight."

"What?" I could barely think since I was just beginning to grasp that Javier was actually here at my doorstep, and that maybe I had another chance.

"Would it be all right if I came in?" he asked with a smile.

Ten minutes later as we sat together on the couch, sipping champagne that I'd had in my fridge. It felt with Javier as it always had. It was as though we hadn't spent any time apart over the last four months.

"I thought you were furious with me," I said.

"I was more hurt than anything else. But then Sebastian told me that in October when he came to tell you that your ex-fiancé was in jail, the first person you asked about was me," he said.

"True," I said.

"When I heard that, I knew then how you really felt about me," Javier went on. "But, I was seeing someone at the time. I tried to forget about you, but I couldn't."

"So you're not seeing her anymore?"

"I broke up with her last month. I tried calling your home number but it just rang and rang."

After Elaine fired me on national TV, my phone never stopped ringing, so I'd cancelled my voice mail and for the last six weeks while I'd been out of Manhattan, my phone had been unplugged.

"So I called Lessie. She told me you were coming back tonight so I booked a flight and here I am."

My heart started pounding faster.

"I have never stopped thinking about you, Sam," he said. I hadn't forgotten his warm, brown eyes, or his warm dimpled smile, just as I hadn't forgotten how easy it was to be with him.

"I couldn't stop loving you." Javier reached over and grabbed my hand. "Sam, will you marry me?"

I knew my answer in an instant. Suddenly, I felt the magnetic north and south poles flip. I heard trumpets and harps and choirs of angels bursting into song. In the frozen mountains of Nepal an explorer stumbled into a beautiful verdant valley and discovered that Shangri-La really exists. Well, okay, not really. But it felt wonderful to finally show my true feelings, what I'd known for months but had suppressed, that I'm crazy in love with Javier.

"Yes, yes I will marry you, Javier."

"So when do you want to get married?" he asked.

"Today is January first, this seems like a good way to start the New Year," I said as we fell into each other's arms.

This time when we made love, I let myself go completely, more than with any other man I'd ever been with. Javier whispered over and over that he loved me and I did the same as we kissed each other everywhere. We came together, and as he held me close, I started crying.

"Sam, what's wrong? What is it *querida*?" he asked, stroking my face.

"I'm just so happy, I thought I'd lost you," I blubbered. "I was so stupid, it took me forever to figure out that I love you."

"It did take a quite a while," he said with a smile. I stopped crying and playfully punched his arm.

"I think I started to fall in love with you the night we had dinner at that Spanish tapas restaurant," I continued. "And then at Summerfest, remember when we were sitting on the rocks by Lake Michigan and you said you wanted to share your life with someone? I thought you were talking about Isabella. But I wanted it to be me."

"And I fell in love with you during our first bachata dance, in my studio. Remember?"

"You made my spine melt that day, of course I remember."

"I could try and make your spine melt again. Horizontal or vertical? I'm ambidextrous," he said.

I laughed. "Both, but horizontal first."

Twenty-six

Black Sand Dreams

The waiter smoothly traversed over the black sand beach carrying a tray with another round of daiquiris. He was built like a bullet train, but none of us were paying him the slightest amount of attention.

"I'd like to propose a toast to Dr. Victoria Huber," I said, holding up my glass.

"Who?" asked Lessie and Elizabeth in unison, leaning forward on their beach chairs, both with blank looks on their pretty faces.

"The woman who said it couldn't be done," I said. "That sociologist who said a never-married, over-forty, professional, single woman has a better chance of winning the lottery than ever getting married. We've all done it."

"But I've been married before," said Lessie.

"Yeah, but you're forty-three and you're getting married again," I said.

"Marty and I haven't picked a date yet, remember?"

"Why don't you get married here, in Hawaii?" suggested Elizabeth.

"That's a great idea!" I said.

"Well, it's not a bad idea," Lessie said. "Let me talk to him about it."

We each sampled our drinks.

Lessie put her drink down and stood up. She shouted to a red-haired, heavily freckled man, sitting in the sand. He was making a sand castle with an eight-month-old girl wearing a flowered sunbonnet. "Honey, can you put some more sunscreen on her?"

He flashed her a thumbs-up.

"Marry him, Lessie. He's in love with your daughter," I said.

"And with me," she said, gazing at the two of them.

Elizabeth sat up and waved to a tall man walking parallel to the ocean and carrying a surfboard. He waved back and then waded into the water, flopped down on his board, and paddled out.

"That's my husband the surfer," said Elizabeth.

Lessie and I laughed. Elizabeth had made a point of referring to Doug as her husband at every opportunity. But they'd only been married for eight weeks so I guess I couldn't blame her.

"Sam, I just remembered, do you know what today is? Besides my *husband's* birthday," said Elizabeth.

"October fourteenth I think?"

"It was one year ago today that your boss fired you on national TV," she said.

I groaned at the memory of the worst day of my life. *Très Chic* had finally folded three months ago. Elaine Daniels was getting divorced from her sixth husband and had filed for bankruptcy. I supposed she was feeling the same way I had on that horrible day last year when it felt as though my life were over.

But she'd brought it all on herself. I didn't feel like gloating. If anything, I felt sorry for her.

"So when is your book going to be done, Sam?" asked Elizabeth.

"Next month, as soon as I go over the galleys," I said.

It wasn't the gossipy tell-all about Elaine Daniels that the publishers had wanted. My book, *Lessons in Love*, was about what I'd learned about myself over the past year. It included plenty of my awful but humorous dating experiences as the Mystery Woman and my discovery of salsa, but also the struggle I'd gone through trying to fit into a mold just to please my boss and my mother. I was uncomfortable exposing my insecurities and incredible immaturity in prior relationships, but I knew that I needed to share an honest and personal account of everything that had happened.

"Hey, that reminds me, you guys know you're my best friends. But I was thinking of dedicating the book to my mother," I said.

"Really, why?" asked Elizabeth.

"Well, I'm hoping it might improve our relationship," I said. After Javier and I had eloped in Las Vegas on New Year's Day, we'd planned our real wedding for this past June in Milwaukee. My mother had wanted it in New York, but Javier and I wanted it where we'd met. I suggested having another ceremony in July in New York, but she was hurt we weren't doing it on her turf first. She'd come to my wedding in Milwaukee, but wasn't happy about it. But it seemed like she was finally starting to come around. She'd actually begun referring to Javier by name and was helping us decorate our apartment in New York.

Lessie and Elizabeth were chatting and laughing when Javier slipped up behind me.

"How's my salsa goddess?" he asked, kissing me on the neck.

"Did you have a nice nap?" I asked him, smiling.

"It was lonely without you," he whispered into my ear. Javier looked out at the beach at Rachel, Lessie's daughter, who was thumping a little red shovel against the sand.

"When are we going to have one of those?" he asked me.

"I don't know. But I'm willing to start trying."

"Me too. How about now?"

JoAnn Hornak has written for *Newsweek*, *The Washington-ton Post*, *Travelers' Tales*, *Milwaukee Magazine*, and www.onmilwaukee.com. An unabashed salsa fanatic, she discovered salsa dancing at forty years old, proving that there is indeed life after the big "4-0".Visit her website at www.salsagoddess.net.